MEMBERS ONLY

COPYRIGHT

Editor: Jenny Sims
Formatter: Melissa Cunningham @bookloveesigns
Cover designer: Shanoff Designs
Photographer: Michelle Lancaster @Lanefotograf
Model: Chase Cassels

BONES

THE DARK KINGDOM

USA TODAY & WALL STREET JOURNAL BESTSELLING AUTHOR

SHANTEL TESSIER

PLAYLIST

"Find Me" by TeZATalks
"Dead To Me" by Melanie Martinez
"Want It" by SoMo
"Blood//Water" by grandson
"King" by Niykee Heaton

PROLOGUE

BONES

Twelve years old

"DILLAN, LET ME tell you what will get you through this life." My father sits across from me at the table while I eat a snack. "Show me a man in love, and I'll show you his greatest weakness."

I frown. "I'm not sure what you mean."

"I mean, he will put her first before anything else, even himself." Picking up his glass of scotch, he throws it back. My father is always drinking. Doesn't matter if it's six o'clock in the morning or midnight. "You and your brother will have a lot of enemies, son. And every one of them will know this."

"Why would we have enemies?" I'm not dumb. I'm old enough to know that my father does some shady stuff with very powerful men who are as rich as they are evil.

He smirks as if what I said was funny. "Because you two will have what others want."

1

"Love?" I question.

"No." He snorts. "Kingdom."

I don't want it, but I keep that thought to myself. He already knows how I feel about the hotel and casino he owns with his two partners—the Three Wisemen. My father just doesn't care. None of them do. I, along with my little brother and two best friends, will have no choice but to take it over one day.

My father holds up the empty glass and stares at it while speaking to me. "Love makes a man weak. Because a man in love would rather save her than himself."

My eyes drop to the table, and I think about his words. "But you married Mom," I say, looking up at him. I would never consider my father to be weak.

The corners of his lips turn up into a sinister smirk. "I didn't say a man didn't need a woman. I said a man in love is a vulnerable one. Although, women are useful for few reasons." His eyes meet mine. "You'll figure those out later in life."

ONE

BONES

Fourteen years later

I SIT AT my desk on the thirteenth floor of Kingdom when my door flies open, hitting the interior wall with a loud bang. I look up to see Luca Bianchi, a longtime friend, barging into the large space.

"Hey ..." I trail off when he shoves his hands in the pockets of his black slacks and begins to pace. His shoes slap on the marble floor. "Luca?"

"What would you do if Grave was in trouble?" he asks, his voice sounding rough.

I place my cell on the desk and lean back in my chair, crossing my tattooed arms over my chest. I get mad at my brother, but he's still my baby brother. "I'd bail him out." No matter the cost or situation. I've been doing it all my life. "Is he in trouble?" I ask, getting worried.

I just saw Grave last night when we had our Sunday get-together at April's and his house. He seemed well. Better than well, actually. He and April announced their engagement. I believe with every part of me that woman saved his life. Grave was headed down a road that

3

would lead him to his death sooner rather than later. But he fell in love, and she demanded better of him. He loved her enough to give it to her.

"No. This isn't about Grave."

I frown. "Is it about Nite?" Oliver Nite-Bianchi is his adopted brother. Luca's parents took Nite in when they found him on the streets. I believe his father did it to grow his army, but in the end, he's provided Nite with a life he could only dream of.

"It's about me." Luca sighs heavily.

My frown deepens. "You need me to bail you out of something? Just name it."

Luca has been a best friend of the Kings since we were young. His father—John Bianchi—is a Don; the ringleader of the Italian-American Mafia. Our fathers were business partners in a sense. We furthered that tradition. I even went into business with Luca—Glass is one of Las Vegas's elite strip clubs—as his silent partner. Well, I say silent, but I'm pretty sure everyone knows and just lets me believe that they don't.

He rips his Armani suit jacket off his shoulders and throws it across the room, where it lands on the black rug. Then he's unbuttoning his white dress shirt.

"Luca ..." I sit up straighter. "What the hell is going on?"

He ignores me. Instead, he continues to undress, kicking his shoes across my room and undoing his slacks while throwing his shirt. Within seconds, he's down to his black boxer briefs.

"What the hell are you doing?" I demand, getting frustrated as to why my friend is undressing in front of me. I've never seen him like this.

"I'm proving to you I'm not wired," he rushes out.

My body tenses at his words. Being part of the Mafia, he knows what's required of him when he's about to spill some information. The Kings use this method too. You never know who might be listening in on your conversations. If you want to be trusted, then you prove your loyalty.

What has he done that he can't get out of? And why in the hell would he come to me for help? Surely, I'm not his only option.

He bends down, digs his cell out of the pocket of his slacks on the floor, and types away before setting it on my desk.

I stare up at him, ignoring the phone. His dark eyes meet mine. If I didn't know any better, I'd say they are watery.

I stand, my concern growing by the second. "Is Haven okay?" His wife is the only person who can make him feel. He's got bodies buried in the desert. For fuck's sake, I've watched him torture grown men without even blinking. It's got to be his wife. She's the only person he gives a fuck about.

Instead of answering, he leans forward and presses play on the video he has pulled up on his cell.

"Number thirty-six," a man on the video calls out.

My eyes fall to watch the screen.

Someone is recording a small room. Several spotlights on the dirty concrete floor shine up on a black brick wall with a single hook.

I sit in my chair and pick up the phone, wondering what in the fuck he's gotten into.

"I said number thirty-six," the man snaps. The phone begins to move around before he holds it steady once again.

A woman is dragged into view by another man. She wears what was once a white lace bralette and matching underwear. They look like she rolled around on the dirty floor. But that's not what makes my heart begin to race. No. It's the fact she's got a black hood over her head, and her wrists are tied together in front of her. The guy slams her back against the brick wall and yanks the excess rope above her head to tie it around the hook. He secures her in place and then steps out of view. She struggles in the position, kicking her bare feet out and twisting her body from side to side the best she can, but it's not much of a fight.

I pause it and look up at my friend. He has his back to me. "Luca … this is sex trafficking," I say bluntly. "What the fuck are you doing? Selling or buying slaves?" He flinches but doesn't respond.

I know his dad deals in it, but this isn't something Luca would ever agree to.

I go back to the phone at his silence and push play again. She struggles with her arms stretched above her head. The pointless fight makes her tired, and her movements slow. The hook is high enough that she's standing on her tiptoes. Her ribs are showing, and the underwear is falling off her narrow hip bones. She's petite. If I had to guess, I'd say maybe five two and a hundred pounds. The way her ribs protrude through her tan skin makes her look malnourished.

"Turn her around," the man recording calls out.

The guy who placed her there grabs her waist to spin her around, and she begins to fight him again. Listening closely, I can hear her mumbling words. They've either gagged her, or she has tape over her mouth. She manages to kick him in the groin, forcing him back.

"Bitch," he growls. Grabbing the hood, he shoves her head into the brick. Her body hangs there—knocked out.

"Hurry up," the guy filming orders.

The other one rubs his dick and then spins her around so her back faces the camera. He steps away while she slumps against the wall. The guy filming snaps, "Remove her underwear."

The man returns to the shot and yanks them down her legs before shoving them into his pocket like it's a souvenir.

I take a quick look at Luca, and he's moved over to the floor-to-ceiling windows overlooking the Strip. He's got his head on the glass, and his eyes are closed. I can clearly see his chest rising and falling with each breath due to the fact his button-up lies on my floor.

I go back to the video.

She still hangs there, unconscious. Now naked from the waist down. Her tan skin would be flawless other than the bruises on her thighs and upper back. Some dot her frail arms. I don't see any visible scars or tattoos.

The black bag over her head represents the fact that looks don't matter. Only her body does. It's what she can offer a man. Shows how she can be used. And the fact that she can't talk also speaks volumes. You can't tell a man no when you have no voice.

And to further their point, the guy slaps her ass. The sound bounces off the walls in the room they're in, making them laugh.

"Next," the guy says, and the one who slapped her ass removes her from the hook on the wall and carries her out of the frame. The video stops.

I run a hand down my face and set his phone on my desk.

Getting up from my chair, I walk over to the floor-to-ceiling windows that overlook Las Vegas. It's three o'clock in the morning. I only ever open the thick black curtains at night to see the lights from the Strip illuminate the town. It's the only time I care to see this city.

"How much?" I ask. For whatever reason, he's decided he wants her.

"Ten million," he answers, opening his eyes and staring out over Sin City. His jaw clenches.

"Why her?" I ask. He's got a wife. Maybe Haven wants her. Maybe she's realized just what goes on behind the scenes of the Mafia, and she saw the video and wants to save her. Women always get emotional.

He pushes off the window and turns to face me. "That woman you just saw is Mia Rosa Bianchi. My baby sister."

TWO

BONES

I SIT AT the table tucked back in the corner of a ballroom in New York City. I come to the city often. Sometimes for business, but mostly for play. This trip is neither one of those. This is an elite auction. Only the wealthiest, most sadistic pricks attend. Tonight, I'm playing the role of one of those.

The large ballroom is dimly lit, and elevator music plays softly from the speakers above. Rows and rows of round tables are on either side of an aisle. A stage stands at the front of the room, and a black satin curtain hangs behind it from the ceiling to the floor. Women wearing tiny black shorts and matching lace bras walk around with trays, serving the guests. Men dressed in three-piece suits that cost more than most homes pass out numbered paddles to each attendee. No names are needed, I was told when I paid my fee to enter. Ten grand was what they charge for a "plate."

"It's for charity." That's what the man said. "To feed the starving children for two years."

I snort, taking a drink of my bourbon. *Really?* Don't they see the irony?

Not that I don't want to feed the starving children in Africa. The

Kings and I do our fair share of donating to charities all around the world. But there has to be a better way for them to collect money other than kidnapping and selling women.

My cell vibrates, and I pull it out of my suit pocket to see it's from Luca.

Luca: Are you there?

Me: Yes. The auction is about to start.

Luca: Thanks again. I owe you.

I DON'T EVEN BOTHER TO RESPOND. *WHAT ARE FRIENDS FOR?*

"Here you go, sir." A man places a small black book down on the table in front of me.

I reach for it, opening the soft leather and skimming it over. It's a menu of the women being auctioned off. I run a hand down my face while I scan the pages. No photos, just names and information about each girl. I should have brought Cross—another King—with me. He would have just set the place on fire, and then we could have rescued all these women. But no one knows I'm here except for Luca. The Kings think I'm in the city to "play." When I told them I had to go to New York, they all laughed and nodded like they thought I was coming to get my dick wet for the weekend.

If only.

My eyes get to the last page, and I read her name—Mia Rosa Bianchi. They made her the main event. No price or starting bid. I'm not surprised. Her name alone is what will bring in the cash. Besides her name, it states the two most important things about her. She's twenty and innocent.

A virgin? Fuck, for some reason, that makes the video of her I watched ten times worse.

The lights dim, bathing us almost in complete darkness, and I notice the numbers on my paddle glow. Now it makes sense. Easier for them to see who is holding up what. The spotlights that cover the stage turn on. The music fades until you can no longer hear it, and a woman who looks to be in her fifties walks onto the platform, microphone in hand. She gives the crowd a smile, dressed in a white satin dress that resembles a wedding gown. It's tightly fitted with a V-neck, showing off her large fake tits and long train, but she has no wedding ring on her finger. Makes me think she's using this opportunity to be the bride she dreamed of. "Good evening, gentlemen. I want to thank you for your generous donations tonight. The auction will begin in ten minutes."

A LITTLE OVER AN HOUR LATER, I'VE WATCHED TWELVE WOMEN being sold. Well, the last one I'm pretty sure was a girl. Definitely under the age of eighteen. And all of them had a smile on their faces. And not the *I'm scared to death* smile, but a genuine *I'm going to serve you. It's my purpose in life* smile. I'm not sure if they volunteered or what the fuck is going on. After all, I thought this was about sex trafficking.

"Next up, we have Mia," the woman's voice announces over the speakers. "Innocent and beautiful. We've saved the best for last, gentlemen."

Men are already gripping their paddles, ready to bid, but no one walks onto the platform.

My hand fists the glass of bourbon before I throw it back. I can't get that video of her out of my mind. I watched it five days ago. What has happened to her since then? How long did they have her before they recorded it?

I stare up at the stage, expecting her to be brought out on her hands and knees in chains with a bag over her head. But that is not what they had planned for her tonight.

A woman is shoved onto the stage. She trips, falling onto her hip. Her palms slap the black stage, and long, dark hair shields her face from the crowd. A black crown that looks dipped in glitter falls off her head and clanks to the floor next to her.

No one makes a sound. She's dressed in a black evening gown. You can't see the front because of how she's hunched over on the stage, but you can see the back. It dips down, exposing sun-kissed skin, and stops at the top of her ass, where two little dimples show. We silently watch as she breathes heavily. Her body shakes, and her spine is prominent. She's even been starved. No physical sign of abuse, though, like I saw on the video. Either they've healed or they have them covered up, which makes me wonder how long ago the video was filmed before it was sent to Luca.

A man storms onto the stage. It's the same one from the video. The one she had kicked in the nuts. "Get up," he orders, grabbing her upper arm.

She tries to shove him away, but he won't release her.

"Richard." Someone growls from beside the stage. "Leave her."

With a mouth set in a hard line, he exits the stage just as angry as he stormed onto it.

Silence falls once again.

She sits there for a few more minutes before she begins to move. She gets to her knees first; long dark curls still cover her face. Then her heels. She sways a little bit but manages to stand and then turns to face the crowd. Silvery-blue eyes—as clear as the sky on a sunny day—glare at all of us from the stage lights that shine down on her. The dress dips low in the front as it does in the back, showcasing two perfectly round tits. They look untouched. The bralette they had her dressed in the video they sent Luca did nothing for them. Her heavy breathing fills the large room as she bends over and picks up the crown that fell off her head. The crowd gasps when she snaps it in half and drops the pieces to her feet.

"You are all bastards," she growls, showcasing a set of perfectly straight white teeth.

Men throw up their paddles, and the bidding begins. Five thousand, ten thousand, twenty thousand, the number rises by the second. Everyone wants her. But I am the one who will take her home.

I stand, buttoning my suit jacket. "Ten million," I call out.

Paddles drop as heads turn to stare at me. Some in shock, others in envy. Who the fuck would pay ten million for a woman they will just throw in a cage? This room might be full of whales, but none of them will dish out that kind of cash for a slave. Not a smart one, anyway. The wealthiest men can be the cheapest at times. And they're not going to pay that much for pussy.

The woman runs onto the stage with her microphone in hand. "The auction has come to a close," she states, unable to contain her shit-eating grin.

I send a quick text to Luca.

Me: She's all mine.

MIA

I'M YANKED OFF STAGE AND ALMOST TRIP DOWN THE STAIRS again. Then I'm spun around, and my hands are pulled in front of me and crossed at the wrists. A zip tie is placed around them and pulled tight, pinching my skin. I reach up and fist both of my hands, landing a hit to his face.

"Bitch," Richard growls and then slaps me so hard it knocks me into a table off to the side of the hallway. It hits me right in my stomach, knocking the wind out of me. My face stings, and I taste blood.

He grips my hair and yanks my head back, placing his face in front of mine. His lips are so close to mine that they almost touch. He lets out a deep breath, and I have to swallow back the vomit from the smell of cigarettes. "Fuck, you're not worth the hassle. No matter how much I'm getting paid to deal with you."

I spit blood and saliva all over him, and that gets me another hit to my face. This time with his fist. So hard it knocks me out of my heels, and I fall to the cold concrete floor. I close my eyes and bite my tongue just to keep from whimpering when my hip hits again. I'm gonna be bruised all over, but I refuse to lie down and take it. I'm going to fight them no matter what. I choose force. They will have to drag my cold, dead body out to the back before I lie down and take whatever these sick bastards have planned. If any of these men think I'm going easy, I'll prove them wrong. I have four brothers. My family is the Mafia, for Christ's sake. I've been fighting them all my life. I can handle a fucking punch and a slap.

"Do I get a discount if my merchandise is damaged?" a deep voice asks from behind me. He sounds anything but concerned about the state he gets me in.

"She spit in my face," Richard whines, pulling a pocket square from his expensive suit and running it over his face while glaring down at me.

I smile up at him from the floor. I go to kick him in the dick, but he takes a step back, expecting it. "Fucking piece of shit ..."

A hand grips my upper arm, cutting me off, and I'm yanked to my feet. "Let's go," the deep voice orders.

"Fuck you." I fight his hold. I can't see his face due to my hair covering half of mine, and he's forcing me to walk in front of him.

A door is shoved open at the end of the hallway, and I try to adjust my eyes to the darkness. It's nighttime wherever we are, and the heat that hits me makes my skin instantly clammy. I go to run off, but the hand on my arm tightens. Nails dig into my skin, and I cry out, my knees buckling as he shoves me through the back door of a limo waiting for us in the alleyway.

Blowing the loose strands out of my face, I look around the inside. It's dark in here too. Purple lights outline both benches at either end and a couch that runs along the opposite side of the bar.

I crawl across the black carpet the best I can to the other side of the car. I plop down on the small bench and turn to face the back door when it closes. Breathing heavily, I shove my hair out of my face the best I can and stare at the man who bought me like I'm cattle he's going to slaughter and feed to his merry fucking men.

The purple lights that line the ceiling illuminate his face. A set of hard blue eyes glare at mine, framed with dark lashes, a straight nose, and chiseled cheekbones. The lack of lighting makes him look hauntingly beautiful dressed in a black suit and matching button-down. He's a wolf in sheep's clothing. A pretty face to hide the evil. There are no Prince Charmings in my world. Only beasts who claw and fight their way through the masses to get to the top.

"Ready, Nigel," he orders, not taking his eyes off mine.

"Yes, sir," says the driver sitting behind me. I turn around to see him just as he closes the divider, closing us in together.

I swallow, turning back to face the monster. "Where are we going?" I ask nervously. Does he live in the States? How far will he take me? I don't have a phone. I don't even have an ID. I was taken with only the clothes on my back, which wasn't much.

I STAND IN THE POOL AT MY FATHER'S VENETIAN HOME IN ITALY. My arms are on the side as I look out over the infinity pool and to the ocean. It's calm at night. It's also my favorite time for a swim. I hear the sliding glass door open behind me, and I look over my shoulder to see one of my older brothers—Matteo—walk outside dressed in his three-piece charcoal suit.

I swallow nervously. He never comes to visit me. He stays in the States. The twins live here, but they leave me the hell alone. I don't even exist to them, and I prefer it that way.

"What are you doing here?" I ask, looking around to see it's just him and me.

"Here on business." That's his cryptic answer.

"Well, the twins aren't home," I say and turn my attention back to the dark ocean.

"Actually ..." I see his shoes come to stand at the edge of the pool out of the corner of my eye. "You're the job."

I DIDN'T HAVE A SECOND TO ESCAPE. HE REACHED DOWN, gripped my hair, and dragged me out of the pool kicking and screaming. Then he placed a piece of cloth over my mouth. I fought him with all I had, but eventually, my body betrayed me, and I was out. When I woke up, I was in a penthouse in New York. I was stripped, washed, and waxed. Touched from head to toe to make me look like a million dollars. To make me desirable. They drugged me. I know they did. I have times that are missing. Days even. I'm not sure how long it's been or if we're still in New York. All I know is that when I woke up, my body was sore, and there were visible bruises that had been there for days, judging by their color.

"Do our family justice," my brother Matteo had said to me before I had passed out in Italy. Then today, I was dropped off at the auction with a hood over my head.

The man sits back in his seat, breaking our stare. His eyes drop down the length of my body and stop on my thigh. My dress had a slit up the side, but since Richard shoved me down, it's ripped clear up to my hip on the right side. You can see the strap to my black lace thong.

He doesn't answer me as his eyes return to mine.

"Hey, jackass?" I snap. "Where the fuck are you taking me?"

He pours himself a drink from the bottle that sits in the glass bucket. "If you won't be silent, I'll make you." He finally speaks directly to me, sounding bored.

Oh, this fucker ... "Gonna beat me into submission? I'll kick your ass," I warn, wishing I still had my high heels on. The sharpness of the heel could come in handy when you want to poke someone's eye out.

"No," he replies in that same tone, but I see a glint in his eyes. Something tells me he's going to be one of those sick fuckers who likes to prove their dominance. He swirls his drink, the ice clanking, and his eyes drop to my exposed hip again. "I'll remove your thong and gag you with it."

My jaw tightens while my tied hands fist in my lap. "Trying to silence me so I can't scream rape?" Typical man who has to force a woman in order for him to feel like he's in control.

His drink pauses in his hand, and he looks oddly satisfied to answer that question. "If I decide to fuck you, you'll choose to remove your clothes for me."

The audacity. I roll my eyes. "Fat chance, asshole."

Taking that drink, he then sets it down at the minibar and begins to unbutton his suit jacket before slipping out of it. He places it neatly on the seat next to him. Then he undoes his cuff links, rolling up the sleeves to his black button-up. Tattoos cover his arms and knuckles—mainly black with very little color to them. I can't make out what exactly they are from here, but I catch sight of a skull ring on his right ring finger. It looks oddly familiar, but I can't place it.

I'm not surprised, though. My brothers all wear a tacky gold ring on their fingers to signify their connection to our world. It's how the cults like to show they have power.

Once satisfied and comfortable, he reaches down and picks up a small lunch box. I shove myself farther into the seat when he comes to sit on the long bench to my right. "Stay away," I order, placing my hands up.

He grips my arm and yanks me from the seat. My knees hit the floor, and my body falls between his open legs. My breathing picks up, my heart now racing with the fear of the unknown. He holds my tied hands in front of him with one hand, and the other goes to the lunch box. He pulls out an ice pack. "Hold this to your face," he orders, glaring down at me.

"What? Am I too ugly for you now that I have bruises?" I snarl. If that's the case, I'll slam my face into the door every day.

He leans down, his face inches from mine. His expensive, suffocating cologne covers me like a blanket, making it hard to breathe. I try to pull away, but he holds me in place. "If you're going to sport bruises, they'll be from my hands. No one else."

I don't look away from his stare and snap, "Prefer your women black and blue?"

He reaches his free hand into his pocket and pulls out a pocketknife. He flips the blade open, and I suck in a long breath. I close my eyes as he lowers it to my face, but I feel the zip tie snap open, my wrists pulling apart in the process. Then he's shoving the ice pack in my right hand. "I won't say it twice," he says before pushing me away.

I fall onto my ass, my back hitting the minibar. He goes back over to his original seat by the door and picks up his drink, dismissing me.

THREE

BONES

I WATCH HER return to the bench seat across from where I sit. She's much smaller in height and overall size than she looked on stage. She's got long, thin legs, and her neck is so fragile I could wrap my entire hand around it—easily breakable. I'm not sure if that's naturally or from malnutrition.

She stares out the window, holding the ice pack to the side of her face. It angers me that the pathetic man hit her. Men like him are weak. He needed his ass beat. I'll do it. Later. Her evening gown was supposed to make her look like a princess, but it's ripped up her thigh, and my eyes keep going to the lace material that covers her pussy.

"Where is home?" she asks, not bothering to look at me.

I take a sip of my drink.

Her head slowly turns to finally look me in the eyes. Her porcelain face is tight, nose scrunched, eyes looking smaller by the second as she glares at me. I half expect her to throw the ice pack at my face. And that turns me on.

Fight me, beautiful.

She sighs heavily, making her chest rise and fall with irritation. "Is it in another country?"

"Does it matter?" I finally ask.

"Yes," she hisses, slamming the ice pack to her lap. "You're kidnapping me."

I bite back a smile. "Honey, I paid for you."

That just seems to enrage her more. She starts speaking a different language. "Excuse me?"

Her words cut off, and she takes in a deep breath, the action making her chest rise again, and this time, I allow myself to watch the way her breasts bounce from the motion, making my cock hard.

"I called you a pompous, self-absorbed son of a bitch," she clarifies with a bite and adds, "in Italian."

I take a drink from my glass and smile behind it. She's exactly what I expected a female Bianchi to be—fucking fire.

My cell rings, and I pull it out of my pocket to see it's Luca. "Hello?"

"So it went well?" he rushes out. "You've got Mia?"

"Yes," I say, taking another drink.

He lets out a long breath. "Thanks, Bones." The sound of appreciation in his voice makes my chest tighten. Why has he kept her a secret all these years? Where the hell has she been? If he cared so much, why did he allow this? Between him and the Kings, we could have protected her. He has to know that we would have done whatever he needed for her. All he had to do was ask. We protect our own. I consider Luca a brother.

I look up at her to see her beautiful eyes already on mine. The soft glow of the purple lights makes them look exotic—like a rare diamond. A look of concern covers her pretty, bruised face. The ice pack is now on the floor—long forgotten.

"You saved her," he whispers, then clears his throat. "But you do whatever you have to do. Do you understand?"

"I understand." I acknowledge him, and her eyes go wide. Her mind thinks the worst possibilities of who I'm talking to and what I'm agreeing to do regarding her.

I'm not her ally. I need her afraid of me. I need her to want to run away from me. She needs to fear for her life. I have to be exactly like the monsters that put her in this situation in the first place.

"Call me when it's done." Luca hangs up.

Locking my cell, I place it next to me where my jacket lies and order, "Come here."

She swallows nervously, and I can hear her breathing pick up. Her eyes dart to the seat next to me. My legs fall open. "Come here." I point at the floor between them. I don't want her ass beside me. I want her kneeling between my feet. I'm going to treat her how she expects to be treated—if I was a man buying a woman to use.

"I ..."

"You don't want me to come get you," I warn, undoing my tie and ripping it from my collar before throwing it too on the seat and undoing the top button on my shirt, needing to be more comfortable. The air in here is too hot, suffocating.

She must see the warning written on my face because she drops to her knees and slowly makes her way across the floor in her evening gown. She stops too far away from me. I reach out, grab her hair, and yank her the rest of the way. She cries out when I bring her face to mine. Her hands go to my thighs, gripping my slacks. She's panting. Those big silvery-blue eyes are large. A set of red-painted, plump lips parted. Her chest rises fast with each new breath she takes. I let my eyes drop to her cleavage and lick my lips, giving her a clear sign of what I'm thinking about.

"Please ..." she begs softly.

My eyes look up at hers. "What happened to that fuck-you mentality? Give up that easily?" I arch a brow.

She licks her lips nervously, but it just makes me hard imagining throwing her to the floor right here and fucking her. I bet she's not even a virgin. Who still is at twenty these days? Especially in a family like the Bianchis. Her father probably sold her to the highest bidder when she was twelve. That's how those sick fuckers work.

"You're very beautiful," I say honestly. No reason to lie to her.

She won't remember much when she wakes up tomorrow anyway. I grip her hair tighter.

She bares her straight white teeth and looks me in the eyes, spitting out, "And you're a sorry piece of shit."

My free hand comes up and wraps around her neck. Her eyes go wide when I squeeze the delicate skin on either side. I don't say anything. Instead, I just watch her. Hating what I have to do to her. It's not her fault. She's a victim of the life she was born into. But this is part of the plan. Her arms fly aimlessly. Her fists hit my chest and arms. She doesn't have the space to really get the momentum to hurt me. Not like she could even if she wanted to.

Her parted lips are starting to turn blue. She could lose consciousness within ten seconds. Five minutes without oxygen for her body to shut down completely. She makes a noise, trying to get in air. Her silvery-blue eyes are drowning in tears that run down her bruised cheeks.

"So pretty," I whisper, watching the life drain out of her.

What would John Bianchi do if I left her corpse on his front door? Exactly like this? With my handprints covering her neck. He wouldn't even care. He allowed her to be sold. But what about Luca? I'd betray him. And Mia? She would be collateral damage—a price to pay that was never her debt to owe.

Her arms fall to her sides, and her body goes slack just as the car comes to a stop. I watch her pretty eyes roll back in her head, and I let her go.

Her petite body falls to the floor at my feet. Her silky tan skin is red with irritation from my hand. She coughs while her body shakes uncontrollably before she begins to cry.

I snort. She's so fragile, like a delicate flower that would be ripped apart by a breeze.

The Bianchi family—John and his brother, Marco, raised their sons to fight the fucking world. How to kill with a knife, a gun, or a fist. But all they teach their women to do is lie down and spread their legs. And to work in the kitchen.

My door opens, and I reach down, grabbing her thick hair and yanking her out of the car.

MIA

I can't breathe. My face pounds like a drum. Blood rushes in my ears. Saliva fills my mouth and runs out of the corners of my busted lips. I can't swallow. My throat is too sore. Raw.

He drags me into a house and up a set of stairs by my hair. I try to keep up, but my legs won't work. So I let him do all the work. I barely feel the sting on my scalp. He shoves me through a door, and I fall flat on my face. My body convulses while I continue to cough.

He leaves me there, and I watch his shiny black shoes walk away from me. I hear the clanking of glass and then ice. He kneels before me, and I look up at him through watery eyes.

"Drink this." He shoves a small glass full of amber liquid in my face. The strong odor smells of bourbon. It's my brother Luca's favorite drink. I've never had a drink of alcohol in my life. I'm not about to start now.

When I turn my face away from him, he holds my chin with his free hand and tips the glass to my lips, forcing me to drink it. It invades my mouth and chokes me. I cough, causing some to drip down the corners of my mouth and onto my chest and dress. But he doesn't let up. He forces me to drink all of it. When he pulls it away and lets go, I bow my head, coughing and gasping for air.

Tears burn my eyes, and I begin to sob. I don't consider myself that fragile, but at this rate, I'll be dead by tomorrow.

I blink the fresh tears away and close my eyes. The room begins to spin. "What ..." My voice is scratchy, and I cringe from the soreness when I speak. I swallow. "I ..." My tongue feels heavy. I open my eyes, and I see a man standing over in the corner that I've never seen before. The guy from the limo kneels before me once again. He looks at me with no emotion. I can't hold myself up on my hands anymore. I go to fall, but his hands go underneath me, and he lowers me flat to

23

the hardwood floor. I blink up at him slowly. Everything is heavy. I look around aimlessly, but all I see are blurry shapes. "What ... happ ...ened?" I've never been drunk, but this doesn't feel right.

I feel his hand cup my bruised cheek and lean into it, a moan escaping my lips at how warm it feels while my body shakes on the cold floor.

His blue eyes are the last thing I see before everything goes black.

FOUR

BONES

HER EYES FALL shut, and I bend down, pick her up in my arms, and lay her on the leather couch. I turn to face a good friend of mine who lives in New York—Tristan Decker—who stands in the corner. "That worked fast," I observe.

He nods. "Told you it would do the trick." He walks over to her sleeping body and runs his hand over her bruised neck before looking back at me. "Playing a part?"

"Something like that." I shove my hands through my hair. I'm not abusive toward women. Do I like rough sex? Yes. But I have never just hauled off and hit a woman or choked one who didn't ask me to do it while we were fucking. I hate that I had to hurt her and make her fear me.

He slaps my shoulder. "Don't get too worked up over it." His eyes fall back down on her. "A pretty woman like her, she wouldn't have lasted a week in someone's cage."

Tristan has seen the darkest side of this life—sex trafficking. He and his brother Avery know what it's like for women to be used and thrown out with the trash when they no longer serve their purpose.

25

Or when they weren't able to survive what their owners put them through.

The door to Tristan's study opens, and Nigel enters. "Sir, the jet is fueled and ready."

"Thanks for the help," I say to Tristan and reach out my hand.

He shakes it. "Call me anytime."

I hope that I never have to call him again for a situation like this. I reach down and pick her limp body up in my arms and walk down the stairs and out the front door to the limo. Nigel opens the back door for me, and I slide in with her.

I go to set her on the long bench seat to my left, but instead, I keep her in my lap.

Eighteen years old

"LUCA?" I CALL OUT FOR MY FRIEND ONCE I ENTER THE HOUSE. *"Luca?" I drop my backpack in the grand foyer and climb the staircase to the right, looking for him.*

He told me to meet him here after school because he needed to speak to me about something. I barge into his bedroom to find it empty. Closing the door, I pull my cell out of the pocket of my jeans and start reading a message I got from my usual fuck while continuing down the long hallway to the media room.

> Emilee: My parents are gone for the night. Come over?

Me: Be there after practice.

*I GO TO HIT SEND JUST WHEN I HEAR SOMEONE BEHIND ME. I SPIN
around to see dark hair fly as someone turns down another hall.*

"Hello?" I ask, pocketing my cell. "Luca?"

*Getting met with silence, I walk back to where I thought I saw
something. Turning the corner just in time to see a door shut at the
very end of the hall. I make my way down to it. "Luca, this isn't
funny," I growl.*

*Once I get to the door, I shove it open and come to a quick stop. A
girl jumps back with a shriek.*

*Who the fuck is this? I ask myself, looking over her. She has her
dark hair down and wears a white sundress. Her silvery-blue eyes are
wide, and they immediately drop to look down at her bare feet.*

*"What are you doing in here?" I ask, taking a quick look around
the room. It has white walls, beige carpet, and a white sleigh bed
covered with pink satin. A tall dresser sits to the right, and that's it.
I've been in this house a million times but never in this room. "Who
are you?" I ask, stepping farther into the space.*

*I've never seen her before. She looks younger than me. "I asked you
a question," I snap when she just stands there.*

*She jumps back but manages to look up at me with her big eyes.
"No one," answers her soft voice.*

I RUN MY HAND DOWN HER TEAR-STREAKED FACE. HER BRUISES
grow darker from that guy's fist. My fingerprints are prominent on
her delicate neck. I should have known then that she needed help.
That something so fragile wouldn't survive in hell. Closing my eyes, I
sigh and hope that this works. Because as much as I want to help her,
she isn't mine to keep.

MIA

I OPEN MY heavy eyes to an unfamiliar room. It's dark, letting me know it's nighttime, but I can make out the bare white walls and matching marble floor from the light on the patio that streams through the see-through curtains covering the sliding glass doors. Placing my bare feet on the cold floor, I see that I'm still wearing the black dress.

Standing, the room sways a little, and I place my hand on the side of the bed to help keep me upright. My head pounds, and blood rushes in my ears.

I reach down, grab the material of my dress, and pull it up to check and see if I still have underwear on. I let out a sigh of relief when I see the black thong is still in place, and there's no blood between my legs. I expected the worst. Why else would the man drug me?

Lifting my head, I drop the dress and listen for any noise in the house but hear nothing. I make my way over to the door and find myself in a hallway. My feet softly step on the floor while making my way to a living room at the end of the hallway.

My feet stop when I see the man from the limo standing outside on the back porch. The sliding glass doors open to the ocean. The soft breeze and smell of the ocean slaps me in the face.

As if he can feel my presence, he turns to face me. He's holding a drink of what looks like scotch in one hand. The other shoved into the pocket of his black slacks. He looks like he did in the limo with the sleeves of his button-up rolled up his forearms, exposing his tattooed and muscular arms.

He steps into the house, and I take a step back.

"I'm not going to hurt you," says that deep voice.

"I don't believe you." I lift my chin, but my knees shake at the way he takes up the space in the room. He consumes it. I have a feeling we could be standing in an open field, and it still wouldn't be enough space.

He smirks, bringing the glass to his lips and taking a drink before placing it on the glass coffee table. "Sit." He points at the couch as he falls into the high-back chair across from it.

The hairs on the back of my neck rise with anticipation of what he plans on doing with me. The urge to run is strong. But I'm not sure where I'd go or how I'd get there. But trying has to be better than the alternative, right?

There's no telling what he plans on doing to me. Wiping my sweaty hands on my dress, I take another step back while he observes me with a look of challenge in his eyes. As if he wants to chase me down. I take another step back and then turn, giving him my back, ready to run out the front door when he speaks. "The closest house is a mile away. Think you can outrun me?"

I swallow the lump in my throat at his threat. His height alone would give him an advantage. His strides would be twice as long as mine. Not to mention the fact that I'm barefoot and he's not. And what would he do once he caught me? Punish me? Drag me back by my hair? He's already done that once. I wouldn't put it past him to do it again.

Turning around, I slowly make my way to the couch and sit down, trying to pull the dress over my thigh so he can't see my thong, but that doesn't really work. The rip is too high.

"You don't have anything I haven't already seen," he says dryly.

Reaching over, I grab the throw pillow and hold it over my lap and catch sight of him rolling his eyes. The action makes him look like a normal man. Not a sadistic son of a bitch who is going to rape me and let his friends have their turn.

"All of your belongings were delivered an hour ago," he states before finishing his drink. He gets up, and I do the same, but he points at me. "Stay seated."

My teeth grind, but I do as I'm told, gripping the pillow for dear life.

He comes back into the room, setting a box on the coffee table.

"This is yours." He opens it up and pulls out a cell phone. "The only contact you will have with the world is with me."

I snort. "Of course, it is."

He looks up at me through his dark, long lashes and then goes back to the cell. Thankfully I've got numbers memorized. Well, not many but the ones that matter. I knew the day would come when my family would take me from Italy, leaving me defenseless. I had plenty of time alone with my phone to memorize the numbers I would need to call for protection when that day came.

"Don't even think about contacting Luca."

My stomach sinks at his words, and he looks up at me again. I stare at him, my spine stiffening and all the air rushing from my lungs.

He holds out the phone, but I don't take it. I can't move. *He knows my brother.* Why and how would he know Luca?

Placing it down on the coffee table, he sits back in his chair, casually dropping his hands on his thighs. The guy is as relaxed as can be, and I'm having trouble breathing. He tilts his head, his dark brows pulling together, and I feel wetness on my face. I'm crying.

"He can't help you," he says. The words are spoken so cold that it causes goose bumps to spread across my body.

"Did... did you hurt him?" I manage to get out.

"No." He shakes his head. "I'm not who you think I am," he adds vaguely.

"You drugged me," I say, my breath catching. "Tried to kill me. Who am I supposed to think you are?"

"I did what needed to be done to get you somewhere that was safe. If I hadn't drugged you, would you have gotten on a plane with me?"

"Fuck no," I snap, feeling anger toward this man now. He's lying to me.

He nods as if happy with my answer. It just proves his point. "This is your new life. And if you want to move forward, you have to let your past go."

No. I refuse to believe that. "But Luca—"

"Luca can't save you." He interrupts me. "I am the only person you contact if you need something."

I snort, but he ignores it.

"You have a new identity. Name, license, social security card ..." he gets up and grabs a box off the kitchen table and drops it on the coffee table. "Everything you need is in here—checking account, birth certificate, and credit card."

"So ..." I run a hand through my hair, trying to comprehend what the hell is going on. My head must still be foggy from the drugs. "You want me to walk away from Luca?"

"I want you to survive," he states. "I didn't pay ten million dollars for you to be kidnapped and die next week because you did something you weren't supposed to do."

I get to my feet, ignoring the way the room sways at the quick movement. "You don't know me." Giving him my back. I start to walk out of the room. "You don't know ..."

"I know your family was selling your body to the highest bidder," he barks out.

I stop slowly, turning to face him to see that he's now standing with his arms crossed over his chest. "Luca was the one who reached out to me."

I shake my head. "I don't believe you. He would have come and saved me himself."

"You were being sold," he growls through gritted teeth like he fucking cares. "He couldn't buy you. He couldn't send Nite to buy you. It had to be me. Someone you didn't know. It had to feel real." Walking over to me, I stay standing in place, letting him get close. He comes to a stop, and I blink, fresh tears running down my face.

"No," I whisper, refusing to believe a damn word this stranger says to me.

It was real. The way he looked at me, spoke to me, and the way he manhandled me. Luca would have never allowed someone to treat me that way, not even a friend of his. This is a way for this man to

31

manipulate me. Make me think I'm safe with him when he's the real enemy. He's probably best friends with Matteo, and they've set me up. Thinking I'll see this as a sense of security, only for them to attack me when I let my guard down. That's why he also mentioned Nite.

"Who do you think called me in the limo?" he asks. Reaching out, his knuckles run down my tear-streaked cheek, making me shiver. "I don't care if you stay here or if you run the moment I walk out that door." Sliding his hand into my hair, he grabs it and gently pulls my head back. Lowering his face to mine, he pauses just before his lips touch mine, and I hold my breath. His pretty blue eyes bore into my silvery-blue ones as he delivers the threat I was waiting on. "But if you leave this house, just be prepared to run for the rest of your life."

FIVE

BONES

I WASN'T PLANNING on waiting for her to wake up. I was going to leave the cash, credit card, and license along with the cell phone on the table with a note. But that didn't seem like enough. First, I needed her to fear me, but now, I need her to fear her past.

She won't survive on her own.

I ignore that, though. She's never had the chance to be independent, but that doesn't mean she can't do it. It just means she needs a little help. I'm the only option for her.

"Will...will you be back?" she asks, stumbling over her words.

"No," I say, letting go of her hair and running my hand through the long curls. "Not unless you need me."

The way her eyes widen lets me know that my words catch her off guard, and I hate that my cock reacts to the way she responds. Like I'm the last person on earth she would call.

She steps back, and I allow my hand to fall from her. She licks her lips. "Where are we?"

"Malibu," I answer.

She lets out a sigh of relief that she's not in another country. As

33

far as I know, she's never been anywhere except for Las Vegas and Italy.

"Promise me," I order.

Her eyes snap up to mine and narrow. "Promise you what?"

"That you won't call anyone other than me." I need to hear her say it. Or maybe I'm just biding my time not to leave her. Once I walk out of this house, she's on her own, and I can't protect her if I'm not here.

"I won't call anyone but you," she says, unable to look me in the eyes. A clear sign she's lying.

Gripping her chin, I shove her head back, glaring down at her. "This isn't a game."

"I'm not ..."

"Quit fucking lying to me," I growl, cutting her off. "You will put others in danger."

She yanks away and rubs her chin. "But you expect me to believe that you don't mind putting yourself in danger?" She snorts. "Yeah, I highly doubt that. You're like everyone else and don't give a fuck about me."

I fist my hands but don't respond because the events that have led us to this moment would prove any argument I have to be a lie.

Crossing her arms over her chest, she pushes her hip out. The one that has the torn slit up her thigh, and I can see her hipbone. My eyes trace along the black lace thong that I know covers her pussy, and I run a hand down my face.

Leave, Bones.

My mind yells, but I can't make my legs move. Once I walk out of my house, there will be no reason to return because I know this woman will never call me for anything. I should have fucking left before she woke up.

"Anything else?" she demands, glaring up at me.

Deciding that's my sign to get the fuck out of here, I start to walk toward the front door. But before I can exit the living room, I come to a stop. Turning back to face her, I notice she stiffens when I look at her.

Knowing this will be my only chance, I walk back to her, and she takes a step back, but thankfully, the couch stops her retreat. "One more thing." I come up to her, cup her face with both of my hands, holding her still, and her head falls back. Silvery-blue eyes the size of quarters stare up at me with mixed emotions—half terror and confusion. I lick my lips. Then I lower mine to hers.

She gasps, her lips parting on mine. I don't force my tongue down her throat or shove her onto her back like I want. Instead, I keep my lips on hers, tasting the bourbon from the drugs I gave her. I let them linger for a few seconds, and when I pull away, I watch her eyes flutter open. She looks dazed, almost in a dream-like state. But I can't ignore the way her body leans into mine as if she needs me to help hold her up.

I run my thumb over her lips, and I'm not even sure she's breathing right now. Without another word, I turn and exit the house, leaving her behind like I was supposed to do all along.

MIA

I STAND ROOTED to my spot in the living room and listen to the front door open and close. The mysterious man bought me, drugged me, and kissed me. And then walked out of my life, knowing I'll never see him again.

I taste the bourbon from his kiss. I've never liked the smell of alcohol, let alone had a drink. He forced some down my throat, and now I lick my lips, savoring the taste.

My knees buckle, and I fall onto the couch, the room filling with my heavy breathing. Reaching up, I run my shaking fingers over my parted lips. Did he know that was my first kiss? Why did he do it? He could have forced me to do so much more. Yet all he did was touch his lips to mine. I wanted to kiss him back. My mind was yelling that would be my only chance at not being myself.

Once again, I'm alone. The fact that he was forward didn't terrify me. It was the way my body reacted. My skin tingled, blood rushing in my ears, and I couldn't breathe.

I froze.

Blinking, I drop my eyes to the phone on the coffee table. Opening up the contacts, there's only one programmed—Dillan. I ignore that number, and my fingers numbly run over the screen, unable to stop myself.

I have no control.

Holding the phone to my ear, it rings once, twice. Just when I think he's not going to answer. It stops, the sound of silence meeting me on the other end.

"He-llo." I swallow the lump in my throat and realize I'm shaking.

"Who is this?" I hear the familiar voice, and I feel my heart pounding once again.

"Mia," I whisper.

"What...?" he trails off. "Mia, why are you calling me?" he growls.

Tears spring to my eyes, and I bite on my nails. "I ... he said not to call you."

"You shouldn't have," my brother snaps.

"Luca." I sniff. "I don't know what's going on. He said you sent him. But he ... he drugged me." My throat closes on me.

He lets out a long sigh. "It was the only option, Mia." His voice sounds pained. "But you need to listen to him." He lowers his voice to a whisper. "This was the only way I could think to save you."

"But ..."

"Please forgive me, Mia."

"Luca—"

He hangs up, and I pull the cell from my ear to see he's no longer there. I feel a tear run down my face as I lean back into the couch and turn the cell off. I won't be calling anyone, ever. I'm on my own.

SIX

BONES

I CHECK MY watch as I'm exiting my private jet back in Vegas. It's a little after six in the morning. The sun is rising, and I'm finishing my third Red Bull of the night. My blacked-out Lamborghini Reventon waits for me inside the hangar. Getting into my car, I hear my cell ring, and I hit answer.

"Hello?"

"She called me," Luca growls in greeting.

I sigh. "I'm not surprised. I expected her to reach out to the one person she *thought* she could trust." Even though I told her not to, I knew she would. She's confused and scared. Probably a nervous wreck that I'm going to show up at the house and force her to do unimaginable things.

He lets out a huff. "I don't expect you to understand, Bones."

"Why don't you try to explain it to me, Luca," I snap at him, hitting the gas and hearing my car roar.

"I did what had to be done." He goes on the defensive.

"Yeah, keep telling yourself that," I say through gritted teeth.

Click. He hung up on me.

Sitting back in my seat, I haul ass down the highway to Kingdom, knowing it's going to be a long fucking day. Just like all the rest.

———

I PULL INTO OUR PRIVATE GARAGE AND EXIT MY CAR. WALKING to the elevator, I scan my key card and ride the elevator up to the thirteenth floor. There has always been a dislike and superstition with the thirteenth floor. Kingdom has four towers, and only tower one has a functioning thirteenth floor. The others jump from twelve to fourteen.

The other Kings and I aren't superstitious in the least. So when we took over Kingdom, we made the thirteenth floor ours.

Getting off the elevator, I take an immediate right, shoving the double glass doors open to our conference room. We've got jammers in here, making any electronic device inoperable. We conduct meetings here with some very powerful people around the world. The last thing we want is for someone to use it against us.

My brother already sits in his seat with a Monster and a Crunch bar in his hands. The guy has never cared about what he puts in his body—drugs included.

Cross sits across from him, flipping a Zippo open and closed like always. He likes to burn shit. His girlfriend's brother sits next to him with a worried look on his face. Derek is afraid of us. For good reason.

Titan sits to his right, arms crossed over his chest and a scowl on his face.

"Did you just get back from New York?" Grave asks as I take my place at the head of the table.

"Yeah," I lie to my brother.

"Must have been an eventful trip," Titan observes, looking over my wrinkled button-up. The guys and I have the Royal Suite on the fiftieth floor, aka the Royal Floor. I'll run up there after our morning meeting and shower.

38

"Let's get started," I suggest, nodding to Derek, ready to get this over with.

"I was thinking." My brother places his tatted arms on the black table, leaning forward. "The other day, I asked Alexa to continue running Crown for me until I could find a replacement."

All four of us Kings run Kingdom together, but the others also have their own responsibilities inside the hotel and casino. Cross has Tit-For-Tat—his tattoo shop. Titan oversees our Queens—our discreet call girls. Men come from all around the world to meet up with our girls. You'd be surprised who will pay to spend the night with a Queen. We have some very high-profile men on our roster. Grave runs Crown—one of our nightclubs. And me? Besides Kingdom, I own several other businesses.

The memory of what he said comes to mind.

We all sit around Grave and April's formal dining room table. A Sunday gathering that has started to seem more like a tradition for us now. We've grown up together, and although we have had our disagreements, we're all a family that seems to keep growing. Grave has April. Titan has Emilee, and Cross has Alexa. I couldn't be happier for my best friends and the life that they have found for themselves.

"Hey, Alexa," Grave starts.

"Hmm?" She looks at him, slowing her chewing.

"Do you mind staying on at Crown? That is, until Lucky's is back up and running, and I can find someone else to take over?"

She looks at Cross, confused, and then back at him. She swallows her food. "I don't mind, but I don't want to take that away from you."

"You're not." He reaches over and takes April's hand, bringing it to his lips. He kisses her knuckles, and she blushes. "I want to come home and be with my wife after a long day at Kingdom."

Alexa starts nodding. "Yes, sure, that's ..."

A silence falls over the room, and April starts laughing.

"No!" Jasmine breathes, her palms slapping the table. "You got married without us?" she asks in disbelief.

"No, but ..." April holds up her left hand and smiles brightly, showing off the massive diamond on her ring finger. *"We have a wedding to plan."*

I always knew Grave wouldn't be able to continue running Crown. As a recovering addict, I thought it would be too much temptation. The alcohol alone would be a distraction. We're not stupid. Although we don't deal in drugs, we know they are passed around inside the clubs.

"I don't understand." Derek looks around quickly. "What does this have to do with me?"

"Well, I want to offer Crown to you," Grave states.

Everyone looks over at the guy, and he sits up straighter. His eyes widen as he points at himself as if there's more than one Derek in the room. "Me?" he asks.

"Why not?" My brother takes a drink of his Monster. "You helped Alexa run Lucky's, right?"

Derek nods, eyes still wide with surprise.

"Alexa will have the new club opened soon, and she won't be able to run both. I don't plan on stepping back into Crown. So ..." He shrugs. "This makes sense."

Some shit went down with Alexa and Lucky's—the bar she was given when Lucky passed away. It's currently under construction. But Cross is determined to have it open and better than ever as soon as possible.

"I've already spoken to the other Kings, and we think it would be a good opportunity for you," Grave goes on.

He had messaged us about this last night while I was sitting on the beach waiting on Mia to wake up. We were all in an agreement that keeping Derek close was a good idea. And what better way to do that than putting him to work at Kingdom. Where we can have eyes on him at all times.

"That's ..." He looks over at Cross, who just stares at him, flipping open his Zippo, not giving his feelings about the matter away. He couldn't care less. If need be, Cross would set him on fire right here and now. "A great opportunity." Derek swallows nervously. "But Lucky's was on a much smaller scale—"

"I spoke to Alexa this morning." Grave interrupts him. "She said that she would continue to work there with you until she opens the new club. That way, you won't be doing it on your own right off the bat. It'll give you time to get some training in."

Derek runs a hand through his dark hair. "That would be great." He nods to himself. "Thanks, guys."

"Then it's decided," I say, ready to get this meeting over with and on with my day. I need to bury myself into my work to get the pretty brunette staying in my beach house off my mind. I want to kick myself in the ass for not setting up cameras there. If I had, then I would have the option of watching her whenever I wanted. No matter how creepy that makes me sound.

Cross closes his Zippo and reaches out, slapping his hand on Derek's shoulder, and he flinches at the contact. "Fuck us over, and I'll kill you. Do you understand?"

"Oh, I would never ..."

Titan gives a rough laugh. "We've heard that before."

"I promise." Derek throws up his hands. "I won't let you guys down."

With that, I get up and exit the conference room, not bothering to say anything else. People can talk a lot of shit. I'm about action, and only time will prove him right.

Making my way back to the private elevator, I step inside and push the button for the fiftieth floor, pulling my cell out of my pocket. I go to her name and hover over it. I feel like I should call Mia. She's probably even more scared now after speaking to Luca. He just reiterated what I had told her—she's on her own.

He was a wreck when he came to me for help. We both knew I was her only hope and that it wasn't a good thing.

. . .

"WHAT DO YOU MEAN SHE'S YOUR SISTER?" I DEMAND. "SINCE when do you have a sister?" Maybe she's adopted like his parents adopted Oliver Nite.

"She's six years younger than us," Luca answers hoarsely. "My mother had a daughter before I was born. My father killed her ..."

"Jesus!"

"After that, she had me, followed by Matteo, then my twin brothers. They went for another boy, and she had Mia." He turns to look at me. His dark eyes are desperate, and it makes my chest tighten. I've seen that look before. He'll do anything to accomplish whatever plan he has come up with. "I was there when Mia was born. My mother begged my father to keep her. And he said that Mia could stay, but a time would come when she would earn her last name."

I run a hand through my hair.

"Her role was to always be a weapon, Bones. He wanted to use her."

"For what?" I ask. "How is he going to use her when no one knows about her?"

"You."

"What about me?" I snap, unsettled by this information and what I saw on the video.

"He wanted her to marry you. So he could have Kingdom."

"This is insane," I state and turn to walk away.

He grabs my arm, stopping me. "You don't understand. In the Mafia, you marry for power. Her name attached to yours gives my father a lot of that. It makes him even more untouchable. She was always a card to be played when he needed to win a hand. And your Kingdom is what he's always wanted."

"I don't believe this," I mutter. It's ridiculous, really.

"He came to me a few months ago and said it was time for Mia to step up and do her part. I blew him off. I've tried to buy time, knowing that you and Mia would never be. But I can't do it anymore, Bones." He punches his bare chest. "I can't save her."

"And?"

42

Running a hand down his face, he sighs. "And Matteo sent me that video an hour ago."

"How do you know for sure it's her in the video?" I reach, trying to think of anything that can ease his concern. "It didn't show her face."

"Because I know!" he snaps and then takes a deep breath. "Matteo called me after I watched it, or I would have been here sooner. Said she was picked up last week. The video was taken in Italy, and then she was placed on a cargo plane and shipped to New York along with the others."

"Why would he call you and tell you this?"

"Because he knows I'm the only one who gives a damn about her and will do whatever it takes to save her from the future my father has decided for her."

I bow my head and rub my eyes. "What do you want me to do?"

"I need you to buy Mia."

"Fuck, Luca," I hiss. "What am I going to do with her?"

"Let her go."

"Let her go where?" He makes it sound like she's a bird I should let fly away.

He turns, giving me his profile view, and looks back over the city. "You've got plenty of vacation homes. I need you to purchase her, then ship her off to one of them."

"I—"

"Don't tell me where you send her." He interrupts me.

"Luca ..."

"Do what you need to do," he adds cryptically.

"What the fuck does that mean?"

"I could send Nite, but Mia knows him. We can't let her know that it's not real. I have no one else to send. And I know my sister, Bones. If you don't buy her and someone else does ... she'll die."

"Luca, this is ..." I begin to pace and run a hand through my hair. "What you're asking me to do is ..."

"I'm begging you, Bones." He grabs my shoulders, bringing me to a stop. This is odd, considering he's still only dressed in his boxer briefs.

43

"I can't save her anymore. She needs you. Why do you think my father is putting her in an auction? To sell her to the highest bidder. If you don't do it, someone else will. And we both know that whoever that is will use her just as that video intended to show."

I don't understand, though. Once I buy her and then set her free, her father will know. He'll be on to us. What will keep him from looking for her? He won't give up that easily, will he? "Your father will know I'm the one who bought her," I argue.

He shakes his head. "It's all anonymous. He'll receive payment, and that's as far as he'll know. It keeps the seller from getting paid and then stealing the product back."

"He'll look for her," I grind out.

"No. Once he's been wired the money, he'll forget about her. He's using his last name to cash in on her."

"I know nothing about sex trafficking, Luca. Even if I wanted to help her, what would I do? Where will she be? How do I get in ...?"

"I don't know any of that." He sighs, his face falling. "Matteo wants me to suffer, knowing that our father is selling her because I didn't keep my end of the deal."

"I can't believe this." I give him my back and start to pace the room. "You should have told me. At least given me a heads-up, so I could have bought her some time."

"I didn't know how you'd react ..."

"We take care of our own!" I yell, getting more pissed off by the second. "You think I would have let this happen had I known the possibilities of what he would do to her?"

"I'm not here to argue with you about the past. I'm here begging you to help me give her a chance at a future. Are you going to help us or not?"

"I'll do it," I growl, not happy with this situation, but what other choice does this woman have? I saw the video, and I know her options are grim.

Silence falls over the room, and then he nods his head before he *starts getting dressed and runs out of my office, not saying another word.*

I sit down at my desk and run a hand down my face. "Fuck!" I hiss.

Picking up my cell, I call one of my friends who lives in New York. He answers on the second ring. "Hello?"

"Hey, I need a favor."

"What is it?" Tristan Decker asks.

"Know of any auctions coming up shortly?" If anyone knows, Tristan does. This is his business. This is his life.

He starts laughing. "Since when are you into buying art?"

"I'm doing a favor for someone."

"Just so happens, a shipment was delivered last week. The auction for the cargo is in five days. Word is a lot of whales will be there to see the art. Are you looking to buy or just observing?"

"Buy. Ten million."

He whistles. "Damn, that is one hell of a favor."

Tell me about it. "I need something for after I've purchased."

"After ...?"

"You know, so I can ship the art to the buyer." I remain talking in code. You never can be too careful these days. Even cell phones can be tampered with. That's why we conduct all our business meetings in a room equipped with jammers.

"Ahh, I have what you need. Bring it by my house after you've made your purchase, and I'll have it ready for delivery."

I DID WHAT NEEDED TO BE DONE. AND I NEED TO LET IT GO. The elevator dings, and I sigh, putting my cell away. The less contact I have with her, the better. She'll never call me, and that's best for both of us.

SEVEN

MIA

Three weeks later

"FIND ME" BY TeZATalks plays in my ears as I approach the beach house. Slowing to a walk, I remove the earbuds and enter through the glass front doors, placing the cell on the table in the foyer. Taking a deep breath to calm my racing heart from my run, I make my way to the kitchen.

The house sits by itself right on the ocean. The back of the house is nothing but floor-to-ceiling sliding glass windows. I leave them open all the time. I like to hear the ocean. The breeze and the smell remind me of Italy. Even though I was trapped in that castle, I miss the view and the warm weather. I wonder if that's why the man who bought me shipped me here?

I dream about him. The way he kissed me, then just left. I hate the way my body reacts to him, even in my sleep. I wake up alone with my skin tingling. So I run. It helps clear my mind. I try to forget him, but it never seems to work. He's still here, demanding attention. His presence fills the large house. His scent lingers in the air. Even the ocean can't mask it.

I go to turn around and enter the living room but freeze. A cold chill runs up my spine and paralyzes me where I stand. Someone's here. My skin tingles, and I break out in goose bumps. I didn't see any cars in the driveway when I returned. But then again, I was only gone for about thirty minutes. I didn't run as far as I had been. "Hello?" I call out.

Silence greets me, and my breathing becomes louder. Blood rushes in my ears, and I swallow. "I know you're there." I can feel it. The coldness in the room. Maybe the man is here to kick me out. Or to take me back to my father. I'll beg him not to make me go. This is the freest I've ever felt in my life, and that's pretty fucking sad.

Laughter comes from behind me, and my stomach drops. Two distinctive sounds that I've known all my life.

I turn around to see my brothers, Matteo and the twins standing there. Matteo leans against the glass door.

"What are you doing here?" I ask, taking a step back. How did they find me?

"Mia?" Matteo, one of my older brothers, sighs, shaking his head. The one who ripped me from the pool and drugged me. "The question is, what are you doing here?"

I look for anything that I can use to defend myself. But even if I had a loaded gun in my hands, they'd still have me dead before I could use it on them. Our father has trained them like dogs. Money. Power. Kill. That's all they know. Pussy is just what they do for fun. *A man can get that anywhere,* my father always says.

Matteo's eyes run up and down my black yoga pants and red sports bra. It makes my fucking skin crawl when he smiles at me like I'm another one of his whores.

"Nice place." Lorenzo nods his head, looking around while walking toward the open kitchen.

"Please leave." I breathe as tears sting my eyes. I don't want them to hurt me, and I also don't want them to destroy this house. It doesn't have any photos or décor, but it doesn't need it. Some things are just naturally pretty.

Matteo rubs his chin, pushing off the glass. "Afraid we can't do that."

"What do you want?" I take a step back.

Matteo yanks me toward him, slamming my body into his. I try to push him away, but he holds me tightly. His hand slides down my high-waisted yoga pants to cup my ass. "Stop!" I shriek in horror, my heart pounding.

"Matteo," Lorenzo says, sounding bored. "She's your sister."

"So?" Matteo leans down and kisses my sweaty neck. I feel bile in my throat. "Pussy is pussy, and my dick is hard at the moment."

I hit my fists into his chest. He shoves me away, making my legs hit an end table by the couch. The sound of it scraping across the floor fills the room while I try to stay on my feet.

He laughs at me.

"We need her to still be a virgin," Gabriel adds, finally speaking. He's always been the quiet one.

Matteo smiles. "You know virgins are my favorite."

"I'll find you one later." He rolls his eyes.

I'm gonna be sick.

"I could fuck her mouth." He shrugs carelessly.

"I'll bite it off," I warn. No way in hell will I let him get that close to me.

He laughs. "There is a device known as the spider gag. It prevents your mouth from closing." My eyes widen that he even knows this. "I could shove whatever the fuck I want into your mouth, and you wouldn't be able to do anything about it."

"Why are you here?" I demand, knowing they didn't come here to fuck me. Even if the sick bastard has considered it.

My father kept me locked away in Italy most of my life with the twins, but Matteo never visited me. I think my father did that for a reason. Or at least I like to think that he tried to protect me from that monster.

Lorenzo jumps off the kitchen counter. "We're here to send you back."

I shake my head. "I'm not going back to Italy."

"You are going to Las Vegas. Back to Bones."

Bones? What kind of name is Bones? Vegas? That's where we lived before my father sent me to Italy. "No ..."

Matteo reaches out and grips my face tightly. His fingers dig into my cheeks, making me whimper. "You will do what you were bred to do and spread your fucking legs," he growls. "Your mouth was made to suck cock, not talk. You are at the motherfucking bottom of authority and will do as you're fucking told."

"He doesn't want me," I try. "He almost killed me." Even though that's true, he didn't for some reason. A part of me knows that he was trying to help me. Why else would he pay all that money, drug me, and then send me away? I've had no communication since that night three weeks ago. I have a cell phone, but it only has one number in it —I'm guessing it's his number since I didn't recognize it. I'm not sure why. I'm sure he had the number to the phone he left me, yet I've had no contact with him. Bones may have spared my life, but he had no plans to ever see me again.

"If you don't go back willingly, we will force you back." He lets go of me.

"Why do you want me with this Bones guy?" I ask as tears build in my eyes. I take a quick look around, wondering why Luca isn't here. He would never let them hurt me. Luca has always been my savior. My protector. He's the only one in the family who seems to care about me.

"Dad wants Kingdom," he states, shoving me away.

My chest tightens at that, knowing exactly what he means. I should have known—the skull ring on the man's hand. I knew it looked familiar. I've met Bones once. A very long time ago. "He's a King," I whisper more to myself.

I know what Kingdom is. My father used to work with Mr. Reed —one of the hotel and casino owners. I might not have been allowed to have a life, but I knew what and who my family was. And my father did a lot of work out of our house. I've seen what he is capable of and know who he dealt with on a daily basis. They were all as sick as him.

"How ... how would my going back to Bones help Dad get Kingdom?" I wonder out loud, trying to make sense of this.

"Because the Kings own Kingdom now. They have for years."

I shake my head, feeling around for the couch before I fall onto it. But what does it have to do with me? "How am I supposed to make that happen by going back to him?"

Gabriel laughs like I just told a joke.

Matteo sighs. "I blame Dad for this. He hasn't taught her shit."

Lorenzo's eyes meet mine. "You seduce him. Make him fall in love with you."

A laugh bubbles up in my throat, but the leveled look he gives me makes me swallow it. "You're serious?"

They say nothing.

"I'll give you two weeks."

Lorenzo snorts, cutting off Matteo. "Two weeks? Be serious, man. This is Bones." Lorenzo looks me up and down, but it's with disgust, not lustfulness.

Thank God.

"He's not gonna fall for her shit in a matter of two weeks. She doesn't even know how to seduce a man." He tilts his head to the side. "I'll give you three months."

"It's impossible," I argue. "No amount of time will help me accomplish that. You guys don't know him—"

"Oh, we do." Matteo interrupts me. "We know what he likes. What he craves. And you're going to be the fucking bitch he needs to break him."

My hands fist in my lap. "He almost killed me."

Matteo smiles. "Girls like you make it so easy to take what we want." He sighs, and I frown, having no idea what he's talking about. "The dude likes a submissive woman."

I swallow, knowing exactly what that means, but I still ask. "Submissive?"

They both nod, but Gabriel's the one who answers. "Bones likes a woman who will crawl on her hands and knees, begging to be fucked."

I can see that. The way he dominated in the limo was all I needed to know about him. He commands the room. "Well, sorry, but that's not me." I may have been sheltered my entire life, but I still had the internet, and the twins always had girls coming and going in Italy. I know what sex is even though I have no experience in it. No matter how many romance novels I've read, they couldn't prepare me for what he wants. I stand from the couch and start to pace the room. "And he almost choked me to death," I snap, trying to come up with excuses as to why Bones wouldn't want me. "What would I even say when I just show back up?" I growl. They're insane.

Matteo waves a hand in the air. "We'll take care of that."

I almost roll my eyes. "How?"

"Don't worry about it."

"You're asking me to do the impossible," I spit out.

"It's not that fucking hard," Matteo snaps, getting irritated. "You lie down and spread your legs. Let him fuck whatever hole he wants, however he wants."

Lorenzo runs a hand through his hair. His tell that he's getting pissy as well.

"I don't want to."

"It doesn't matter what you fucking want!" Matteo shouts. "You will go back, and if you don't go willingly, I'll drop your ass off at his fucking doorstep, naked and crammed in a box!"

I bite back a few choice words, not wanting to get hit. It's been nice not having a hand to my face. "Why does Dad want Kingdom so bad, anyway? It's just a hotel."

That gets them to laugh. "Again, Dad has taught her nothing," Matteo adds.

"And he has three other business partners." There were three other Kings; Bones had a brother who went by Grave, then two others. They said the Kings own it now. That makes four of them. "Dad getting Bones's cut isn't gonna help him."

"Let us worry about that," Lorenzo says.

Matteo gives me that slimy smile again.

"What?" My heart races as they exchange a look. Are they going to hurt the Kings? That's the only way they would get all of it.

Gabriel nods once to him.

"What?" I demand.

Matteo takes a step toward me. "We're here to help you, sis."

Fear cripples me at his words. He's never called me that before.

"What are big brothers for, anyway?"

"Make it good," Lorenzo tells Matteo

"Make what good?" I tremble, my legs buckling.

"You'll see." Matteo smiles right before his fist hits the side of my head.

My body hits the hard and unforgiving floor, and my ears begin to ring. I curl up in a ball as I feel a shoe hit me.

A hand fists my hair, and my head is jerked up. Matteo kneels before me, screaming in my face, but I can't hear him. The pain is too consuming, the ringing too loud. I taste blood, and my stomach heaves as I swallow it. Thankfully, the darkness takes me sooner rather than later.

BONES

I'M SITTING IN my office; it's almost midnight, and I'm finishing an email when my door opens. I look up to see Titan enter. He plops down in the seat across from me and places his hands behind his head with a shit-eating grin on his face.

"What do you want?" I ask, not in the mood.

"You've been pissy for the past couple of weeks. More than usual. What gives?"

"Nothing," I lie.

Honestly, I don't know what the fuck is wrong with me. I've just been in a funk. But it's been longer than two weeks. It started after I promised Luca I'd do him a favor. How was I supposed to know it was for his fucking sister? I thought it would require some bullets, a little blood, and maybe digging a grave. But no. It was much deeper than I could have imagined.

I flew her to California and left her at my beach home. I've had it for years and never once used it. One of the things they don't tell you about being a multibillionaire is that if you want to stay that way, you don't get time off.

I've never been much of a vacation type of guy anyway. I prefer to keep my head in my work. I want to know every little thing going on in my business at any given second. But ever since I dropped her off, she's been on my mind.

The way her body melted into mine when I kissed her. It was as if she had no control. Just like me. It's had my mind in the gutter ever since.

"I'm about to head home." Titan stands, getting my attention. "Need me to do anything before I leave?"

I go to tell him to get the fuck out of here, but my cell rings. I pick it up to see it's Lane, a doctor we use for Kingdom. He cares for our Queens and any other time we find ourselves in a situation that requires a doctor. I frown.

"What is it?" Titan asks.

"Not sure." Holding up my cell for him to read the screen, his brows pull together. I hit answer before it can ring again. "You're on speakerphone, Lane. I'm here with Titan," I inform him in greeting.

"Bones." He sighs and adds, "Titan."

"What's going on?" Titan asks him. "Everything okay?"

"I thought you guys should know that Luca is on his way."

"What do you mean *on his way*?" I ask. "For what?" He should be working at Glass right now.

"I have to make this quick," he rushes out. "The ambulance should arrive any second."

"What the fuck are you talking about?" Titan snaps impatiently.

"Haven called me from Luca's cell. Said she found him at Glass. Thankfully, I was already here at the hospital tonight. Picked up an extra shift," he rambles.

"Get to the fucking point," Titan demands.

"All I know is multiple gunshots wounds."

"Fuck." Titan falls into his chair.

"I've done my best to keep it under wraps and quickly assembled a team that I know is the best and will keep their mouths shut. But I suggest you get here ASAP and bring NDAs. The last thing you want is for the world to know he's been shot, putting Haven in more danger than she already is." He hangs up.

"Motherfucker!" Titan jumps up from his chair and rushes out of my office to go get what we need. I find Haven's name in my phone and call her.

She picks up immediately. "Bones—"

"Lane called me." I get to the point and hear her sniff. "Titan and I are on our way. Don't speak to anyone, do you understand?" She needs to understand how dire this situation is. I can console her later.

"Y-Yes." She sobs out. "There was so much blood—"

"Not a word, Haven." I interrupt her, needing her to get her emotions under control for one second. She can cry on my shoulder when I get there. "This is important. We cannot let anyone know that he's there."

"I won't," she agrees with a sniffle.

"Be there shortly." I hang up, grab my keys out of my desk, and run to the elevator, where I meet up with Titan.

EIGHT
MIA

I SIT ON the beach with my knees pulled up to my chest, enjoying the night breeze. I'm not sure of the time. It's dark. The water looks black. It's been a few days since my brothers showed up and threatened me. I haven't slept a minute. Too afraid they're watching me and will return when they see I haven't left to go do what they ordered.

I'm starting to feel delirious. I think I'm seeing things that aren't really there. I can't be sure. One minute, the figure is standing in the corner of the bedroom, and the next, it's gone.

Dillan had left me with money and a credit card, but I'm not sure where to go. I walk into town. It's just a couple of miles away, and I enjoy the sun and fresh air. Well, I did.

When I woke up from my beating, I crawled to the bathroom, took a hot bath, then got into bed. This is the first time I've ventured out of it since. I needed to see the ocean, hear the waves, and breathe the fresh sea air. The beautiful house has been tainted. It's no longer safe, and I have no idea where to go.

My body hurts. Sometimes it's hard to breathe. I had a headache for a day straight, but it finally went away. I'm not sure how much longer I can do this. Stay up and worry about when they'll show up again.

I'm tired. Exhausted.

I need to call Luca. Dillan and Luca said not to call him, but things have changed. Dillan said Luca had him take me to keep me safe. I'm no longer safe. I'm not going to call Dillan. But maybe Luca can talk to him for me? If I call Luca and tell him everything, he could warn Dillan what my brothers and dad plan on doing. Tell him everything that I know so he has a heads-up. I don't want Dillan to die or to put the other Kings in danger. I'm not a killer like my father raised my brothers to be. But mainly, I don't want to see my father win. He doesn't deserve Kingdom. And if I don't get it for him, he'll go a different route.

Making up my mind, I push myself up to stand and make my way into the house on wobbly legs. I keep all the lights on at all times. I stumble down the hallway to the last door on the right. My cell sits on the nightstand. My only way to communicate with a world that keeps trying to get rid of me.

I haven't tried to call Luca since he told me not to. I just pray that he answers. Maybe I'll feel better after I talk to him. Maybe I'll be able to sleep once I hear his voice.

It rings once … twice … and I bite my busted lip. My stomach falls at the thought he'll ignore me.

"Hello?" a female voice answers.

"Haven?" I ask, my heart racing. Why is she answering his cell?

"Yes." She sniffs. "Who is this?"

"It's me, Mia." The fact that Luca didn't have this number saved in his phone just further proves what he had said to me when I called him. He had no intention of ever talking to me again. "I was calling to talk to my brother."

"Oh, my God …" she chokes out. "Mia. Luca … Luca's in trouble."

BONES

"Here," I say, handing Haven a cup of coffee.

"Thanks." She takes it with a yawn while wiping her tear-streaked face with her free hand.

I hand Emilee—Titan's wife—hers, and she thanks me before she returns to rubbing Haven's back.

We've been at the hospital for hours now. The sun will be coming up soon, and I'm on my third cup of coffee. The caffeine doesn't seem to be working. I'm not usually one of those guys who needs a lot of sleep, but the adrenaline has worn off, and it took what little energy I had left with it.

They have us sitting in a private room. When we arrived, a nurse was already sitting with Haven and got us up to speed on his condition. Titan took the time to get NDAs signed by anyone who had seen or heard that Luca was here except for those working on him at the moment. They will have to sign once he's out of surgery.

I walk over to the seats across from Emilee and Haven, sitting next to Titan.

"Who do you think did this?" he asks me softly so the girls can't hear. We don't want to worry Haven. But I'm sure the thought has already crossed her mind—is she next?

I shake my head, unable to answer that. *The list is a mile long.* You're not a part of the Mafia without having a hit out on you. Leaning in, I make sure to speak equally quiet. "Once we get word on his condition, I'll go up to Glass and see what I can find."

Our friend was shot. Multiple times. As far as we know, he didn't fire his weapon, which makes me think it was personal. Whoever did it knew where he'd be, and they wanted him to feel comfortable. Not aware of any threat. Otherwise, we'd be taking care of the dead body of the sorry bastard right now instead of waiting on word if Luca is going to live or die.

"You shouldn't be there alone. I'll go with you," Titan states, then pulls away, leaving no room to argue with him.

My cell rings, and I pull it out of my pocket to see it's Grave.

"Hello?" I answer, standing and walking out of the room, going down the quiet hall so the others can't hear my conversation.

"Any word?" he asks in greeting.

"No. He's still in surgery," I answer, leaning back against the wall.

He lets out a long sigh. "April is having someone open the flower shop for her. We'll be on our way shortly."

"Okay." I nod to myself.

"I spoke to Cross, and he's on his way. Should be there any moment."

Grave and Cross were already at home in bed when Titan and I arrived at the hospital. We tried calling them both, but they didn't answer. My brother puts his phone on silent when he goes to bed. If he's not at Kingdom, he's checked out. He actually likes spending time with his future wife—his exact words to me when I asked him about his phone not being on when I tried to call him one night.

"I spoke to Nigel an hour ago. He's taking care of everything up at Kingdom until we get there." There's nothing we can do for Luca here, but we're not going to leave until we know he's out of surgery. Even then, he's not going to be in the clear, but we're not leaving Haven here alone.

"One sec, babe." I hear him call out to April. "Okay, she's about ready," he informs me. "We'll be there soon." He hangs up, and I pocket my cell.

Walking back to the room, I sit down next to Titan just as the door opens behind me. I jump up and turn around, expecting it to be Lane, telling us how the surgery went or a nurse to update us, but I freeze when I see the small-framed brunette running in.

My heart picks up at the sight of her. "Mia?" I question, thinking I must be wrong. Maybe lack of sleep is making me see shit.

She stops, her long dark hair slapping her in her tear-streaked face. "Bones?" Her silvery-blue eyes widen when they meet mine.

She called me Bones, which means one of two things. Either she's realized who I was or she's known since I bought her in New York, and she pretended not to. I'm not sure which one I want to be true.

"What are you ...?"

"Mia!" Haven stands, interrupting Mia when she sees her. "Oh, my God. I'm so glad you made it." She runs over to her, pulling her in for a hug.

What the fuck is she doing here? That is all I can think while staring into her watery eyes. They stay glued to mine while her arms cling to Haven. As if she thinks her sister-in-law can save her from me.

"Tell me he's okay," she asks Haven, swallowing.

"He's in surgery," Haven answers, still holding on to her. "They won't tell us anything new."

Mia's eyes are still on mine, and I fist my hands, trying to figure out how she found out about Luca and why she would come here. She had to know her father was the one selling her. What if he were here? Why would she chance her freedom when Haven could keep her up to date with Luca's condition?

"Who the fuck is Mia?" Titan asks. With his arm on the back of my chair, he's spun around to look at them.

"I'm Luca's sister," she answers him, her eyes finally leaving mine to meet his.

I run a hand through my hair, trying to get my thoughts in line. She can't be here. She has to go.

Emilee looks surprised, and Titan looks confused. Nite looks about as shocked as I do that she's here in the flesh.

"Why are you here, Mia?" I ask, stepping around the row of chairs over to them as my shock wears off. I didn't drug her and ship her off into hiding for nothing.

"My brother was shot," she snaps, finally pulling away from Haven. "Where else would I be?"

"How did you even know—"

"I told her." Haven interrupts me.

I fist my hands. "I told you not to say anything."

"She's his sister," Haven says defensively.

"You need to go," I grind out, gripping her upper arm.

"Dillan, no ... I have to stay here." She sniffs, calling me by my first name. "I have to be with him. This is my fault."

What does she mean it's her fault? Why would she think that? "Mia ..."

"Let go of her, Bones," Haven demands, trying to pull Mia's arm free of my grip. "You're hurting her," she adds and jerks harder.

I let go and walk over to Oliver Nite-Bianchi—Luca's adopted brother—who is already pushing a sleeping Jasmine off his shoulder and getting to his feet. "I want her gone," I tell him.

He nods.

"Bones?" I hear Haven call out, but I ignore her. She's not going to change my mind.

"Now." She can't be here. What if Mr. Bianchi arrives? Her life is in danger, and I made a promise to my best friend, who may lose his life. I'm going to fucking keep it. "I want her on the jet and ready to go in an hour." I'll send her to Alaska even if I have to buy property there to keep her.

"Bones?" Haven orders.

"What?" I snap, turning to face her.

"Something's wrong," Haven cries while holding Mia.

My eyes go to her, and she's breathing heavily, her hand pressed into her side. "Mia?" I step up to her, and she looks up at me. Her pretty eyes meet mine before they roll into the back of her head, and her knees start to buckle. My arms go out, catching her before she can hit the floor.

NINE
MIA

I OPEN MY heavy eyes, my vision a little blurry. Reaching up, I rub my eyes and open them again. This time, I see I'm no longer in the waiting room but lying in a hospital bed. I sit up, and the room spins. "What?" My hand goes to my pounding head. "What happened?" I ask myself.

"You passed out," a voice announces from my right.

Looking over, I see the back of *Bones* standing at the window that I hadn't noticed. Lying back into the bed, I sigh, running a hand through my hair. "Why am I in a bed? Dear Lord, did they admit me?" Please, no. I need to be with Luca. Not here in a bed of my own.

He slowly turns to face me, hands in the front pockets of his jeans. His eyes drill into mine as if I did something wrong. *He knows.* "Not yet." He finally speaks, breaking the tense silence.

"Yet?" I shriek. "I can't—"

"They wanted to run some tests first," he adds, leaning back casually against the windowsill and crossing one ankle over the other.

I look up at the ceiling, unable to meet his intimidating stare right now. Once again, I'm vulnerable. I don't have time for this, and neither does Luca. I knew going three days and nights without sleep would catch up with me. "Luca?" I manage to get out even though my chest tightens. I've done this. Haven will never forgive me. I'll never forgive myself. I should have run the moment he left me in California. But I have nothing to my name. Not my real name. Dillan tried to give me everything that I needed, but I've never been fully on my own. I wasn't sure what to do or where to go. No job experience. No life skills that any adult would need to survive. I was raised to depend on someone else for survival.

"Still in surgery," he answers.

"How long has it been?" I swallow the knot in my throat.

"Almost six hours."

I bury my face in my hands, trying to calm my racing heart. Six hours? I know nothing about surgeries, but that seems like a long time. "This is all my fault."

"Why are you here, Mia?"

I open my eyes to see he has moved to stand at the foot of my bed. His dark blue eyes glare at me.

"I ... Luca—" My heart pounds in my chest at my betrayal. At what I've done. I can never take it back. I should have taken my brother's promise as what it was—a threat. I just never thought they'd go after Luca. But now it makes sense. He's been the one on my side. Why not take out my only ally?

He crosses his tatted arms over his chest at my lingering silence. "I'm going to ask you one more time. Why are you here?"

I fist my hands. "I told you. My brother was shot."

He tilts his head to the side. "Let's try this again. You show up with bruises in multiple places, a busted lip, and a concussion, and you expect me to believe you came back for Luca?" Shaking his head, he adds, "For the last time—why are you here?"

"What?" I breathe. I press my hand to my sore side and close my eyes. *Run tests. They know.* I hadn't thought about what I looked like when I ran to Las Vegas to be with my brother and sister-in-law. I haven't looked at myself in days, knowing it isn't a pretty sight.

"Mia." He snaps my name at my silence.

64

I bow my head and whisper, "I didn't tell them anything." He has to know I was never going to do it. That's why Luca is in surgery in the first place.

"Who?" he demands.

I want to laugh that he hasn't put it together yet, but why would he? He doesn't know my father's plan for me. For him. He's just as in the dark as Luca was.

I lift my chin and look up at him standing at the end of my bed. He's got his tatted arms crossed over his chest and legs spread wide. He's dressed in a black T-shirt and faded blue jeans. His jaw is so sharp it could cut glass. He looks extremely pissed. And he's going to want to kill me after I tell him what I know, but he deserves to know the truth. I may have been born into the Mafia, but I don't live by their moral code. I will not die protecting my father's secrets. "They came to me. Told me this would happen."

"Who the fuck is *they*, Mia?" he growls.

I ignore his impatience. "They want Kingdom," I say instead.

He snorts. I guess this isn't a surprise. Like my brother has a long list of enemies, I'm guessing the Kings do as well.

"Mia!" he shouts, and I flinch.

"My father," I rush out, looking at him through my dark lashes, and add softly, "he wants *your* Kingdom."

He just stares at me with a look of annoyance in his cold eyes. I'm nothing more than a problem for him. Just like I am for everyone else.

Licking my busted lip, I sigh. "A few days ago, my brothers came to me—the twins and Matteo—and told me to go back to you. To do whatever was necessary to make you fall in love with me and marry me." I sniff. "My father wants you dead along with the rest of the Kings. He wants your Kingdom," I lower my voice. "And he wants me to do it."

His silence continues.

"I wasn't going to do it." I shake my head, unable to meet his eyes after my confession. How stupid my father must think Bones is to fall for me—a woman he didn't even know existed. He knows that I have no experience. He kissed me, and I froze. I didn't even know what to do. I have nothing to offer other than my body. A woman is only good for one thing in my family. And I'm sure Bones gets that anywhere. "I swear. I—"

"How are you feeling, miss?" a nurse enters the room asking, and I'm thankful for the interruption. It's hard to breathe in here with Bones also occupying the room. I need some space and fresh air. It's like I'm back in the limo with his hand around my throat.

"Fine." I throw the blanket off me. "How is Luca?"

"He just got out of surgery and is being moved to the ICU. The doctor will come and speak to you further about it."

I nod.

"This is good news, miss."

"Thank you. May I see him?" I ask.

She gives me a kind smile. Practiced to perfection. I feel she'd give me the same if she had to tell me he'd passed away due to his injuries. "I'm sorry, but not at the moment."

The door closes, and I'm left alone with him once again. I can't even meet his eyes now. Too ashamed. Embarrassed. Luca is all that I have, and my own family wanted to take him from me. How far will they go now if Luca dies? They'll blame me for that as well.

BONES

"Say something," she whispers, keeping her eyes on the bed.

I have nothing to say. I know what her father wants. Does she think he just decided to take what's mine? He's not going to get it. No matter how much pussy he tries to throw at me.

I uncross my arms and run my hand through my hair. My newest concern is her and my best friend, who is fighting for his life.

Three days ago, they showed up and smacked her around. Informed her she would pay the ultimate price for not obeying their command. "Why didn't you call me?"

Her eyes slowly look up to meet mine.

"Why didn't you call me when they showed up at the house? I told you to call me if you needed anything." I had only left her one number in her cell, and it was under Dillan. I was afraid if she knew me as Bones, she would have been too afraid to reach out to me. I thought Dillan made me sound more relatable and kind. Thinking about it now, I realize that sounds stupid since I almost choked her out and then drugged her.

"You kidnapped me. Drugged me," she growls, hearing my thoughts, and my eyes narrow on her. "Then shipped me away. Why would I call someone who didn't want anything to do with me?"

I fist my hands. I did that to save her. To get her as far away from me as possible, yet here she is with bruises. They used Luca to get what they wanted. How far are they willing to go?

She glares up at me, looking so small in that big bed. Her dark hair is down and tangled in multiple places. Her silvery-blue eyes look dull and tired. Her pouty lips are dry. She looks as malnourished as she was when I bought her. Why hasn't she been taking care of herself? "How long were they there?" I ask instead, needing to know the details.

"I don't know." She shrugs. "After he shoved me to the floor and kicked me, I passed out. When I woke up, they were gone."

My jaw clenches. "Did they all touch you?" Three men against a woman is horrible enough, but then for it to be someone her size? Not to mention they're her fucking brothers. They wanted to scare her, rough her up, but not to the point of killing her. No, they wanted her to come crawling back to me, pretending to need help. Giving me the chance to be the savior and fall for the damsel in distress. And when she didn't, they went after Luca, knowing that would do it. It's the one person who means anything to her. He's never betrayed her—not like the rest of her family has anyway.

She shakes her head. "Matteo did all the work."

Just then, the door opens again, and Haven runs in. "Oh, my God, Mia." She rushes over to her bed and hugs her tightly. "The nurse told me you were up and talking," Haven adds. "I had to see you."

I turn and exit the room and begin to pace the empty hallway. Looking up, I see Lane walking toward me, still dressed in his bloody scrubs. I swallow, meeting him halfway.

"Luca—?"

"He's stable. For now." He places his hands on his hips, and I let out a long breath. "But he's not out of the woods."

I nod, figuring that would be the case. "And Mia? Were you able to look at her test results?" I didn't want anyone else looking at them. One less person we have to give an NDA to.

I already knew nothing was broken, but they ran other tests as well once it was clear she had been beaten. Add the fact that her brother had been shot. I wanted him to be very thorough.

"Rape tests came back negative, along with pregnancy test. As you were told earlier, she most likely had a concussion from the head laceration found, but it's too late for us to tell now."

I didn't expect her brothers would rape her, but you never fucking know. I wouldn't put anything past them at this point. "Anything else?"

"She was dehydrated, and my guess is she hasn't slept in days. Maybe due to the attack. Victims react differently to any kind of trauma. Add sleep deprivation, starvation, and stress regarding Luca, and that could be your cause of the fainting."

"What do you suggest for recovery?" I ask. My concern now is to make sure I keep her safe. I can't allow her and Luca to both die.

"Honestly, it won't take her long to bounce back. She needs to eat regularly. Even if she's not hungry. I'm going to write her a prescription for nausea pills in case she gets sick. The best thing for her now is rest."

I nod, stepping back.

"I need to speak to Haven."

"She's in Mia's room." I point at her door, and he walks past me to speak to them privately.

Leaning back against the wall, I close my eyes, running a hand down my face. Now what the fuck do I do?

"He's been placed in a private ICU room," Titan speaks, walking down the hall to me. "As you requested. And in his own wing. NDAs have been signed."

I nod toward Mia's door. "Lane is speaking to Haven and Mia now."

His eyes slide over to it, but he doesn't bring up the elephant in the room—who is she, and how do I know her. Instead, he says, "I'm going to order around-the-clock private security for Luca."

"You can never be too careful," I agree with him.

"And her? Want the same?"

"She won't be here much longer." She'll get released today. There's nothing they can do for Mia. She should have sought immediate treatment when she was assaulted. I would say that the fact Luca was shot helped her. Otherwise, she would have passed out alone in my beach home. But then again, he was shot because of her, or so she thinks.

Hearing the door to Mia's room open, I look over to see Haven exit and literally charge toward me.

"You and Mia can stay at my house," I tell her. Titan, Grave, and Cross will be next door. It's our very own private, gated community. No one goes in or out without the Kings' knowledge. "Your house won't be safe, and someone needs to watch over her." I'm never home anyway. I live at Kingdom.

"I'm not going anywhere," she states.

"Haven ..." I grind out her name, not in the mood to argue with her.

"When I'm not in Luca's room, I will be at our house."

"I'm afraid you can't stay there," I tell her. Luca is going to live, and I can't risk the Bianchi brothers going to their house and hurting Haven. Luca wouldn't want to live if his wife was killed.

"Then I'll stay here with Luca," she offers. "But I think it'll be fine. Honestly, I'll have Nite hire extra security for the house. He can stay there with Mia."

"No. Haven ..."

"I understand that you've never loved anyone, *Dillan*," she snaps my real name, and my jaw tightens. "But my husband has been shot! And I'm not fucking leaving him." With that, she stomps off down the hall.

Titan arches a brow as if to ask me what I expected her to do. Not everyone is as coldhearted as me. Instead of defending myself, I walk away, needing to get a few things in order for Haven since she's going to be stubborn. But she was right about one thing, Luca's and her house needs extra security. Even though Mia thinks this has to do with her, it doesn't mean that whoever did this doesn't have other opportunities in mind.

TEN
MIA

I'M PULLING MY socks and shoes on. The doctor came and saw me an hour ago. He filled Haven and me in on Luca and said that the paperwork had been started for my release. He gave me a couple of prescriptions but said the main thing I needed was rest.

I'm not going to get any. Not when my brother is here in a drug-induced coma. Haven has been keeping me updated since the doctor informed us what happened to him. Turns out, Luca had been shot twice. Once in the chest and the other in his leg. That's why surgery took so long. They thought he was going to lose his leg but were able to save it. He's stable, but it's still an uphill climb.

The door opens, and I look up to see Dillan entering. I finish tying my tennis shoes and grab my purse off the bed. "I'm leaving."

"You'll wait for the nurse to escort you out in a wheelchair," he replies flatly.

I push my hip out. "I'm fine."

"It's hospital policy."

"Oh." I've never been in one before. He could be lying to me. I look up at him, and he's staring at me intently. Blue eyes scrutinize my busted lip and ratted hair. I tried to brush it, but it needs to be washed. I have long, thick hair. It's always tangled easily.

"Do you have any news on Luca?" I ask, wondering why he's back in here. I haven't seen him since he left when Haven came to see me.

"You're coming home with me," he states.

I laugh at that. A deep, doubled-over laugh that makes my already sore side hurt. "I would have never guessed you to be a comedian, Bones."

"I'm serious, Mia."

My laughter stops. His eyes give nothing away, but his fisted hands do. He doesn't want me to go with him as much as I don't want to be around him. "I don't need your help," I growl and head toward the door.

He steps in front of me, making me halt. "Actually, you've proven that you can't take care of yourself."

"I don't need a babysitter," I snap.

He steps forward, closing the small distance between us, and I tilt my head back to look up at him. His height is intimidating.

I hate the way my stomach flutters when he's this close. That all I can think about is the kiss he gave me before he turned and left me behind at his beach house. And the way he stared at me in the limo. The way his eyes looked over my body like he wanted it. Feeling anything for him is a big no. Not like he'd feel anything other than annoyance for me, but still. My family will make sure that I'm never happy. And I hate the fact that I even like how he stared at me—I'm not a piece of meat. Not to him, not to anyone. But when you've been ignored all your life, the first sign of any attention makes my body heat rise.

"When was the last time you slept?" he demands.

I frown at the odd question. "I just woke up ..."

"You passed out," he corrects me. "When was the last time you ate anything?"

Huffing, I cross my arms over my chest. "You are not my ..." I trail off.

"Not your what?" He smirks, liking the fact that he intimidates me.

Fuck him. "I almost said father. But in a way, you're just like him." I'm not going to hold back when it comes to this King. I don't have to. If I piss him off, maybe he'll let me go.

That smirk falls off his face, and he steps even closer, his chest now bumping into mine, and I hold my breath. "Be very careful about what you say, Mia," he warns.

It just makes those butterflies intensify. "Why?" I ask, straightening my shoulders, not willing to back down from him. Weakness is deadly in my family. And no matter how terrified I am of him, I won't show it. "Are you going to ship me away again?" Please do. It'll save us both a lot of trouble.

I watch the way his blue eyes darken while he glares down at mine, hands fisted by his sides, and I know by the way he's breathing that he's trying to calm himself. I can only imagine what kind of man he is when he doesn't hold himself back.

"Do it." I bait him. "Put your hands around my throat and choke me out. Just like you did the last time I was with you." Dillan is a fucking bastard. I remember the stories about him and the Kings as kids. It was my thirteenth birthday when my father shipped me away. The Kings and Luca were six years older than me. Well, except for Grave, who was a year younger than the rest. He was only five years older than me. But I overheard stories about the Kings, and they were already tearing up Vegas. It wasn't hard to figure out what kind of men they would grow up to be.

He lifts his hand, and I flinch. That smirk returns to his lips. He opens his fist and runs his tatted knuckles down my face. The skull ring is cold against my skin. My breathing hitches, and my knees threaten to buckle. The last time he touched me, he kissed me. My lips part on their own at that thought. "If that's what will get you some rest. I'm a problem solver."

My heart begins to pound in my chest at how easily he threatens me. That memory of him choking me out in the limo comes to mind. He was strong, and I was too weak. I swallow the fear, trying to calm my heart and arch a brow. "Then fucking do it." I'm not sure if I want him to choke me or kiss me. At this point, I think I'd welcome either one.

The door opens, and I step away from him, taking in a shaky breath. His hand falls to his side. "Hello, miss." The nurse from earlier enters with a wheelchair. "You ready to get out of here?" She smiles at me, then looks at him. "I've been told by Dr. Lane that she's going home with you."

My stomach sinks. *The doctor?* What did he say for the doctor to allow this?

"She is," he confirms.

"Great." She nods once. "If you want to pull your car up to the entrance, we'll meet you out there."

He exits the room, and I sit in the wheelchair with my purse on my lap. "Have you seen Haven Bianchi?" Maybe if I can find her, I can talk her into going to her and Luca's house.

"Yes, ma'am. Bones spoke to Dr. Lane, and he pulled some strings. Luca was placed in a private ICU room in his own wing, and she is going to be staying with him."

Bones spoke to Dr. Lane? Haven gets to stay with him?

I slump back in the wheelchair and cling to my purse. Why would Dillan do that for her? Maybe it's for Luca? All of them are friends. I'm the outcast. The burden.

She pushes me out into the harsh afternoon light. My eyes squint to see a matte black car sitting at the entrance. Looks like something he would drive. Sleek and expensive. Probably a limited edition. I'm sure it cost him what would feed a small country for a year.

"Here we go," the nurse says cheerfully. She's happy that I get to leave the hospital. That's their goal. I want to trip and fall flat on my face, so she'll have to admit me again. At least that'd mean I'd get to stay closer to Luca.

I stand from the wheelchair, and he walks around the front of his car to open his passenger door for me. I fall into it, and he slams it shut. Just further showing me how aggravated he is about this situation.

I look over the black interior and close my eyes. The car smells like his cologne that night in the limo. Clean, like fresh linen. When his hands were on me, his face inches from mine. Then I remember the kiss. It would be innocent to someone else but to me? Goose bumps rise along my arms at that thought, and I shiver. It was my first. I doubt he knows that. And if he had, I doubt he would have done it.

He gets in the driver's seat and pulls away from the entrance. I hold in a sigh at how close I am to Luca. At least I know Haven is with him. Luca wouldn't want to see me anyway, even if he was conscious. He'd be so disappointed in me right now for multiple reasons.

"Why did you talk the doctor into letting Haven stay in Luca's room?" I ask him. I feel like Dillan isn't the type of guy to lie to you. He'll tell you the truth no matter how much you hate to hear it.

"Because she wanted to be with her husband," comes his cold reply.

"Well, I wanted to be with my brother," I snap at him.

He ignores me, placing his left wrist on the steering wheel. My eyes slide along his tatted and muscular arms and notice the way his black T-shirt is tight against his broad shoulders. My eyes continue to the ink on his neck. It comes all the way to his defined jaw. It makes him look evil and sexy at the same time. Like something forbidden but unable to stay away from. The type of guy any mother wouldn't want her daughter to date. Not for love anyway. No, a man like Dillan is a fuck you and leave you when he gets bored—which probably wouldn't take long. I'm sure his phone is full of women he could call at any time, and they'd crawl on their hands and knees for him to give them a second of his time.

When he turns his head, his blue eyes meet mine for a quick

second before he looks away, catching me staring, but he remains silent.

Closing my eyes, I lean my head back on the headrest and take in a deep breath. It's going to be a very long stay in Las Vegas because I'm not leaving until my brother wakes up, and I won't be running away after that either. This time, he'll have to be the one who physically ships me away.

BONES

I PULL THROUGH the black iron gate of our property that has a gold K in the middle. The Kings and I have a compound of over two hundred acres with our own private security, where we each built a house. We used to live at Kingdom, but the others have fallen in love over the past year and now spend their nights here rather than at Kingdom. Except for me. I prefer our Royal Floor on the fiftieth floor over living here.

Pulling up to my house, I drive under the breezeway and around the back into the garage. I shut off the car and look over at Mia. Her head rests on the headrest, tilted to face the passenger window.

I sit and wait for her to look over at me. To give me that glare she does so well, but it doesn't come. "Mia?" I ask, reaching out to her. I place my hand on her shoulder, giving her a soft shake, and her head falls to face me, hair covering most of it. I push it back behind her ear. "Mia?" I ask again.

Her plump lips are slightly parted, and her eyes are closed, her long thick eyelashes resting on her bruised cheeks. My eyes drop to her chest, and I watch it rise and fall evenly with each breath. She passed out.

A part of me is relieved. She needed this, and I didn't want to choke her out to accomplish it. The fact that she challenged me in her hospital room to do so turned me on. And I hate that. Mia Bianchi is not for me. Even if I want her. There isn't a man on this planet who would say she's not attractive. There's a reason her father kept her hidden from the world all of her life—because she is a weapon. To use at his convenience.

I get out of my car and walk around to the passenger side. Opening up the door, I bend down and place one arm under her legs, the other behind her back, and lift her out of the car, closing the door with my hip.

I enter my house through the garage, passing the laundry and mudroom. Walking farther down the long hallway, I push open the last door on the right—my bedroom.

I lay her on the bed, and she doesn't even move. She's on her back with her arms out to her sides. I walk to the end of the bed and remove her shoes and socks, placing them on the bench. Then I walk back over to her. I stare down at her face and run my thumb over the split on the corner of her lip.

I kept my word to Luca, got my hands on a ticket, flew to New York, bought her, met up with Tristan, drugged her, and shipped her off. Yet here she is, sleeping in my bed in Las Vegas. She wears a pink T-shirt and denim shorts. Staring down at her body, I look over her legs. She has a bruise on her knee. A small one on her thigh. And I know under her shirt, she has more.

And that brings up another question—*how in the fuck did they know where she was?* And why? Luca said that they wouldn't want her. That his father wouldn't care where she went as long as he got his money. So my question is, who is actually after her? Her brothers or her father? As bad as it sounds, why did they stop? Mia had said that she passed out, and when she woke, they were gone. If it's all about the money, her father has already been paid the ten million. Why not kill her right then and there?

I guess I could have hidden her better and not sent her to one of my vacation homes. It's my fault. She said they told her to return to *me*. But the auction was supposed to be anonymous. How do they know I was the one who bought her?

I thought shipping her away was the right thing. I run my knuckles over her chin and down her neck. I can feel her pulse, slow and steady.

Now what the fuck do I do?

ELEVEN
MIA

I WAKE IN a dark room. I sit up and run my hands down my T-shirt. I'm still dressed, but my shoes and socks are gone. My hands roam along the bed next to me for my phone but don't find it. Leaning to the other side, I find a nightstand and touch something that feels like a lamp. I twist the knob at the top, and it lights up the room.

Walls the color of a thunderstorm rolling in. Black hardwood floors with a dark gray area rug. A black four-post bed sits in the center. I lie on top of black silk sheets and matching pillowcases.

I get out of the bed and sway on my feet. Thick black curtains run along the far wall. I walk over, shoving them open to reveal an Olympic-size swimming pool and hot tub attached, but I can't see much else. It's too dark.

"How long was I asleep?" I ask myself through a yawn.

"Almost twelve hours."

I spin around at the sound of his voice and place my hand on my chest as he enters a set of open double doors. "Dillan," I breathe. "What are you doing here?"

"I live here," he states, bringing a tray over to the side of the bed. He sets it down and then starts to walk over to me.

I stand like a statue, trying to remember what happened last. I was at the hospital. They discharged me ... car ride ... I closed my eyes just for a second—that's the last thing I remember. "How did I ...?" I stop that stupid question. There's only one way I got into this house— he carried me and removed my socks and shoes. The thought makes my cheeks redden. I keep finding myself in vulnerable positions with him.

He stops before me and reaches out, running his hands down my side, and I hold my breath, hating that I like the way he's always touching me. "How do your ribs feel?"

My eyes lift to his when his hands pause, but he doesn't pull them away. He's the first man to ever touch me at all, in the limo, California, here in his room. My heart races, and the blood rushes in my ears. I hope he doesn't notice how my breath hitches at the contact. "Fine," I lie. My side still hurts. "Why did you let me sleep for so long?"

"You needed it." He steps back, his hands falling from my body.

The fact that he no longer touches me allows me to think clearly and helps me remember why I'm here, making my eyes narrow on him. "I need to be with my brother."

"I just hung up with Haven. He's not any worse, not any better. And you can't go see him."

I let out a long breath. "I don't need your permission to do something."

"Technically, I own you," he says as if he's talking about buying a car. Like I'm something so insignificant that can be bought and sold like an object.

My blood instantly boils at those words. "Don't say that." I manage to get out through gritted teeth.

"Or what?" He tilts his head.

This has been my life for twenty years. Men owning me. First my father, but then he sold me, hoping that some bastard would buy me and he could take over their fortune. I'm a card to be played. A toy to be used. Just because Dillan doesn't share my blood doesn't mean he has any less power over what I do, who I see, and where I go. I'm just as powerless with him as I have been all my life.

"That's what I thought," he says before turning his back to me and exiting the room.

I bite my lip and turn to face out the window again. I miss Italy. I didn't realize how much I loved that prison. I spent most of my days in the pool. Maybe that's what I need. Silence.

I unlock the sliding glass door, walk outside and begin to remove my clothes. I need to feel free. I need to clear my head. This is the only place I have to do it.

BONES

I WALK BACK into my master suite to go take a shower. I've been in my study here at the house for the last twelve hours while she slept. I need to go to Kingdom, but my ass could use a shower first. I go to enter the bathroom but stop when I look through the sliding glass door to see she is by the pool.

She has her back to me while she stands at the edge of the shallow end. She reaches down and removes her shirt up and over her head. Her hair falls down, covering her bruised back. Then she pushes her shorts down her thin legs and kicks them to the side, exposing a black cotton thong.

I walk over to the sliding glass door and watch as she slowly walks down the steps, sinking her injured body into the water. It's dark out, but the pool lights illuminate the water. She slowly sinks into it, holding her breath. Pushing off the wall, not swimming very far and pops her head up, taking in a breath before turning around and coming back, knowing her body is in no condition to go all the way to the deep end.

She pops out again, her head back, and she pushes her dark hair from her face. I see her flinch at how sore her body must be while trying to take it easy. I should go out there and pull her out of it. Tell her that she's not allowed to swim yet. Her body needs time to heal. But I don't. Instead, I stand here watching her like a weirdo.

Her eyes open and lock on mine. She ducks into the water, covering her chest. I hate to tell her I've already seen her practically naked in that video her brother showed me.

I shove open the glass door and step outside into the hot night. "I'm going to go into Kingdom for a few hours. We'll go up to the hospital to grab the car when I get back."

She frowns. "What car?"

"I assume you drove my car." She tilts her head to the side. "The one I had parked at the beach house." I have a Bentley Continental GT that I leave there. I'm quite glad that she drove it back. It just sits there and never sees daylight. It needs to be driven. She can drive here while she stays with me.

"Oh." Her eyes lower, and drops of water run off her long lashes. "It's still there."

"At the hospital, yes, I know."

"No, it's still in Malibu."

I frown. "Then how did you get here?"

"Haven sent me their private jet. That's why it took me so long to arrive. I had to wait for it to pick me up in California."

It's only a little over an hour flight, and the drive time is about five hours. But it would have been easier to drive than wait for the jet to arrive. "Why didn't you just drive?" The keys were there hanging in the garage. I didn't want her to be stranded.

"I don't know how," she whispers.

"How do you not know how to drive?" I snort.

She still hovers under the water, right up against the side, shielding her body from me. Her arms still cover her breasts, and her hair floats around her like a black cloud. Her silvery-blue eyes meet mine. "I was never offered that opportunity of freedom."

I run a hand through my hair. *Jesus!* Why didn't Luca at least teach her these things? Everyday options that we take for granted.

"I'll teach you." I decide. The woman needs to know how to drive a damn car.

Her eyes light up, and she stands to her full height, so the water comes to her chest instead of her neck. A smile so wide that it lights up her gorgeous face. Fuck, my dick twitches in my jeans. "You will?"

I clear my throat. "Of course. Everyone should know how to drive a car."

She bites her bottom lip, and her eyes look up at me with a softness that makes my chest tighten. "Thank you, Dillan," she whispers, and my breath catches at the way she says my name. It's the first time without a bite. Plus, no one ever calls me by my name. It's always Bones.

I wave her off. "I'll be back in a few hours." Then I turn and walk out of the bedroom, not even bothering with that shower. Because if I do, I'll be jacking off in there imagining her topless in my pool.

I'M SITTING BEHIND MY DESK WHEN TITAN ENTERS MY OFFICE. "You're here early this morning." We haven't even had our daily meeting in the conference room yet.

"What do you want?" I ask without even looking up at him.

"What's wrong with you?" he asks, sitting down.

I place my elbows on the desk and glare at him. "Last chance. What do you want?"

He just smirks. "So Mia?" I sigh, knowing this conversation would come. "Who knew that Luca had a little sister."

Yeah, who the fuck knew? "I didn't." *Lie.* Even if I didn't remember her, I knew she existed. I just never would have guessed she was a Bianchi.

Reaching up, he runs his hand down over his face. "What are you going to do with her?"

"Excuse me?" I ask, blinking. He makes it sound like she's something I can just return.

"Well, the world has no idea she exists. How are you going to keep that under wraps?"

I sit back in my seat.

"Look ... by the way I saw you and Nite react to her running into the hospital, you two knew she existed. I'm not even going to ask how. But she's obviously been in hiding. Now she's out." He spreads his tatted arms out wide. "The Bianchis have a lot of enemies—case in point, our friend is currently in a coma after being shot—and Mia making her presence known to the world could cause even more problems. For her. For you. The Bianchis in general."

I never thought about that. Luca said she was to be used as a weapon, but what would happen if someone actually got their hands on her? Her father wouldn't give a shit what happened to her. He proved that by selling her off to the highest bidder. She said he wants Kingdom, but the dots don't line up. If someone else had bought her, who knows where she'd be right now. He got his money already. Did her father send her back here because he knows I was the one who purchased her? Names were never used in the private auction. I didn't have to sign anything. We paid our table fee in cash, and that was that. The wire transfer was untraceable. If someone were to leak any information about the auctions—you'd be killed. No questions asked. So that makes me wonder how they know I did it.

I try to tell myself she's not my problem, but then I think of Luca. I can't allow someone to use him against her like that. I can't go to her brothers for help. They already gave her a timeline before they came after her again.

"Call a meeting," I tell him. "The conference room in thirty. And text Nite. I want him there too."

He nods and gets up without saying another word. Picking up my phone, I make a couple of phone calls.

An hour later, I walk into our conference room to see my brother, Titan, Cross, along with Nite already seated at the custom-made black table that easily sits twenty people. A skull is carved out of the middle, and Kingdom is written in gold at each end. This is where we conduct all our business meetings. We've got jammers blocking any type of electrical devices in here.

"You're late," my brother announces, checking his watch.

I snort. Like he's never been late for a meeting before. Hell, there were days that went by, and none of us even knew where he was.

"What's this about?" he asks when I don't acknowledge his previous statement.

Cross gives a chuckle. "I can guess."

Sitting at the head of the table, I toss some folders onto the center and speak. "We've got a problem."

"Well, you'll have to be a little more specific." My brother laughs, reaching out for one.

"The Bianchis," I add.

Grave's jaw sharpens, opening it up. "What about them?"

"Mia is meant to steal Kingdom," I announce.

Silence falls over the room, and each one looks up at me. Then the Kings start to laugh, and even Nite smiles. The guy is mute. We all have our weapon of choice, and he's picked silence. "How's she going to do that exactly?" Cross questions.

"She's supposed to marry me," I answer.

All laughter comes to a stop, and I lean back in my seat.

"Wait ... what?" Grave asks, his eyes quickly scanning over the papers in front of him, double-checking it's not a marriage license or something. Making sure I haven't lost my mind.

Cross shakes his head.

"You're serious?" Titan sounds skeptical, not even bothering to pick his folder up.

I nod. "Luca came to me about four weeks ago. Showed me a video of Mia. She had been sex trafficked—"

"Fuck," Titan hisses, interrupting me.

"Told me she was being shipped to New York. I made a phone call, got an invite to an auction, and bought her," I explain in the simplest way possible.

"Tell me you're kidding." Grave growls. "Why are you giving us medical records then?" He gestures to the open folder in front of him. "Who do they belong to?"

I go on. "I shipped her off to live in my Malibu home. Everything was going well. Then three days ago, Matteo and the twins somehow found her at my beach house. Told her to come back—her father wants Kingdom, and he's going to use her to get it."

Cross pushes his seat back and stands over by the floor-to-ceiling windows. Pulling his Zippo out, he starts fidgeting with it.

"Then ship her back," Grave demands. "Somewhere they won't fucking find her."

That's not going to work. "She refused them." He snorts, not believing that. "When she told them no, they gave her three months to make me fall in love with her, marry her, and her dad will have Kingdom."

Titan scoffs. "Shit don't work that way."

Grave places his elbows on the table and runs his hands through his hair. "Unless she married Bones, and then he kills them both off." He shrugs. "Then he's got a forged trust that leaves his shares of Kingdom over to him and of course whatever he makes up on Mia's behalf."

"It still doesn't work that way," Titan argues.

"It'll work however John Bianchi wants to spin it," Grave snaps at him. "Look at what George did to Emilee."

Titan's jaw sharpens at the mention of his wife and her father. "You guys are looking at this the wrong way." He shifts in his seat. "John has nothing if he doesn't have Mia. So ..." He lifts his hands out wide. "He can't get what she doesn't have access to."

"Just what are you suggesting we do exactly?" Cross asks, spinning around to face us.

"We take care of—"

"Don't you dare say we kill her," I interrupt him.

Titan sighs. "Don't tell me you haven't thought about it."

I ignore that comment. "No. We're not killing her. She's innocent."

Grave snorts. "So she says." My brother argues.

I fist my hands on the table. "She refused to return to Las Vegas after they assaulted her, and then three days later, Luca is shot. Don't you think that's a big coincidence?"

Nite just stands there, staring at the table, and I can see his mind trying to play catch up. See if there's anything he missed.

"Wait a minute." Grave lifts his finger. "Are you saying that you think Luca's brother shot him to lure her back here?"

"That's exactly what I think." I nod.

"The Bianchis are ruthless," Titan adds.

"Are these Luca's medical records?" Grave asks, frowning and picking his folder up once again. "Did they fuck him up before they shot him?"

"No. They're Mia's."

"What do you mean?" Cross growls. "And why do you have them?"

"I spoke with Lane. They beat her up and left her there at my beach house. Mia thinks that because she didn't come running to me in Vegas, they went after the only person she loves."

"So what do we do?" Cross asks, flipping his Zippo open and closed.

"It's simple. Bones doesn't get married. John can't do shit without that connection," Grave answers. "I mean, he's not going to marry her." He laughs like that's absurd.

"Then you're putting a timeline on Mia's life," Titan argues as if he cares if she dies. "If she was given three months, then what will happen at the end of that time?"

"We'll worry about it then." Grave shrugs, looking at me. "But in the meantime, I'd hide her so fucking well that even you forget where you put her."

I sit down and sigh, knowing he's right. I can't protect her. Not like she needs. The more miles between us, the better. If she stays here, her brothers will think she's just useless and kill her. If I send her away, they'll think she's useless and kill her. Or worse, sell her again.

"Hear me out," Titan goes on. "What if he did marry her?"

Grave snorts, and Cross laughs.

"I'm serious," he argues. "You marry her but have an airtight prenup. A spouse can only get a percentage of what you have once you get married. He had Kingdom shares before he married her. Therefore, she can't touch it."

"Too risky." Cross shakes his head.

"Is that what you and Emilee did?" Grave arches a brow, looking at Titan. "Did you do an airtight prenup?"

"No," Titan growls as if that's ridiculous. "I married my wife because I love her, not because I was cornered."

"Bones isn't backed into a corner," Grave argues. "For all we know, Mia is lying." He points at me. "How many women have tried to get what we have? A lot. It's not uncommon for women to use their pussy for a payday."

A silence falls over the room while everyone stares at him. He arches a brow. "Are you all suggesting that April got pregnant on purpose?" he demands.

"You said it." Titan shakes his head. "Not us."

Grave shoves the papers off the table and starts to climb up on it to get to Titan, but Cross grabs the back of his shirt, yanking him back.

"You motherfucker—"

"Enough!" I shout, interrupting Grave and standing from my chair.

Titan sighs. "None of us think that April was trying to trap you." He throws his hands up in surrender. "But this affects us all. If John gets one foot in, he will find a way to get it all."

That's why I told them. I've always been a very secretive person. What I do is no one else's business, but this does include them. We are all equal partners. If one is attacked, we are all under attack.

"Maybe we're looking at it from the wrong angle," Cross says slowly, shoving Grave into his seat. "We find who went after Luca first. You said that Mia has a timeline?" He looks at me, and I nod. "Then we've got time there. But whoever shot Luca could be getting away as we speak. So let's start there first and then circle back when need be."

"Where do we start?" Grave asks, placing his hands in his hair. "We have nothing to go on."

"Glass," I answer when everyone looks at me. "That's where he was shot. We've got surveillance. If no one saw anything, the cameras did." I've been too busy since I brought Mia home from the hospital that I haven't had the chance to go to Glass yet. I was going to watch the cameras there, but I can do it from here just as good.

We all enter my office, and I pull up the surveillance at Glass on my computer. After logging in and going back to yesterday, we watch it as the screen goes black.

"Well, that's convenient." Cross sighs.

"Here ..." I take a piece of paper from the black Kingdom stationery—it's got a gold circle and K in the middle—and I write down an address. "Titan, you and Nite go get him and bring him back here. We'll meet you downstairs."

"Got it." Titan nods before he and Nite turn and exit my office.

My brother turns to face me. "You've never been that guy who thinks with his dick, so don't start now." Then he storms out.

"Ignore Grave," Cross tells me, and I wave off his concern.

But little does he know, my dick is screaming pretty loud right now. And all I can think of is Mia lying naked in my bed underneath me with my hand wrapped around her throat again.

TWELVE

MIA

I DIDN'T SWIM for very long. My side hurt too much to actually enjoy it. Instead, I sat in the shallow end, just soaking up the night heat.

Getting out of the shower, I enter his bedroom and see a door to the right. Hoping it's a closet, I smile when I'm right. It's large—the floor is white marble with a black inlay design in the shape of diamonds, and it's cold on my bare feet. To my right is a set of dresser drawers. I open the top one up and see watches of various colors and sizes—all expensive designer brands. The second drawer is full of cuff links. Shutting it, I turn and look around to see the rows and rows of clothes hanging. To the left is nothing but shoes—everything from tennis shoes to boots to dress shoes. Some are still in their boxes.

Stepping up to one of the racks, I run my fingers over the dress shirts, feeling the softness of the fabric. I come to his T-shirts and drop the towel from around my chest. Standing up on my tiptoes, I remove a black one. It says Kingdom in gold letters on it. I slide it on. One shoulder hangs off, the sleeves come down to my elbows, and the hem reaches mid-thigh. It's huge, but I have nothing to wear here. Plus, it's really soft and smells like him.

When Haven told me what happened to Luca, I panicked, grabbed what I could, which was only my phone and purse, called an Uber, and got to the private airport as fast as I could. I don't know how I'll get my stuff here.

Opening another drawer, I find his boxer briefs. I don't have any extra underwear, and I refuse to go without. I pull on a black pair and roll the band down a few times, hoping that will help keep them up.

Exiting the closet, I turn off the light and then leave the bedroom. It's on the first floor. I walk down the hallway to an opening. It's the living room. It too looks like no one is ever here. Bare, dark gray walls, and no throw pillows, blankets, or decorations of any kind.

I turn around the corner and walk up the stairs. My bare feet sink into the plush carpet while my hand grips the dark banister. I make it to the top and take a right. The second door on the left is partially open, so I step inside.

It's a media room. I recognize it because my father's house in Italy had one. It's got a huge screen at the front of the room. Three rows of five black leather chairs that have blue neon lights underneath them.

The back wall has shelves of movies on it. I walk over, scanning the DVDs, and come across what looks to be a photo album. I remember my mother saying that she would make me one but never did. Not sure why I'd need pictures to remind me of a nonexistent childhood.

Picking it up, I sit down on the floor cross-legged and open it up. The first page has a picture of Dillan and a woman. I've seen her before. At the hospital. Dark hair, blue eyes. I don't know her name. But she's standing in a hallway with him. Looks like a school, but I can't be sure. I've never been, just from what I've seen on TV shows. He's got his arm over her shoulders. She's holding a Louis Vuitton purse in one hand and her cell in the other. She's got a bright smile on her face. He stares at the camera, looking almost numb. The flash illuminates his hard blue eyes and sharp jaw. He doesn't have any tattoos that I can see—not like he does now—and it makes him look so young. He's wearing a white T-shirt with jeans. She's dressed in designer heels, a skirt, and a sweater. She's leaning into him, both arms wrapped around his waist.

I flip the page and see another picture of him. He's on a baseball field this time. Dressed in a blue-and-white uniform that says Wildcats on it, he's got a bat in one hand, a ball in the other, and he's smiling. One that shows off his dazzling smile and two dimples. He's beautiful.

Turning again. I see another picture, and I frown. He's wearing a T-shirt like I have on, but it's white with black letters reading Kingdom across the chest. He still doesn't have any visible ink. He stands there with my brother Luca in a hallway next to a set of glass double doors. I tilt my head to the side. "Why does this look familiar?" I whisper to myself. "Like I've seen this before." I didn't know him. I never met the Kings ...

Twelve years old

I WALK DOWN A HALLWAY AND COME TO A STOP WHEN I SEE A GUY standing at the other end.

Luca has a visitor? It's not uncommon for my brothers to have friends over. But I'm always told to stay in my room whenever they have someone over.

His body stiffens, and he starts to turn around, but I run down the hallway and into my room. "Hello? Luca?" he calls out.

I slam the door shut.

"Luca, this isn't funny," he growls.

The door is shoved open, and I jump back with a shriek when the boy enters my space.

Blue eyes quickly scan the room and then land on me, and I drop mine to my bare feet.

"What are you doing in here?" he asks. "Who are you?" he questions, stepping farther into my room.

"I asked you a question," he snaps when I don't answer.

I jump back but look up at him, my heart racing. My breathing is erratic. No one is supposed to know I exist. I'm going to be in trouble. If I'm lucky, maybe he won't say anything. "No one," I answer softly.

He goes to open his mouth, but I hear my brother. "Bones?"

The boy turns to face Luca, and I shut the door, locking myself in.

"Who the fuck is in that room?" I hear the guy ask my brother.

He sighs, repeating my words. "It's no one ..."

"I saw her. Luca, your dad wouldn't have a 'no one' in this house. Especially a child. Who the hell is she?"

"It's complicated," Luca answers.

"Then simplify it for me," Bones demands.

"I—"

"Boys." I hear my father interrupt them.

"Bones." Another male's voice comes from the other side that I don't recognize.

"Father." I hear the guy named Bones respond.

"We're headed to Kingdom. Have some business to handle. You guys will come," the man he called Father orders.

"Dad, I have baseball practice in an hour," the kid argues.

"And I don't give a fuck!" the man snaps. "That shit isn't important. Kingdom comes first no matter what."

"Yes, sir," the kid known as Bones growls.

I hear their shoes slap on the floor and then silence.

Opening my door, I peek out through the crack to see I'm alone once again. Closing it, I lean my back against it and slide down to my butt and let out a long breath. My dad will be so pissed if he knows someone saw me.

THAT WAS DILLAN! I NEVER KNEW WHAT HAD COME OF THAT— Luca's friend seeing me. My brother had come home later that evening, bloody and in a bad mood. I didn't dare talk to him after he'd spent time with our father alone. The blood never bothered me. I knew we were a Mafia family. I grew up thinking that everyone's dad got "rid" of any problem that came their way. That it was perfectly fine to walk into a room and see cash lying around with drugs and guns. I knew not to touch them. Luca taught me everything I needed to know about our family. Our parents moved back to New York—where our father was from—when I was very young. My father would go back and forth quite a bit, but my mother rarely did. From what I would overhear, she was too busy drinking and popping her pills to stay up during the day and sleep at night. She had four boys that my father wouldn't allow her to control. And me? Well, I didn't exist to anyone. Except Luca. He made sure that I had the best nannies who would teach me about the world. When I moved to Italy at thirteen, they followed. What they didn't teach me, I learned from TV and books. I may not have ever graduated high school, but at least I knew how to read. That was the one thing Luca was adamant that I learned when I was younger. My father didn't care if I even knew how to tie my shoes. To him, my only reason for existence was to eventually use for his benefit. And women don't need brains to lie on their backs and spread their legs.

Turning the page, I see another picture of Dillan. He's in a hospital bed. He's got his right arm in a cast, and just like before, he looks void of any emotion—a broken soul. The girl is with him again. She sits on the side of his bed, talking to another girl. She's got bleach-blond hair. I know her too. She was at the hospital last night. She was sleeping on Nite's shoulder. He had moved her off him when Dillan ordered him to get rid of me. Again.

This does nothing but prove how much of an outcast I am. They've all been friends for years. And I'm just Luca's sister who no one knows existed.

BONES

My office phone rings, and I pick it up. "Hello?"

"Sir, Nite and Titan are in the meat locker and ready for you," Nigel informs me.

"Thank you." I hang up and exit my office, stopping by my brother's. I enter Grave's to find him sitting at his desk, leaning back in his chair with his black combat boots propped up on the surface and talking on his cell phone.

"It's whatever you want," he says, smiling. "If you want that, then get it." He snorts. "Of course ..."

I clear my throat, and he drops his feet, sitting up straight.

"Hey babe, I have to go. Yeah, be home soon. Love you." He hangs up quickly.

I exit and stop by Cross's office. "They're here." I pop my head in, and he's typing away on the computer, giving me a finger for one second.

Making my way down the hallway, I come to the front of our office and push the button on the elevator. It opens, and I step in and turn just in time to see Grave and Cross coming toward me, so I hold it open for them.

Standing silently in the glass box, I push the button to take us down, and my brother turns to face me. *Here we go.*

"You don't actually believe her, do you?"

"I do." The poor thing isn't lying.

"She's a Bianchi," Grave adds. "We don't fuck with them."

"Luca ..."

"We've been friends with Luca since we were young. We don't do business with Matteo or the twins. And we sure as fuck don't get in bed with a Bianchi that we never knew existed."

My jaw tightens, but I don't say anything. He's right, but this is different. She's different. I have blood on my hands, but I'm not going to add hers to it. "I made Luca a promise," I say through gritted teeth.

"Yeah, well ..." Grave looks over at Cross. "We all know how easily those are broken." The elevator dings before the door slides open and Grave storms out.

I look over at Cross, and he's flipping his Zippo open and closed. If he's affected by what Grave just said, he doesn't show it. Cross made Grave a promise not to sleep with his fiancée's best friend. Of course, Cross broke it and slept with Alexa, and she's recently moved in with him. I like her, and Cross loves her.

Grave had always been high on drugs or drunk off his ass. Now that he's clean and sober, I think Grave just feels out of control. Things are taking place that he doesn't have a say in.

We walk down the hallway and enter the metal door at the end of the hall, stepping into the meat locker. Nite and Titan are already inside with Jeremy.

The man jumps to his feet. "Bones ..."

I raise my hand. "Sit down."

Jeremy licks his lips nervously. "Bones ..."

"If you don't sit down, I'll break both of your kneecaps," Titan warns casually.

Letting out an aggravated breath, Jeremy does as he's told.

"What happened?" I'll give him one chance to tell me how things went down last night. Let's see what he does with it.

"What do you mean?" he asks, tilting his head to the side.

Reaching into the pocket of my jeans, I tell him, "That was not the correct answer."

Titan grabs his arm and stretches it across the table as I flip open my pocketknife and stab him in the hand with it.

His shrill scream fills the concrete room as blood instantly pours onto the surface. I yank it free and wipe the blood off on my jeans before shutting it and placing it back in my pocket. Titan lets go of him, and he falls out of his chair like butter melting to the floor, cradling his left arm to his chest, crying. Then Titan bends down, grabbing his shaking body, and rips his shirt up and over his head.

"Put his hand on the table," I order.

Titan picks him up with his hands under his arms and sits him back in the chair. Snot and drool run down his face and naked chest while Nite steps up behind him. Titan hands him the shirt, and Nite wads it up before cramming some of it into Jeremy's mouth while holding it in place.

Grave stands beside the table, lifts up his shirt, and removes his studded black leather belt from his jeans. He then wraps it around Jeremy's forearm and pulls tight, cutting off the blood supply. Cross comes up to the front of the table and removes his cross necklace and lighter. He runs the flame along the metal while Titan unscrews the lid to a water bottle and pours it over Jeremy's wound, washing away the blood. He cries into his gag when Titan takes his own shirt and wipes off the water with the edge of the fabric, drying it off.

Cross flips the Zippo closed and then presses the cross to the knife wound on Jeremy's hand. He sobs behind the gag as Cross does it several times before it's cauterized. Then everyone lets go of him and takes a step back.

"I have all night," I tell him.

Trying to catch his breath, he yanks his shirt from his mouth. Watery eyes meet mine. "I didn't—"

"The cameras don't work." I interrupt whatever lie he was about to tell me. Although I wasn't lying—I do have all night—that doesn't mean I want to spend all night here.

"A man came in," he rushes out, holding his arm.

Ah, now we're getting somewhere. "And?"

"And he asked me if you were available."

My brows rise. "Me?"

He nods quickly and sniffs. "I told him no, but Luca was there. Up in the office. And he asked me what time we closed." He closes his eyes tightly and starts sobbing again.

"And?" I snap, making him jump.

"He paid me a thousand dollars in cash to cut the security tapes," he admits shamefully.

I reach up and rub my chin. "You let someone shoot Luca for a thousand dollars?"

"No. No." He shakes his head quickly. "Shoot? He didn't say that. He never said that he was going to hurt Luca."

"What the fuck did you think he was going to do?" Cross snorts.

"He wanted to talk to Bones. He asked for him by name ..."

"Everyone knows who the fuck Bones is." Titan slaps the back of his head.

"But why did he think I'd be there?" I speak my own thoughts. If someone wanted to talk to me, they could have shown up here at Kingdom or called me. The Kings don't hide. We don't have to.

"Seriously?" Grave arches a brow at my question. "How long do you expect us all to pretend that you don't own half of Glass?"

"It's not public knowledge." I ignore his previous question.

"The Bianchis know," Titan speaks.

"Did you know the guy?" Grave asks Jeremy.

"No. Never seen him before."

My eyes go over to Titan, and he shrugs, thinking what I am. Everyone in Las Vegas knows who the fuck the Bianchis are. So if it wasn't one of Luca's brothers, then who the hell was it? I take the pocketknife out and flip it open once again.

"What are you doing?" Jeremy tries to jump up from his seat, but Nite holds him in place by his shoulders while standing behind the chair. "I told you everything I know."

"You did," I agree. "But you also sold Luca out for a thousand dollars, and I can't have that." Whoever shot Luca knows this guy is weak. They put a target on his head, maybe on purpose. Either way, he can't be trusted. Not with my business and not with Mia's life.

"Wait. Wait." He lifts his hands in surrender. "I can help you—"

"No, you can't." I interrupt him. "Nite."

He grips his hair and yanks Jeremy's head back while I reach out and slice the blade across his neck from ear to ear. His body jerks as blood pours from the wound and down his bare chest.

One problem down. Just a hundred more to go.

THIRTEEN

MIA

I STAND AT the kitchen island when I hear a door open and close. Dillan is home. My eyes snap up, looking around, knowing it wasn't the front door. He must be coming through the garage. This house may be large, but it's eerily quiet and gives me goose bumps. It almost has an abandoned feel to it. I'm afraid I won't be able to sleep once I lie down. I might have to stay up several nights just in order to sleep for one.

I stand still, trying to calm my breathing. All of a sudden, I'm nervous. I keep playing that one time I saw him over and over in my head. Although he said he knew Luca, did he know who I was when he bought me in New York? He had to have remembered me, right? But why didn't he just tell me? So much could have been explained. I would have seen him as an ally, not a wealthy sadistic man who was buying me as a toy to sexually torture. I would have begged him to call Luca before he left me in Malibu. Maybe Luca would have actually spoken to me.

I could kick myself for not recognizing him in the limo. He looks different but also the same. It's hard to explain.

His shoes slapping on the marble floor let me know he's getting close, and I rub my sweaty hands on the T-shirt ... shit! I realize I'm barely dressed. I did my laundry but hadn't changed yet. I'm still wearing his damn boxers.

I could go do that real quick. Sidestepping the island, I go to leave the kitchen just as he steps in under the archway. He comes to a stop at the same time I do when he sees me. Blue eyes drop to my bare feet and run up over my legs, chest, and face. When his eyes meet mine, he's practically growling.

I don't have time to process why he's mad at me because all I can think about is he's covered in blood. It's not on his hands or arms. I can tell by the line on his forearms that he's washed them clean. But it's splattered on his tattooed neck and clothes. This is what I imagined a Dark King would look like—they slaughter their enemies. I step toward him. "Dillan ..."

He takes a step back, and I stop once again, not sure what I am going to do. I've grown up with this. Blood doesn't scare me. I once watched my father and Luca kill a man because he was two grand short on a loan my father had given him. "Are you ... are you okay?" I manage to get out.

He slowly nods. "Fine," he clips, and his eyes drop back to my legs.

I realize once again that I'm wearing one of his T-shirts. "Sorry," I mutter, grabbing the hem and trying to stretch it longer than it already is. It just makes the neckline dip low, exposing more of my chest. "I don't have any clothes here. What I wore is in the dryer. I hope you don't mind ..."

"It's fine." He looks away from me, his eyes going over all the food I made.

"I thought you'd be hungry," I say softly, unable to meet his stare. This is so awkward. I have never wished I was locked away in our house in Italy more than I do right now.

There's a long pause before he speaks again. "I'm going to shower." I watch his shoes turn and hear him walk away.

I lean against the island and let out a long breath, telling myself that I'm a goddamn Bianchi, and I won't let the fact that I have a pussy allow him to treat me like I'm a fucking flower.

BONES

REACHING UP, I grip the back of my shirt and rip it up and over my head while storming down the hallway to my bedroom, trying to ignore what I just saw.

She's in my kitchen, pretty much naked and cooking.

My cock is rock fucking hard while my mind runs through the different positions I could fuck her in.

"Dillan?"

I come to a halt and turn around to find her in the hallway, following me like a lost little puppy. She stands there dressed in one of my Kingdom shirts and nothing else. I wonder if she's wearing a bra. My hands itch to find out. Instead of tearing the shirt off her, I grip the one I just removed from myself.

"What?" I bark, and she jumps.

"I ..." Her silvery-blue eyes take in my bare chest and arms. They slowly run over the ink I've covered myself in over the past few years. Most people don't understand it, but I don't give a fuck. "Um, I just wanted to see if you were okay." Those beautiful eyes reach mine again, and I arch a brow. *She cares if I'm okay?*

Deciding to test the waters, I take a few steps, closing the distance. She doesn't retreat. I reach up and push some hair behind her ear. "Aren't you afraid?" Most women seeing a man who bought, drugged, and shipped them away would be terrified if they ever saw that man again.

"I've seen blood before, Dillan. And I know enough about the Kings to understand what you're going to do to make sure Luca is safe."

Of course, she has. Even though her parents got rid of her, she was still here until she was thirteen. She's seen enough. Knows enough. "I'm fine," I tell her.

"Can we go see Luca after your shower?" she asks, her big eyes full of hope.

"No." I take a step back.

Her shoulders fall. "What? You said ..."

"Forget what I said," I tell her, turning to finish walking down the hallway and into my room. "You're not going to the hospital. You're not even going to leave this house." I enter the bathroom and shut the door, but it immediately flies open, and I turn around to see she's stepped inside as well. "Mia ..."

She slaps me across the face. "I will not ..."

I wrap my hand around her throat and shove her into the wall by the door, slamming her back into it. Breathing heavily, I glare down at her. The woman shows no fear. She can't be more than five two and a hundred pounds. I've seen grown men more afraid of me. "You do not have a say here. Do you understand?" I ask through gritted teeth.

"I will not be your prisoner," she spits out. Her hands come up to my bare chest, and she tries to push me away.

I step into her, pushing my body flush with hers, pinning her to the wall. "No one knows you exist." Her body softens against mine, and her lips part as if that fact never occurred to her, and now that she realizes it, it's crippling. "I had everyone at the hospital sign NDAs to ensure no one speaks of you." The Kings were right. If the wrong person knew where she was, it'd be over. And Luca would never forgive me. "So either you hide here in my house, or I ship you off again." I lean my face down to hers and inhale her hair. It smells like my shampoo. Fuck, the thought of her naked in my shower makes my pulse race. "And I send you somewhere that you have no chance of escape." Pulling back, I look down at her, and her silvery-blue eyes are swimming in tears. They search mine for any sign that I'm bluffing. I'm not. Shipping her away would be the best thing for both of us. Not only because of her life being in danger but also because my cock is hard, and all I want to do right now is rip off that shirt, bend her over, and eat her pussy. "Do you understand?"

She sniffs and lifts her chin; her hands grip my forearms, digging her nails into my skin. "Capisco perfettamente." She speaks in Italian, and my cock jerks inside my jeans. Something about the way her voice sounds when she speaks Italian makes my knees go weak. Straightening her shoulders, she repeats in English. "I understand perfectly, *Bones.*"

I don't miss the fact that she calls me by my nickname. She's treating me as a King. Good. I'm not her friend. Releasing her neck, I take a step back. She lets go of my arms, and she reaches up to rub her now tender skin. I wasn't holding her that tight. Not like last time.

The first tear falls down her face, and I watch it roll over her lip and chin before it falls onto the shirt. She just stands there, staring at me, looking defeated. Her mind is finally telling her that she will have no freedom here either. It's Italy all over again. But at least she was alone there. Here, she has me—her own personal security guard in a gated prison.

We all do what must be done. My father once told me. I had to learn that the hard way, and so will she.

"Get out," I order as she continues to just stand there.

She blinks, and fresh tears run down her face. Slowly, her eyes rise to meet mine, and they grow cold with a look of pure hatred in them. My name was just added to her very long list of people she hates. Which is fine, as long as I'm at the top. I'm a competitive person. "Luca lied."

I tilt my head to the side with that statement. "About?"

"You. The Kings. He said you were different than my family, but you're not. You're all the same. Controlling and manipulative." She pushes off the wall, taking a step toward me.

The corner of my lip turns up. "I do whatever needs to be done. No matter the price."

To that, she says nothing. My eyes drop to her bare legs again, and my cock reminds me that it still thinks the idea of her and me naked is the best way to handle the situation. I have to agree. Reaching down, I undo my belt, and she stiffens. My eyes find hers once again. "I'm going to shower. Either you get naked and join me or get the fuck out." I unbutton them, followed by the zipper.

She lets out a huff and then spins around, storming out of the bathroom and slamming the door shut. I meant that more as a threat than an invitation. But I'd be lying if I said I'm not disappointed she didn't take me up on it.

FOURTEEN

MIA

"**I** SAW HIM," I growl at Luca while he stands in my bedroom. Running a hand through his hair, he sighs. "I told him you were no one."

I flinch at his words even though it's the same thing I told the strange man who stood in my bedroom yesterday. "He's a King." I heard Luca call him Bones. And although I've never met the Kings, I know who they are.

"Yes," he agrees. "But he won't be a problem. He let it go, and he's got too much going on to remember you."

His words make my chest tighten. I'm always forgotten. I should be used to it by now, but somehow, it still hurts to know how easily someone can forget you exist. "But what if he does remember me?" I ask, trying not to let him hear the hope in my voice.

"If he does, he won't say anything," he assures me. "The Kings are nothing like our father. Or our brothers, for that matter." Walking over to me, he gives me his kind smile that always makes me feel safe. "The Kings will not use you against Father. They are not those kind of people. They're the good guys."

. . .

I SHOULD HAVE KNOWN LUCA WAS LYING. THE KINGS WERE only eighteen when I first saw Dillan. Now they're grown men, running a Kingdom. They will do anything to get rid of any threat that comes their way, and I'm that to them now.

I sit at his island with a piece of lasagna in front of me. I haven't touched it because I'm not in the mood to eat anymore. Dillan just told me I'm a prisoner. Again. At least in Italy, I knew what to expect. I looked forward to Luca's visits. For once, I'm in the same state as him, and I can't even see him. What if he doesn't make it? I won't even get to say goodbye. I can't take that as an answer.

I hear Dillan entering the kitchen, but I refuse to look up or acknowledge him in any way. Fuck him! Fuck the Kings and fuck my family. They can all go to hell.

"Here." He drops a box in front of me, making a slapping noise. "Where's your cell phone I left with you at the beach house?"

I look up at him through my lashes, hoping the bastard catches on fire with my glare. "Going to take that freedom away from me too?"

"Yes," he states, holding out his hand to me.

My jaw tightens, and I slap my hands on the kitchen island, standing to my full height. He is easily over six feet tall. But I've been small all my life. That doesn't mean I'll let someone bigger run all over me. "If you want it, you'll have to take it." It's not like I have anyone to call other than him and Haven anyway, but still, it's the point. He's trying to isolate me from everyone. Maybe he wants me to go insane? It's some reverse psychology bullshit. I've seen it on TV.

His bottom lip starts to twitch, and then he begins laughing at me —like throws his head back laughing.

I walk around the kitchen island and shove him.

His laughter stops, and he grips my wrists in his strong hands, yanking my body into his. He's freshly showered, and the scent of his body wash fills my nose. It smells like cedarwood. Much more refreshing than the smell of blood from when he first arrived. He looks down at me, and I can still see the laughter in his pretty blue eyes. He thinks this is funny.

"Mia ..."

"I won't let you do this!" I argue. "I will go see Luca. And I will talk to whoever I want."

Letting go of my wrists, he reaches over and picks up the box he had set down in front of me. Placing it in my hands, he takes a step back, crossing his arms over his chest.

"What's this?" I ask, staring down at it.

"Open it," he orders.

Letting out a huff, I rip the lid off and pause at what I see before looking back up at him. That same gorgeous smile he had in that picture with the baseball bat is on his face right now. God, he really is gorgeous for a man. More than any man should be.

"This is your new phone," he states, taking the box from me and removing the black device. "I want your old phone because I was afraid that maybe your brothers put a tracker on it when they went and saw you. This one ... I had delivered while at Kingdom. And ..." He pushes a button on the side, and I hear it come on. "It has everyone's number in it. I charged it earlier in my office while at work, so it's good to go."

I bite my lip nervously as he hands it to me.

"Emilee just lives next door, and so do Alexa and April. Jasmine isn't far away."

Tears sting my eyes, and my breath catches in my throat. This is about as much freedom as I've ever had. I look up at him.

"I don't want to isolate you, Mia." He reaches out and cups my face with his warm hand, and my pulse starts to race at his tender touch. "But I will protect you. Even if that means doing things that you don't agree with." With that, he pulls away and turns to exit the kitchen.

"Dillan?" I call out.

"Yeah?" He turns around under the archway.

"My old phone is on the nightstand charging."

He nods once and then turns, disappearing once again.

I fall onto a barstool at the island and open my contacts. They're all there. Jasmine, Haven, April, and Alexa. Along with Cross, Grave, Titan, and Bones. Luca is also there and Nite. A guy named Nigel. I remember him from the limo. He was the driver.

I hold the phone to my chest and smile as I hear it ping several times in a row.

I open a message that says **BITCHES** at the top and read over the chat.

Jasmine: Breakfast in the morning?

April: I'm down.

Alexa: Of course.

Jasmine: Empire?

I SIGH, KNOWING THAT NO MATTER WHAT EMPIRE IS, I CAN'T GO there. Although Dillan was nice enough to give me a phone with everyone's number, I have no doubt that he won't allow me to leave the house to be with the girls.

Emilee: No. I heard Mia can't go out in public.

· · ·

April: We can do it at mine? I'll cook.

Sounds good.

THEY ALL RESPOND WITH.

Jasmine: See you all at six.

I SMILE AT THE FACT THEY THOUGHT TO INCLUDE ME IN something so simple. Breakfast. Just girls getting together to hang out before their day starts. How did they get this number? Bones must have given it to them before he even brought it home to me.

I feel like I should be nervous because I don't know any of them. I didn't see Haven reply to them, but maybe that's because she's staying at the hospital with Luca.

I lock the screen and put it on the kitchen island, that smile still on my face. I have plans with the girls in the morning, and it doesn't even matter that I don't know them.

BONES

I WATCH HER from around the corner. She sits at the island, smiling down at her phone. One of the phone calls I made this evening was to get her a new one. I had no clue what all her brothers did to keep tabs on her when they showed up in California. The least they could have done was get her number. This was my best option.

I'm cutting off any contact she has with the world other than what I approve of. And that will be a very tight circle. My circle.

Pushing off the wall, I walk back down the hallway to my bedroom. I pick up her old cell phone off the nightstand and head out to the garage. Grabbing a hammer, I set it down on my tool bench and bang on it until it's in fucking pieces.

Then I walk over to the sink, fill it with water, and drop it in. You can never be too sure. Entering the house once again, I go back to my bedroom to find her standing at the end of my Alaskan king-size bed.

She still wears my shirt, and my cock reminds me that the hand job I gave myself in the shower was not nearly good enough. "What?" I growl, irritated with myself.

She crosses her arms in front of her and drops her face to the floor. It reminds me of when I saw her all those years ago, back when I had no idea who she was. I should have made Luca tell me. But our fathers ended up taking us to Kingdom, and let's just say there were other things on my mind. And over time, I just erased that memory. I believed her when she said she was no one. It was almost as if I had dreamed of the interaction between us.

"May I go to breakfast in the morning with the girls?" she asks softly. Her eyes rise, and she looks at me through her long, dark lashes.

I hate that my mind instantly pictures her on her knees looking up at me like that. "No."

Her head snaps up, and she lets out a huff at my refusal. "The girls were messaging, and they want to have breakfast at Grave and April's house so I can go."

I run a hand through my hair. "That's fine." A smile grows across her face. Just like the one when she was in the pool and when I told her I'd teach her how to drive. "But come right back here afterward."

She nods in understanding. "Thank you."

My chest tightens that she's fucking thanking me to walk across the driveway to go to breakfast with some women she doesn't even know. "You're welcome," I say awkwardly.

"Were you hungry?" She changes the subject.

"No." I'm starving, but I'm not telling her that. I have to be up soon. Right now, I just want to go to sleep and forget about the half-naked brunette in my bedroom.

"Oh, okay." Her face falls. "I'll go clean up the kitchen." She walks past me but stops at the door. "Where are your blankets?"

I turn to face her. "Blankets? For what?"

"I need a blanket for the couch." She points back behind her to the hallway. "I toured the house this evening, and this is the only room that you have any furniture in. Well, besides the living room."

"I'm never here," I say defensively. Like I need to explain why I have a ten-bedroom house but only enough furniture to fill up a one-bedroom apartment. I don't want to make her sleep on the couch. The poor girl has been through so much already. "You can have my bed," I tell her.

"Oh no, that's okay," she rushes out. "I can sleep on the couch."

"It's decided," I growl. "You'll sleep in my bed." With that, I give her my back and enter my bathroom, slamming the door behind me. Walking over to the sink, I turn on the faucet and splash some water on my face.

Hearing my cell ring in the bedroom, I go back in there and pick it up off my nightstand to see it's Titan. The Kings and I very rarely get much sleep. Our bodies are just used to it by now. "Hello?" I snap.

"I just got a call, and it looks like we need to go to the Airport," he says in greeting.

"For what?" I ask, looking at the clock to see it's almost two a.m.

The Mason brothers run the Airport. Three people I despise. But we ended up making a deal with them recently. We went into business with them for diamonds in order to help out Cross. It's not the call I would have made, but it is what it is.

"Turner had a guy come in to fight tonight bragging about robbing a strip club a couple of nights ago."

I frown. "But as far as I know, nothing was stolen from Glass."

He sighs. "I agree, but it's something worth looking into. Even if it's not Glass, we may get a lead on something we can use."

"I'll meet you outside in five," I hang up and walk over to my closet. Grabbing a Kingdom hoodie, I slip it on, pocketing my cell. Then I walk into the kitchen. My feet stop on their own at what I see.

Mia has her back to me, standing at the dishwasher. She's bent over, placing dirty dishes in it. The shirt of mine she wears rides up, exposing her bare thighs to me. Her skin looks like it's been kissed by the sun, and they look so smooth. I imagine walking up behind her and running my hands up her legs, reaching underneath the shirt and pulling my boxers down that I can see from here to expose her pussy to me.

"Dillan?"

I blink to see she's now turned around, looking at me. "I have to go." I clear my throat.

She frowns but doesn't say anything.

"I'll be back later." With that, I turn and get the hell out of my house, thanking my lucky stars that the Mason brothers need to see me. Maybe I like them after all.

Titan already sits outside of my house in his car. I fall into the passenger seat of the candy apple red Maserati. "Grave didn't answer his phone," he informs me.

"He's probably asleep." I look over at his house, and not a single light is on. Grave would stay awake for days or sleep for days when he used. Now that the kid is clean, he sleeps whenever he can.

"Cross is meeting us there. He's up at the club with Alexa helping her get it ready for the grand re-opening."

We pull out of the gate, and I lean my head back, closing my eyes for a second. It's a mistake. Because all I picture is me and Mia in my kitchen. Her body laid out on my dining room table like a feast, and my head between her legs with her hands in my hair ...

"You okay?" Titan asks, bringing me back to reality.

"Yeah." I lie and sit up straighter.

"We're going to get to the bottom of this," he assures me. "We'll find out who the fuck shot Luca."

Right? That needs to be my main focus. Not the gorgeous brunette whose father runs the Italian-American Mafia. "It's not adding up."

"Which part?" he asks, getting on the highway.

"All of it." I shrug. "Mia was so sure that it was her brothers who shot Luca. The timeline adds up with that."

He shifts in his seat, and I look over at him. "What?" I demand when I see his hand tightening on the steering wheel.

He gives me a quick glance before placing his concentration back on the road. "Do you really believe her?"

"I do." I nod and look out the passenger window. "I saw the look on her face at the hospital. Poor thing was scared to death."

"Just marry her then."

My head snaps back over to the left, and I glare at him. "You can't be serious?"

He shrugs. "Not like you're saving yourself for someone special." Titan chuckles. "Throw the biggest fucking wedding of the century and marry her. Give them a show and rub it in John's fucking face. And if what her brothers tell her is true, then her father will make his move, and we'll be ready." His eyes meet mine, and I see just how serious he is before he turns back to the road. "He may be John Bianchi, but we're the motherfucking Kings. And that means something."

THE AIRPORT IS JUST THAT—ONCE AN AIRPORT THAT WAS abandoned years ago. That Tanner, Turner, and Trey Mason own. It's their Kingdom. But where we cover our illegal activities with shiny and expensive things, they don't even bother to cover how corrupt they are. It sits on the outskirts of Las Vegas on two hundred acres. It has five stories of the original airport, and the hotel next door has been transformed into apartments they rent out called the Mason Towers. Where the bomb shelter once was underneath the airport is now their own personal dungeon.

The cops don't come here, no matter what. The Masons have them on their payroll, along with many other important Vegas names. Their father used to run it, then handed it over to them. Just like our fathers gave us Kingdom.

I never wanted this life, but I'm not the kind of guy to half-ass anything, so I devote my life to our business. It's given us a life that most only dream of.

"Titan, Bones." Turner Mason nods to us as we enter their office. He's stuffing a black duffel bag full of guns that sit lined out on a table. Turner is the middle brother. He's their muscle, hitman, and runs for the Cartel. Out of all the Mason brothers, you don't want to piss him off. I've never liked him. Or any of them, for that matter. Trey and Grave got into some trouble in the past, and Tanner, the eldest brother, took the fall for them. He spent some time in prison but recently got released. Of course, I didn't find out until it was too late. My brother chose to keep his illegal activities a secret from me. None of us actually know what went down to this day.

"Titan said you have someone for us?" I get to the point.

He nods. "Tanner has him down in the basement."

Titan and I go to exit the office just as the door opens, and Cross enters with Grave. "You didn't answer my call," Titan says to my brother.

"Sorry, phone died. But I was at the club with Alexa and Cross. What do we have?"

"We were just headed to find out," I answer, shouldering past him and out of the room.

Making our way to the bomb shelter, we stay silent. I don't have much to say, and my mind is still going over what Titan said in the car about marrying Mia. He made it sound like marrying her was a business transaction. Write up a contract, sign it, and then throw a big party. He was right when he said I wasn't saving myself for that special someone. I told myself that I'd never get married. A life of a King isn't an easy one. Why bring a woman into it? She'd expect too much from me and eventually a family. I don't want to be my father. I don't want to see my son have to live the kind of life I have. Or a daughter? What the fuck would I do with a daughter? I'd be a horrible husband because Kingdom would come first. And the same as a father —my kids probably wouldn't even know who I am. Doing Luca a favor and having Mia take my last name are two very different things.

And let's not forget what my father told me—*show me a man in love, and I'll show you his greatest weakness.* I can't say he's wrong because Titan, Grave, and Cross will do anything to make sure nothing happens to their Queens. Even if that means dying for them. I'm not saying that's a bad thing. If you love someone, you should do anything for them. I consider all the Kings my brothers, even Luca and Nite. So my father's words make sense because I would not only kill for them, I'd die for them.

"Everything okay?" my brother asks me.

"Fine," I growl. Fuck, why does everyone care how I feel right now? I liked it better when they were all single and too busy with their own hectic lives to pay attention to me. Now that they've all locked down some pussy, they're in my business like it's their own life.

"Where's the girl?" Grave goes on to ask as if she's too insignificant to remember her name.

"My place." Where else would she be? Does he expect me to keep her by my side with a leash attached? I have to hide her, so I sure as fuck wouldn't bring her here.

"I told him he should marry her." Titan laughs again like it's a joke.

"That's the worst idea you've ever had." Grave snorts.

"It's a means to an end." Titan shrugs. "John would come out of hiding along with his sons—"

"Speaking of sons." Grave interrupts him. "Luca would kill Bones once he wakes up. There's a reason they've been hiding her."

"I don't see it being a problem." Cross finally speaks. "Bones told us that Luca sent him to help her. It's obvious he trusts him with her."

He shouldn't have. I haven't stopped thinking about fucking her since I forced her into the limo.

"Yeah, well—"

"Can you guys just shut the fuck up?" I snap, cutting off Grave.

Thankfully, they listen.

Exiting the elevator to the bomb shelter, we make our way through the old tunnels. After passing the jail cells lined up on either side, we enter the door at the end into the one cell where they keep their special guests. We've been here recently when Cross needed answers.

A guy sits tied to a chair. Tanner Mason has his back to us, arms crossed over his chest. As we enter, he turns to face us. "Kings." He steps to the side. "Have a gift for you."

Grave snorts. "It's only a gift if he has something to tell us."

The guy looks up at us through his busted face. I'm not sure if the Masons did that or if it was from his fight here. "Heard you were bragging about robbing a strip club," I say.

He lifts his chin and glares up at me.

"All of a sudden, he's got nothing to say." Tanner smirks. "Let's fix that." He walks behind him and grips a handful of his hair, yanking his head back.

Grave grabs his face, squeezing hard enough to force his mouth open, and he holds his free hand out to Cross. "Give me a knife."

The guy starts thrashing in the chair.

Cross retrieves his pocketknife and flips it open, handing it over to Grave. He holds it up to his chin.

"Okay, okay—" the man rushes out. "It wasn't Glass." He looks at me.

I tilt my head to the side. "Which one was it?" Being a King, we hear about everything that happens.

Grave takes a step back, letting him go. "It was Mansion. A friend of mine works there and helped me set it up."

I rub my chin. "So you know nothing about Glass and Luca Bianchi being shot?"

His eyes widen, and they dart around the room. "Luca was shot? Fuck, man, is he okay?"

Titan gives me a "told you so" look. Everyone knows Luca, and no one would dare go after him unless it was his own family. That was why Luca didn't draw his weapon. He never saw it coming.

Cross has already pulled out his cell and has it to his ear. I look over at him. "Thank you." He hangs up. "It's true. Mansion was broken into, and over a hundred grand was taken."

Dead end. Fuck! Not sure what I was expecting to find, but a part of me already knew what the outcome would be.

"What do you want to do with him?" Tanner asks.

"Let Nicholas know where to find him." Nick owns Mansion. He can take care of his own mess. He can pay us later for handing him over.

"Wait. No!" the guy rushes out, and we ignore him, turning to exit the cell while he tries to save his own ass.

"What do we do now?" Cross asks, pocketing his cell.

"Go to bed." Grave yawns. "I'm not like you guys. I need sleep."

FIFTEEN

BONES

TITAN PULLS INTO the back of Glass. Getting out, we both walk up the metal stairs to the second floor, and I use my key card to unlock the door. Pushing it open, we step into the hallway, and I look over the blood smeared across the carpet.

"Fuck," Titan hisses, letting the door close behind him.

"Haven told us that he was unconscious when she found him." We spoke to her the entire time on the way to the hospital. She was all alone and terrified. We wanted her to know that we were on our way. She told us that she found him lying facedown in the hallway. As if he had crawled across the floor. Which doesn't make any sense. Why not call one of us? What was he going to find in the hallway to save him?

We follow the blood smear into the office and see the massive blood stain in front of the desk. We've dealt with blood all of our lives, but it's different when you know it belongs to someone you consider family. The fact that whoever it was, was looking for me makes it worse.

"Blood splatter on the desk," Titan observes.

"Maybe he was standing in front of it," I offer. By the way the blood covers the carpet and desk, you can tell he wasn't sitting in his chair.

"Where was his weapon?" Titan walks around the desk and starts opening drawers.

"It was on him." I spoke to the detective that showed up at the hospital when we arrived. He promised he would find out who did this, but we all know that the police won't be able to do shit. They can't control the Mafia. Plus, they are easily bought. I told them to stand down, move along, and stay the fuck out of our way. He looked more than happy to oblige and accept the stack of cash we handed over. "Haven took it from his holster and gave it to me while at the hospital. It's in my safe at home."

Titan nods. "Did he get a shot off?"

"Nope." I checked. There was still one chambered, and the magazine was loaded, safety off like always.

Titan sighs, running a hand down his face. "Lane said that the bullet in his leg entered from behind. But the one in his chest entered through the front."

I nod, crossing my arms over my chest.

"So maybe he was standing, facing the desk. Someone came in and shot him in the leg. He turns around, and they shoot him in the chest."

"Makes sense. But if they already had the advantage, why wait for him to turn around to shoot off the one in the chest? Or why go for the leg and chest at all? A shot to the back of the head, and he would have dropped dead."

"Maybe they didn't want to kill him?" he suggests.

I shake my head. "No. I think they wanted him dead. But I also think they wanted Luca to see who they were and suffer. Like a last fuck you." I flinch at my own words.

Titan notices and sighs. "This isn't your fault," he offers.

I give a rough laugh that holds no humor. "Of course, it is. They were here for me."

"We don't know that."

"Jeremy—"

"Jeremy was a piece of shit, and we can't trust a damn thing he said to us," Titan interrupts me.

"But what if he was right? What if this doesn't have anything to do with Mia?" I offer. "And everything to do with me."

He shakes his head. "It's too coincidental. It has to be connected somehow. But I'm afraid only Luca can help us figure it out."

I spoke to Haven earlier, and he's still in his drug-induced coma. They ran some tests, and I'm waiting to hear back from her regarding brain activity.

"What are you going to do about the club?" Titan goes on.

"I have a crew coming first thing in the morning. It was closed today and will be closed tomorrow as well. They said they could get everything ripped up and replaced tomorrow afternoon. Then It'll be open as of tomorrow night again. Right now, nothing has been released about what happened to Luca. I'd like to keep it that way. If I shut down the club for too long, people may start to ask questions. Plus, I can't do that to the girls." Exotic dancers choose Glass because we take care of them. Some have children, sick parents to take care of, or are paying their way through college. I won't let this hinder their income.

He pushes up off the chair and stands. "I'll help you. Just let me know what I need to do and when I need to be here."

"Thanks. I appreciate it," I say, knowing damn well I'm not going to let him help me. If this has to do with me, I won't put anyone in danger. I'm still standing, which can only mean one thing—whoever it was will come after me again.

———

TITAN DROPS ME OFF AT HOME, AND I ENTER THE HOUSE TO FIND it silent and dark. I make my way down the hallway to my master suite and slowly open the door. She has the curtains open to the sliding glass doors, the back porch lights giving the room a soft glow.

123

Unable to stop myself, I walk around the side of the bed and see her sleeping, the covers pulled up to her chin. Her lips are slightly parted, and a few strands cover her pretty, porcelain face. I reach out and push them away, letting my tatted knuckles feel her soft skin.

"Dillan." She moans my name, and my cock strains against the inside of my jeans.

Fuck, I haven't had sex in almost four months. It was before I watched that video of her in my office. I can't even tell you how many times I've jerked off to the thought of her since I left her in California. It's pathetic, really.

"Yeah, I'm back," I tell her, expecting her to open her eyes and wake up, but she doesn't. Instead, she sucks in a deep breath and starts gently snoring.

She's out.

My phone vibrates in my pocket, and I pull it out to see it's Titan telling me he's showering and then heading up to Kingdom.

Deciding I need to do the same, I turn my back on her and head to the bathroom. It's almost four in the morning. I have a long day ahead of me and don't have time to be distracted by her. I know she'll be here when I return because she has nowhere else to go.

MIA

I went to sleep by myself, and I woke up alone. Not like I expected Dillan to be home. He practically ran out of his house when he came home to find me in nothing but his shirt.

Looking at my cell, I see it's five till six. After dressing in my clean clothes from when I arrived, I walk outside of his house, feeling the warm air on my skin. I can't say that I missed Vegas because I was a prisoner here too. At least in Italy, I had free rein of the house, and I got to go shopping. No one knew who I was there. Not like they knew my family here. My father was always in the headlines in the US. People knew he was in the Mafia and doing illegal shit. He was arrested multiple times, but nothing ever stuck. My mom or one of my brothers—once they were old enough to drive—would go bail him out. I think the system just wanted his money. They would see an opportunity to look like they were doing their jobs while getting a fat payday.

The rising sun allows me to see the massive, exclusive cul-de-sac. I was asleep when he brought me here, so I didn't get to see the house from the outside. Four houses sit in a horseshoe, but the houses are far apart. They're surrounded by a tall rock wall with a black iron gate with a golden K in the middle. A guard shack sits there with their security. In the center of the houses is a big clubhouse.

I'm not sure which house I'm going to. Stepping down the six stone steps, I see a car enter the gate at the other end of the property. It's a white sports car that pulls into the first house to my right. The driver's side door opens, and a redhead steps out. She looks over at me and pushes her big, square sunglasses up to the top of her head. "Mia?" she calls out.

I lift my hand and give an awkward wave as if there's another woman standing outside of Bones's house that could possibly be named Mia.

She gets back in her car and starts it up. I stop walking and watch her back up, and she comes over to the front of his house and opens the passenger door for me. "Get in."

I slide inside and reach out my right hand. "Mia," I introduce myself nervously.

Her eyes look down at my hand, and I think she's about to laugh at me, but instead, she grabs it, then pulls my body across the center console and hugs me. Her short red hair smells like peaches. "I'm Jasmine." She pulls away.

I nod. Thought so. She was the blonde in the photos from when they were in high school. Or maybe they were from college. I couldn't tell. But she was also at the hospital, sleeping on Nite's shoulder when I arrived.

"Well, Mia, it's nice to meet you." She throws the car in gear and drives around the half circle back to the house she was originally at.

"You too."

Getting out, she looks at me over her shoulder. "Do you know any of the girls?"

I shake my head. "Just Haven." And I don't even know her that well. Luca brought her home to Italy once. I loved her immediately but never got to see her again. Not until the hospital yesterday.

She gives me a smile. "She won't be here today. But I promise we're harmless."

I enter the house with her, and she calls out, "The life of the party is here."

We make our way to the kitchen, and I see a woman standing at the stove. Her dark purple hair is up in a messy bun. She wears a pair of denim shorts and a white tank top. She takes a quick look over her shoulder—her ice-blue eyes meeting mine—and she smiles. A piercing of diamonds hangs from her nose. "Good morning, ladies."

"April, this is Mia. Mia, this is April," Jasmine introduces us. "Grave's fiancée."

I nod at her. "Hello."

"Hey, make yourself at home," she says, going back to her cooking.

"Where are Emilee and Alexa?" Jasmine asks, tossing a strawberry into her mouth while leaning against the large island.

I stand awkwardly over by the table, wanting to offer my help but also not wanting to overstep. I'm not sure if these women have invited me because they feel obligated or are just truly interested in getting to know me.

"Emilee should be here any moment. Not sure where Alexa is," she answers.

"She's probably still in bed. She was up at the club late last night."

"Yeah, Grave and I went up there to help her and Cross with a few things. But the Kings ended up having to go to the Airport," April adds. "Grave didn't get home until almost four. He was home long enough to shower and took off for Kingdom."

"I'm here! The party can begin." A brunette enters the room, and I know who she is. She's in the pictures with Bones that I found. And she was with another one of the Kings at the hospital. My eyes catch sight of the diamond on her finger, telling me she's either engaged to one as well or already married.

"About time." Jasmine grabs a bottle from the brunette's hand. "Let's drink. Mimosas all around."

"Hi." The girl comes over to me and reaches out her right hand. "I didn't get to properly meet you the other night." She smiles shyly. "Emilee."

"Mia." I reach out and shake it. "It's nice to meet you."

"I wish it was under better circumstances. I'm so sorry about Luca. Have you spoken to Haven?" she asks.

"No." I sigh. "I don't want to bother her." She knows I'm here and will contact me if she needs me.

Emilee nods.

"Speaking of here," Jasmine wipes her mouth with a napkin. "Where have you been?"

"Jasmine. That's none of our business." April scolds her, swatting her arm with a spatula.

"What?" She jumps back, laughing. "You're all thinking the same thing."

"It's all right." I give her a soft smile. "I've been in Italy."

"All your life?" Jasmine asks

"For the most part." I pull out a chair and sit down at the table.

Jasmine grabs a jug of orange juice out of the fridge and pops the cork on the champagne she took from Emilee. "And you came back because of Luca?"

"Yeah." I look down at my hands. All these women are obviously very close with Haven and Luca. I don't want them to know that I'm the reason he's in a coma. "I had called Luca, and she answered, telling me what happened to him."

"Speaking of what happened ..." Jasmine speaks, pouring some drinks into flutes. "Does anyone know if the guys found out what they wanted at the Airport?"

Emilee shakes her head. "I was asleep when Titan returned, and he was gone before I woke up."

"I spoke to Grave before he left this morning," April states, piling some bacon on a towel-covered plate. "They confronted a guy who the Mason brothers were holding, but it just wasn't what they wanted to hear."

The door opens again, and then a bleach blonde enters the kitchen. She has her hair up, pieces falling out everywhere, dressed in a Kingdom T-shirt with black sweatpants on along with what I'm guessing is her makeup from last night. She's got a cross tattoo on her inner wrist that looks like it's on fire. I notice she doesn't have a ring on, and I didn't see her at the hospital the other night.

"What the hell happened to you?" Jasmine laughs, looking over at her.

"I'm exhausted." She falls into one of the chairs at the table. "I haven't been to bed yet."

"Mia, this is Alexa, Cross's girlfriend." Emilee introduces her.

I nod. The cross on her inner wrist now makes more sense. I bet it has to do with Cross. "It's nice to meet you."

Her blue eyes meet mine and soften. "I'm so sorry to hear about Luca."

"Thank you," I whisper, pushing some loose hair behind my ear awkwardly.

Every time someone mentions his name, my chest squeezes to the point it's hard to breathe.

Alexa's cell phone rings, and she pulls it out of her pocket. "Hello?" She answers, placing her elbow on the table and her face in her hand. "Fuck," she hisses. "I forgot. I'll head there now." Hanging up, she drops her phone to the table.

"What is it?" Jasmine asks.

"I forgot that the contractor was going to be at the club today. I've got to go—"

"I'll meet him," she offers, walking over to her. "Go home and get some rest. You're going back tonight after Cross gets off, right?"

Alexa bites on her bottom lip for a second and then nods. "Yeah. Thanks. It shouldn't take him more than twenty minutes. He just wants to go over a few changes that we made. There's an extra set of updated drawings there for him to take."

Jasmine rubs her back, and Alexa lays her head on the table. Jasmine looks at me. "Want to go with me?"

"I ..." Pausing, I can't make myself tell her no. She just offered up my freedom like it was nothing. As if anyone can get in a car and go wherever they want.

"She's not supposed to be seen in public," Emilee reminds her.

"It's not public." Jasmine rolls her eyes. "It's a club. That's closed. Not like it's a Saturday night and the place is packed. The contractor isn't even going to think twice about her being there."

I stand from the table and nod my head. I want to get out. Even if it's just to be alone somewhere else. Bones doesn't own me no matter how much he thinks he does. So what if he paid ten million for me? I'm not for sale. I am allowed to have a life and make my own decisions. And I'm starting with this one. "I'd love to go."

SIXTEEN
MIA

THIRTY MINUTES LATER, she's pulling up to a club. A guy is already there waiting on her outside.

"I'm so sorry," she tells him, opening the door.

"No worries," he says, entering with us. Jasmine was right. He doesn't pay me any attention.

I look around the large open space and a mirrored wall behind the bar. It's got a stage at the front for live music. There's a main bar to the right and what looks like a smaller one on the other side, next to the stage. It looks unfinished to me, which makes sense since she's giving the contractor the updated plans, but what do I know about running a club? Absolutely nothing.

Alexa was also right; the man didn't stay very long. He went over a few things with Jasmine while I wandered around, and then she walked him out.

"This place is nice," I say as she returns from locking the front door after the guy leaves.

"Thank you. It just needed some love," she says vaguely, and I don't push her any further to tell me what happened to it. Not my place. "I'm going to run downstairs to Kink really quick. Is that okay?"

"Of course." I nod.

I follow her down a flight of stairs and through a door. "Wow," I say. It's like night and day from upstairs. This is something I'd imagine you'd see in New York. Black and white leather walls with silver buttons on the material. "What is this place?" I ask.

"This is Kink. Alexa, Bones, and I own it."

"Dillan?" I ask, surprised.

She nods, flipping some light switches on. "Technically, he's our silent partner. Since some men still believe women aren't allowed to do anything on their own, we had to have him on the paperwork."

I nod like I know what she's talking about, but I don't. I'm not a businesswoman. "So what is it exactly?" I go on as she walks into an office and sits at a desk.

"It's a sex club—BDSM."

"BDSM?" I ask slowly.

"Yep." She smiles up at me proudly. "Anyone can do anything they want with whoever they want as long as they sign the consent forms." Wiggling her eyebrows, she adds, "As many cocks as a woman could need." Waving her arm out, she looks down at her paperwork. "Feel free to look around if you'd like. This will only take me a minute."

When your family chooses to make you disappear, the time goes by excruciatingly slow. I found the best way to pass the time was to read. I found dark romance to be my favorite. I love when the heroine falls in love with the villain. The forbidden love that you're not supposed to want. I may not have ever had sex, but I read about it in books. I understand that not everyone has that kind of sex life, if any. But that doesn't mean I don't know anything about the BDSM lifestyle.

Curious to see the club, I exit her office and walk down a hallway. At the end, I take a left and enter the open dance floor/bar area with black barstools and a black marble bar top. A mirror runs along the wall outlined in twinkling white lights. This looks to be further along with construction than the club upstairs.

I walk across it to the other side and down another hallway. Square windows allow you to see into different rooms. I walk into the first one on the right. A black leather table has what looks like leather belts for restraints placed strategically along the table. I run my hands over it, feeling how soft it is.

The back wall is white leather, and it, too, has restraints that hang from it in various places—wrists, ankles, neck, and waist.

"What the fuck, Jasmine?" I hear a familiar voice yell.

"She's fine, Bones." Their voices grow nearer. I step out of the room into the hallway just as I spot them coming toward me. "See. She's in one piece, and there's no one else here." Jasmine comes to a stop with her hand on her hip.

BONES

I GLARE AT Mia as she stands in the hallway, dressed in the same clothes she stormed into the hospital wearing. It reminds me that I still need to get her belongings from my beach house. "What the fuck are you doing?" I snap at her.

She takes a step back but lifts her chin. "How did you know I was here?" Her eyes go to Jasmine, who shakes her head.

"I asked you a question." I avoid answering hers. "I told you to go straight back to my house after breakfast."

"Don't talk to her like that," Jasmine snaps at me from behind. I turn to face her, and she continues, "She's a grown ass woman, and she can do whatever the fuck she wants."

Ignoring her, I turn to face Mia once again.

"I'm sorry," Mia says in a small voice, looking down at her hands.

"Don't apologize to him, Mia. You owe him nothing." Jasmine growls.

I spin around to face Jasmine again. Grabbing her upper arm, I drag her back into her office and slam the door shut behind us.

"What the fuck is wrong with you?" Jasmine shouts at me.

"Do you have any idea what you're doing?" I get in her face. "You're putting her in danger."

"Danger from what?" She scoffs. "The only danger I see for her is you."

I step back and run a hand through my hair. Cross had spoken to Alexa, who had informed him that Jasmine and Mia had gone to the club, and I was livid. On top of everything else going on, I had to chase them down. "You don't understand, Jasmine." I sigh. "Just leaving my house puts her at risk."

"Then explain it to me." She places her hands on her hips.

I fall into the chair in front of her desk and look up at her. "We think it was one of the Bianchi brothers who shot Luca." Her eyes widen. "In an attempt to lure Mia back here."

"I—"

"She passed out at the hospital because the Bianchi boys had assaulted her a few days before Luca was shot. She needs to stay hidden for now. No one can know of her. Not yet. Not until we have a lead on who the fuck shot Luca and how I can protect her. Do you understand that?"

She falls into her seat and nods. "I'm sorry, I didn't know ..."

"Now you do. So instead of giving me the 'she doesn't answer to me' speech, please stay out of it." With that, I get up and exit her office in search of Mia. I find her in the last room to the right.

She stands in front of an iron railing, running her fingers along it.

I lean back against the padded wall and cross my arms over my chest, watching her. Her breathing picks up, and I would give anything to hear what she's thinking.

Looking up, she meets my eyes, and her cheeks turn red. Licking her lips, she asks, "You own part of Kink?"

So she's been talking to Jasmine. "Just on paper." When Jasmine came to me with her idea, I told her that I would help her in any way that I could. I believe in what she and Alexa are doing. I have no doubt that they can run this place and make it very profitable. But as always, someone was in their way, and they needed someone with a dick.

"Have you-are you into this kind of stuff?" Her eyes roam over the bench that sits in front of her.

"I've been a member for a while now," I answer honestly. I joined the New York location after Tristan and Avery Decker took us there while we were trying to find a lead for Titan and Emilee.

She swallows, her eyes dropping to the floor.

I step into her, and they snap up to mine. Reaching out, I tuck her hair behind her ear, letting my fingertips run down her neck, feeling her pulse race.

My eyes search hers while my dick hardens in my slacks. I'd love to tie her down in one of these rooms, put a do not disturb sign on it, and keep her here. Make it her new prison. Her own hell. That would ensure her safety. No one would ever think to look for her here, and I'd get to use her however and whenever I want. It's a win-win for me.

"Dillan." She breathes my name, licking her lips nervously.

My hand slides to the back of her neck, tangling in her hair, while the other wraps around her waist, pulling her into me. Her eyes grow heavy when she feels my cock pressed into her lower abdomen. I'm not going to pretend I don't want her. That's idiotic. "Has anyone ever kissed you other than me, Mia?" I ask, licking my lips.

"No," she answers breathlessly.

So innocent. So pure. Wish I knew why that turned me on even more. "Have you ever come for a man before?" Obviously, if she's never been kissed, I doubt one has ever gotten her off.

Her cheeks redden, and she goes to look down, but my hand in her hair tightens to keep it in place, forcing her to look up at me.

That, right there, is why I asked her that question. Because I wanted to see the look of want in her eyes. Hear the little whimper that slips from her parted lips. She may be innocent, but it's not by choice.

I lower my lips toward hers, and at the last moment, I dip my face to her neck and press mine to her skin.

Her body softens against mine, her hands gripping my shirt, trying to pull me even closer to her. And I know if I wanted to, I could have her right here and right now. But I don't have time for that. I have to remind myself that she is not for me.

So I release her and take a step back. Then I turn and walk out of the room, listening to her following me.

SEVENTEEN

MIA

I SIT IN Dillan's passenger seat, my legs rubbing together. Unable to get comfortable. My skin feels clammy, my pussy throbbing, and I can feel the sweat bead on the back of my neck.

Kink got me all worked up.

I don't know why.

Bones likes a submissive. Matteo had said to me. I knew what he meant, but I didn't put much thought into it. Now it's all I can think about.

I catch him looking at me for a quick second before he places his eyes back on the road. He's taking me home. Like a child in trouble, he's driving me back to his house, where I'll spend all day alone. I'm probably grounded and won't be able to spend time with the girls.

I'm being punished for wanting a normal life. For wanting a little bit of freedom.

Hell, I'm a twenty-year-old goddamn virgin. I've never even used any toys. The only thing I've ever had to get me off was a shower-head. Well, I also used the jets in my father's hot tub a few times, but that wasn't the most comfortable.

He almost kissed me in Kink. I've never known that kind of need. My body was vibrating. My thighs clenched. But instead, he kissed my neck and then pulled away. He's playing with me. Probably thinks it's funny. I'm just a game to him. If he has to take care of me, he might as well get some fun out of it.

My eyes go to look over at Dillan out of the corner of my eye, trying to stare discreetly. He's wearing a black button-up with black slacks. The sleeves of his shirt are rolled up to show off his ink-covered arms. And he's got the top two buttons undone.

He's unbelievably attractive. The kind of sexy that you know your mother would hate if you brought him home. But he's also scary. Like walk faster down an alleyway if you saw him alone type of scary. That's what makes it so interesting. When you stare at him, your heart starts to race out of fear and anticipation.

A pair of black shades covers his face, but I can see the side view of his lashes when he blinks.

The sound of his phone ringing in the silent car makes me jump. **Grave** lights up his dash. He reaches out to the screen on his dash and hits answer. "Yeah?"

"Find her?" His voice fills the car, and I roll my eyes.

Great. Now they all think I'm a runaway.

"Yes. We're on our way to the house now," Dillan answers, changing lanes on the highway.

"Okay. How long before you get back?"

"I'm going to work from home today," he announces.

"What?" I bark out.

The unintelligible sound that Grave makes tells me he's just as pissed that Dillan is staying home to babysit me like a child.

I slump down in the seat and watch the city roll by while we drive down the highway.

"What about tonight?" Graves growls.

"I have to be at Glass by seven. Then I'll meet you guys there around midnight." Dillan hangs up without a goodbye. I have a feeling it's more, so I can't get any information out of their conversation.

"I don't need a babysitter," I say when the silence fills the car again.

"Yet here I am taking you home in the middle of the day," he speaks.

It's actually not even eight in the morning yet, but I don't correct him. I stay silent the rest of the way back to his house. The moment he pulls into the garage, I jump out and run to the bathroom.

Standing in the shower, I hold the sprayer in my hand, debating whether to put it between my legs. To get off. It's been so long since I felt anything. Since I was able to get any type of satisfaction from anything.

Why don't I use Dillan? It's not like I'm trying to trap him. Or take over his business to give to my father. And I know he understands that; otherwise, he would have shipped me off on the first plane out of here when I came running back. Or killed me already.

You know they're my favorite. My brother had said. It's as if they hold being a virgin over our heads. Like being a virgin is something they can take at any time. I'm not holding it for someone special. I just haven't had the chance to be with anyone.

I tried once, but Nite shot me down. He was always there and watching over me. He was the only guy I was around who wasn't actually blood. Even if my mom and dad had adopted him. But too much had happened. I'm the reason he no longer speaks. So any chance I had there is gone. But Dillan? He's something new. Something I can use to my advantage. Others have taken advantage of me, so why can't I get something for myself now?

Making up my mind, I place the showerhead back in place and start soaping up my body, knowing exactly what I'm going to do.

I'm twenty motherfucking years old. Not a little girl. It's time I act like it.

I walk through his closet. I reach out, running my fingers along his button-ups. Picking out a white one, I pull it off the hanger and

139

slide it on. The sleeves are too long, and the hem almost reaches my knees, but the material is soft and cool against my skin.

I don't drink, but I wish I had something to take a sip of right now. Just to calm my nerves. I hate how nervous I am. Men like Dillan sleep with experienced women. I make my way upstairs, running my hands along the banister. Making it to the top of the landing, the softness of the carpet almost tickles my feet.

I look to my right and see his office door cracked. Taking a deep breath, I push it open and step in.

He's sitting at his desk, his phone in his hands, and he's typing away on it. I have a moment of panic. What if he doesn't want me? This is stupid. Why would he want me? I have nothing to offer him. But isn't that what we're taught from a young age—to use our bodies?

He looks up, his eyes meet mine, and he stops typing.

Refusing to back down, I force my legs to take me over to him. Dillan isn't the kind of man who wants a timid woman. No. Many women would give anything to be where I am right now, and I refuse to be a girl anymore.

If I decide to fuck you, you'll choose to remove your clothes for me. That was what he had said to me in the limo that night. I had no idea how right he was, and I refuse to take no for an answer.

His eyes drop to my bare feet and slowly run up over my legs as I come to stand by his desk. His neck tattoo moves as he swallows, but other than that, he's completely still.

I can't explain it, but the way he looks at me gives me the courage I need.

Stepping between his desk and chair, I lean my ass back against the surface, facing him. He leans back in his chair, his eyes meeting mine, and I swallow down the knot in my throat.

His phone falls to the floor. "Mia—"

"I want you," I say, interrupting him before he can turn me down. I'm going to become a woman today. Even if I have to beg him, I will get what I want. My father taught my brothers to take what they wanted. It's time I live up to the Bianchi name.

"We shouldn't," he protests, but the way his blue eyes darken when they drop to my exposed legs tells me he's fighting a battle I'm about to win.

Reaching out, I grab his hands from his lap and place them on my bare thighs underneath his shirt.

He doesn't pull away. Instead, his fingers dig into the sensitive skin, making me shiver. "Are you saying you don't want me?" I hold my breath, waiting for him to answer. He could deny me, and it would make our bad situation worse. Because I'd have to run away due to embarrassment.

He slowly stands, his hands making their way up to my waist, pulling the shirt up in the process. He towers over me. "It'll hurt."

"First time for everything," I say. Everyone has to have sex for the first time. I want mine to be with him.

His eyes search mine, and doubt fills my mind once again. He doesn't want me. I'm an inconvenience. A temporary problem that he's trying to get rid of.

When he removes his hands from underneath my shirt, I feel tears start to sting my eyes, but he reaches up and rips it open. I gasp as the buttons go flying across the room, exposing my body to him.

His hands go back to my waist, and he runs them up over my ribs. My heavy breathing fills the room. My first instinct is to cover myself up. A man has never seen me naked before, and his blinds may be closed, but the lights are on. He can see every inch of me this close.

I reach out and wrap my fingers around the edge of his desk to keep them in place. I can't give him a reason to stop now or make him think I'm not ready.

"Fuck," he groans. "You're so goddamn beautiful, Mia."

I shudder at his words while his hands come up to my breasts. I'm on the smaller side at a B cup. I hate it. I've always felt self-conscious about them.

"Dillan," I pant, my hips bucking on his desk, needing him to do something, but he's just staring at my body.

His hand slides around to my back and up to my neck. He grips my hair and yanks my head back, and I cry out in his office, sucking in a breath.

He lowers his lips to my neck and tenderly kisses my racing pulse.

Letting go of the desk, I grip his forearms. "Dillan, please," I beg, almost in tears. My pussy is throbbing, my legs shaking. I'm embarrassed and turned on.

His free hand grips my hip, and he wraps my leg around him, the movement causing my ass to slide toward him, and I feel how hard he is in his slacks. "Oh, God," I whimper.

His lips trail up my neck to my jaw, and then he's on my lips. I open up for him, letting him take control and have his way with me.

His tongue enters my mouth, and mine meets his with need. I want to taste him. To know what it feels like to be wanted.

He drops his hand from my hair, and they both grip my ass, lifting me off the desk. I wrap my arms around his neck while my legs tighten around his waist.

He carries me over to the couch and lays me down on it. His lips come free of mine, and I suck in a breath as he falls to his knees at the end of the couch. My heart starts to race. I'm not nervous. The complete opposite, actually. I'm starving for something that I never even knew existed.

Slowly, he's pressing my shaky legs apart, and my hand instinctively covers my pussy.

He drops his head to look down at me. "You can't be shy now, Mia." He grabs my hands and removes them. My eyes are fixated on his as they take me in. His tongue runs across his teeth. Dropping his right hand to my pussy, he runs his knuckles over it, his skull ring cold against my burning skin. I suck in a deep breath at the feel of it.

He adjusts himself, lowering his chest to the couch, his head close to my pussy. "Dillan—" I gasp. "What ...?"

"Are you telling me to stop?" he asks, looking up at me through his dark lashes.

"No," I whisper.

Keeping his eyes on mine, he runs his tongue over my swollen clit.

My hips lift on their own, and I slap both of my shaking hands over my face—embarrassed and impatient.

"Relax, Mia." He gives the inside of my thigh a soft kiss, and I feel my entire body tremble. "This part isn't going to hurt at all."

His hands slide underneath my thighs, throwing my trembling legs over his shoulders. His fingers dig into my ass, picking it up off the leather just a bit. I drop my arms to my sides and take in a shaky breath, looking up at his ceiling.

My hips thrust on their own when I feel his tongue on me again.

I realize I'm gasping for breath and try to even out my breathing as I feel his tongue. This time, he pushes it into me, and I moan at the sensation of what I can only explain as heat and energy. Everything begins to tingle, from my fingertips to my toes.

My back arches, and my hands go to my chest on their own, cupping my breasts. He continues to kiss me in the most intimate way, and I begin to drown. Warm water rushes through my body, taking over. I close my eyes, and reaching out, I find his head. My fingers thread through his hair, and I pant. Hips bucking, lips parted, and body convulsing, I hold him, praying it never stops.

I can't speak. I'm not even sure I'm breathing. Everything seems to go dark, like the wave has pulled me below the surface, holding me down. Then it explodes. My pussy pulses, and my body breaks out in sweat and goose bumps.

Before I can recover, he pulls his head from my shaking legs and starts to undress.

BONES

I LICK HER off my lips, staring down at her on the couch. Her heavy eyes meet mine, but she looks far off. Dazed.

"Amazing," I whisper, my hand cupping her right breast. A rough moan escapes her parted lips.

Sitting up, I grab my painfully hard cock in my hand and stroke it a couple of times, feeling the five barbells along the shaft—my Jacob's ladder. I've never slept with a virgin since being pierced, so I'm not sure how they'll affect her being her first time. But regardless, the sex alone will hurt her.

That's why I ate her out first. I wanted her to be relaxed and already satisfied just in case this hurts her too much, and she tells me to stop.

Her heavy eyes close, and I lean down, pressing my body to hers. My hands come up to her hair, and I pull her head to the side, my lips finding her neck, trailing kisses up to her ear. "Last chance."

"Please?" she begs, the heels of her feet digging into my back as she wraps her still shaking legs around me.

Leaning up on my left elbow, I reach between our bodies with my free hand and grip my cock. I press into her soaking wet pussy, slowly pushing the tip inside without even bothering to use a condom. Any rational thought leaves my mind at the moment. She's finally giving me what I've wanted ever since I saw her in New York. It's like she's granting me a wish, and I'm going to be the asshole who takes full advantage of it.

My face drops to her neck. *"Fuck."* It's been so long since I've been with a virgin. I forgot what it felt like. There's the resistance, her tight cunt gripping my dick in the best way. It makes my breath catch. Pushing my hips forward, I enter her a little more.

She arches her neck, a shaky cry coming from her lips.

"Stop?" I question.

She reaches up, her hands gripping my face, and pulls my lips down to hers. I open up, deepening the kiss immediately, swallowing her cry while I push into her simultaneously.

Pushing all the way into her, I stop and pull my lips away. My head drops to her neck and softly kisses the damp skin, giving her a second to catch her breath. And myself as well. She's so fucking tight; I want to explode right now.

She opens her eyes, and tears run down her face.

"Mia—"

"Don't stop," she interrupts me, breathing heavily.

I pause, my hands cupping her face. "I'm hurting you."

"I'm fine," she reassures me, her body arching, pressing her chest into mine.

My cock throbs inside her, and I groan. My mind tells me to stop, but someone has to be her first, and I want it to be me. She chose me. I looked up from my phone to see her enter my office, and I thought I was seeing shit from lack of sleep. I tried to deny her. To tell myself not to do it. Women like Mia bring men to their knees. Already I'm not thinking clearly. Not using a condom. I always use one. She's a virgin, so I'm guessing she's not on birth control. But that's not going to stop me from coming inside her. No way will I pull out. I wanna see that pretty pussy leaking my cum.

Sitting up, she reaches for me, thinking I'm stopping. "Dillan—"

Pulling her legs from around my hips, I shove my arms behind her knees and push them open wide.

She arches her neck, crying out, and I start to move. My breathing accelerates when my eyes drop to look at my cock inside her wet pussy covered in her cum. There's a little blood, and I lick my lips, imagining placing my head back between her legs, but I refrain. I'm afraid if I stop, she'll change her mind.

"Oh, God..." She trails off, her hands pushing against the cushions on the couch.

"I'm not going to stop," I warn her.

She shakes her head quickly, causing her hair to stick to her tear-streaked face.

My hips begin to move aggressively while I lower my lips to hers, swallowing the cries as I try to stop myself from coming too soon.

EIGHTEEN

MIA

I LIE ON Dillan's couch in his study, my breathing starting to return to normal, but my legs are still shaking. Almost comically. I bring them up, bending my knees, and it just makes them shake worse.

He stands and picks me up. I lie limp in his arms, not even able to ask what we're doing or why he's carrying me downstairs. Entering his bedroom, he lays me on the bed and goes to his bathroom. He exits with a towel a second later.

"Spread your legs," he orders, standing next to the bed.

I swallow nervously and do as he says. Covering my face with my hands, I flinch when I feel the towel on my pussy. I want to cry. It's so sensitive right now. I wonder if it will always feel this way.

He pulls the towel away, and then I feel his hands on my wrists. He removes them from my face and hovers over me. His pretty blue eyes roam my face before dropping to my trembling lips. When I think he's about to kiss me, he stands and reaches out his hand to me. "Come on."

He helps me off the bed and leads me to the master bathroom.

Then he opens a door at the end of the bathroom. All it has is a toilet. I walk inside, and he closes it behind me, securing me inside alone.

I use the restroom and bite my bottom lip to keep from crying out when I wipe. I'm so sore.

Once I finish using the restroom, I open the door and step out to see him sitting on the side of the tub. He has the water running.

He stands, and my eyes drop to his dick. It's still hard and has a little blood on it—my innocence. Something that I never thought I'd be able to give away. Something that my father was trying to sell to the highest bidder. I've been sheltered all my life, and I finally got to give myself away. My value just dropped, and I couldn't be happier about that thought. Even if Dillan was the one who paid for it.

"Mia," he softly says my name, and I blink, interrupting my thoughts to see he's now standing in front of me with his hands on either side of my face.

I notice my breathing has picked up again. His thumbs rub my cheeks, and I realize I'm crying, and he's wiping the tears away.

His dark brows pull together, and his eyes search mine before he lets out a long breath. "I shouldn't have—"

"I don't regret it." I know what this looks like. That I'm an emotional wreck right now. I couldn't even tell him how many times I cried myself to sleep in Italy. How lonely I was. How I felt like death would be the only release I'd ever get.

"I do." He sighs.

My chest tightens at his words.

"I should have told you no."

I fist my hands, shoving him away from me, and I take a step back when he doesn't budge, his hands falling to his sides. "I'm sorry I forced you to do something against your will," I say through gritted teeth. "It won't happen again." Passing him, I go to storm out, but he grabs my upper arm, spinning me around. "Fuck you—"

He yanks me to him and slams his lips to mine. My arms wrap around his neck, and I press my body into him, moaning into his mouth. His hands grip my ass, and he lifts me before setting my ass on the cold marble counter.

I pull away, panting. "I thought you didn't want me?"

He places his forehead to mine, taking a second to catch his breath. "You deserve better, Mia." Pulling away, he stares down at me, his pretty blue eyes full of sympathy. "I'm no better than them."

Wrapping my legs around his hips, I pull him against me, my fingers grabbing his hair. "I'm so tired of people telling me what's good for me. When do I get to choose?"

He runs his tatted knuckles down my cheek before pushing pieces of matted hair behind my ear. "If you had an option to choose, it wouldn't be me."

"Dillan—"

"You haven't had the chance to see the world, Mia. To experience what other women have. But I promise you that I will show it to you."

The world? Right now, I'd settle for the hospital to see my brother. "And?"

"And what?"

"Then what?"

He tilts his head to the side. "Then you can choose."

NINETEEN

MIA

I LIE IN Dillan's bed with a bowl of ice cream in one hand and the remote in the other, flipping through the channels. It's been a week since I practically threw myself at him in his office. He made a phone call and had all of my stuff delivered from his house in Malibu. I already have what little there was put away in my very own closet. I was surprised when he showed me he had a his and hers. Of course it was empty—just like the rest of the house.

I'm always alone. Dillan is very rarely home. He had told me that once, but I have a feeling he's also staying away to avoid me. Either way, I'm lonely at night. Just like I was in Italy.

I've become friends with the girls, but April and Emilee are home with the guys at night while Jasmine and Alexa are at the club and Kink working. They are getting ready for their grand opening soon. I'm still not allowed to go out in public, so I have to hide out here.

Deciding on a cooking show, I lean my back against the headboard and toss the remote beside me on the bed while I start to eat my ice cream just as my cell rings.

Picking it up off the nightstand, I frown when I see it's a blocked number. Dillan told me he had saved all the numbers I needed for this new phone. But maybe it's a private line from Kingdom, and he's calling me from it.

Hitting answer, I smile. "Hey?"

"Hello, *sis*," a familiar voice whispers.

My back stiffens. "How did you get this number?" I ask, my hands instantly shaking.

Matteo chuckles. "Do you really think that dark castle he keeps you in will save you?" I swallow nervously, looking around the dark room. The only light is from the TV. "We're always watching you, Mia."

"What do you want?" I ask, trying to swallow the knot that forms in my throat. I hate how right he is. No one can hide or run from my family. I'm no different.

"Tick tock," he says vaguely.

"What does that mean?"

"It means that you're running out of time. Make Bones—"

"I can't." I interrupt him. We might be having sex, but that doesn't mean anything. He won't love me. My brothers don't know that I've told him about their plan. But even if he wasn't aware, he still wouldn't fall for me.

"I have an incentive for you. Check your messages."

I pull the phone from my ear and stare at it when it vibrates, alerting me of an incoming text. I open it up and play the video. And just when I think Matteo can't be any worse of a human, he proves me wrong.

"Make it happen, Mia. Or we'll give you away for fucking free." He hangs up.

BONES

I WALK INTO my house and rip off my black leather jacket, checking my watch. It's a little after six in the morning, and I'm exhausted. Having to divide my time between Glass and Kingdom this week is wearing me thin. Titan is helping with things at Kingdom, but he's growing irritated at the fact I won't let him help at Glass. And that's not adding Kink to my schedule. I may be a silent partner, but Alexa and Jasmine want my opinion on the build. Which I'm more than happy to help out with. And just yesterday, I had to make a mad dash up to Kink because Jasmine threatened to kill the plumber.

I turn the knob to my master suite slowly so I don't wake up Mia. But stepping inside, I realize she's not in here. I frown, walking over to the bathroom door and pushing it open as well. I hear the shower running. I go to look away but realize she's dressed in a T-shirt of mine and a pair of cotton shorts, sitting on the floor, under the sprayer.

"Hey?" I walk over to it and pull the glass door open. "What are you doing up so early?" I'm not even going to ask why she's wearing clothes in my shower.

She has her back against the tile, her knees pulled up to her chest, and her head down on her knees.

"Mia?" I call out her name, but she doesn't move.

I reach out to feel the water, and it's ice cold. "Christ," I hiss, reaching over and turning it off. I yank the towel from the rod and open it up. "How long have you been in there?" I demand.

Still no movement or response.

I step into the shower and bend down. Wrapping the towel around her, I place my hand under her chin, forcing her to look up at me. Her eyes are red and puffy, her lips a light shade of blue, and I notice her small body shaking. "What happened?" I rub the towel along her arms, trying to warm her up.

"He called me," she whispers.

My hands slow. "Who?"

"My brother."

How did he get the number? "What did he want?" I'm guessing it's not Luca because I spoke to Dr. Lane last night, and he was still in a coma.

"Sent me a video."

Letting go of her, I step out of the shower, praying it's not the one I've seen. Her phone is on the counter, and I open it up, prepared to go to her messages, but she already has it opened, and it's paused on a video of her in a darkly lit room. "Fuck!" I hiss, turning and throwing the phone. It hits the wall and shatters the screen. Spinning back to face her, I see she's staring at it on the floor. "I'll get you a new one."

"It won't matter." She lowers her head again to her knees. "He's watching me."

I storm back into the shower and grab her upper arms, yanking her to her feet. Now is not the time for her to close off or give up. I need her to tell me everything that she knows. "He said that?"

She tries to pull away from me, but I just dig my fingers into her arms more, refusing to let her go. "Please...?"

"Mia!" I snap her name. "This is serious. What did he say?"

She lifts her eyes to mine, and she sniffs. "Tick tock."

Letting go of her, I sigh, running my hands through my hair. I know exactly what the fuck that means. They gave her a timeframe, and although she still has time, she's not moving fast enough for them. If they have eyes on her, then they expect a show, and they're not seeing one. "Then we give them what they want," I state, knowing what needs to be done. Titan was right in a sense. I have to buy her some time while waiting for Luca to wake up. At this point, he's our only hope.

"What do you mean?" she asks, her lips and shoulders shaking. I don't miss the fact that my T-shirt she wears is wet and clinging to her body. I can see her hard nipples poking through the fabric.

"He wants a show, so we'll give him one. We go public and make them think wedding bells are in our future."

"No." She shakes her head, her wet hair sticking to her face. "No, Dillan. We can't ..."

"Yes, we can."

"Wedding? Are you serious? He'll kill you the moment he knows we're married," she growls.

"We won't do it tomorrow. Or next week. We don't even have to announce an engagement. Just make it look like there's a possibility for one." All we have to do is look like we're in love. That will satisfy John for a little while.

"My father will push for a quick wedding."

I understand that she's been kept in the dark all her life. And even though she wasn't allowed schooling, she's smart. But she doesn't understand how things work. Even if we did get married, her father wouldn't gain access to Kingdom immediately. Like she said, he'd have to kill me first. Or both of us. Either way, we'd be dead. "I don't give a fuck what he wants," I decide to say.

She sighs. "Obviously, you do, or you wouldn't be doing this. You're not even thinking."

"I'm thinking of ways to save your life," I bark, confused as to why they would send her that video. They can't release it to the public because that would expose their illegal operation. Why hide her for so long to expose her in their sex trafficking? It's an idiotic move. "They put their hands on you. They shot Luca. What do you think they'll do next?" I gesture to her body and quickly look away, trying not to get a hard-on right now.

"Oh, so I'm supposed to believe you care about me?" she snaps.

"I don't," I lie. I keep reminding myself that I made Luca a promise, and I intend to keep it. But she doesn't need to know that. "You should be thanking me."

She snorts. "Thanking you? For what? Kidnapping me? Drugging me? Dumping me off in the middle of nowhere and leaving me defenseless?"

My teeth grind. "No one was supposed to know where you were."

"Well, someone did!" Her voice rises.

"Mia—"

"I didn't start fucking you to give him what he wants." Now she's screaming at me.

"I never said you did." I haven't thought once that she's carrying out their plan. Mia is easy to read. And allowing me to fuck her was a fuck you to her father. It was the only situation she had control over.

"I won't let him win. He doesn't deserve that ..."

"Calm down." I grab her arms and yank her wet and shaking body into me, her wet clothes soaking mine.

"I'm not them." She stares up at me with tears in her eyes. "They won't use me." She sniffs. "Not anymore. I won't do it, Dillan."

I kiss her wet hair, trying to think of a plan. I always knew I had to come up with one. I just figured I'd have a little more time.

"I just need to disappear," she whispers.

"No," I argue. "We're not doing that again." I can't keep track of her and be here for Luca while running three businesses at the same time. *You also can't continue to fuck her if she's away.*

"It's pointless. No one can beat them." She pulls away from me and takes the towel, wrapping it around herself though she's still fully dressed. Dropping her eyes to the marble floor, she says, "Ending it would be best."

I frown. "Ending what?" She doesn't answer me. She just continues to stare at the floor. "Mia?" I step into her, lifting her chin to where she has to look at me. "Ending what?" I demand this time.

"I don't expect someone like you to understand where I'm coming from."

"Try me." She can't possibly be talking about dying. My lack of sleep is fucking with my hearing. It has to be.

She licks her lips. "When they showed up at the beach house, Matteo grabbed my ass and spoke about fucking me until one of the twins stopped him." She swallows. "Yeah, I'd rather die right now than have my own brother rape me." She pulls away from me, and my hand drops to my side like a rock off a cliff. "I can't keep running. They will find me. And Matteo will get whatever he wants." Tears build in her eyes. "Don't you see? I'm just alive to do my father's bidding. Once I'm your wife, your life is over, and mine will be too."

"I can save you." I say the words before I even think them through.

She steps back into me, the corner of her plump lips lift, giving me a sympathetic smile, and she places a hand on my racing heart. "My life isn't worth the cost."

At this moment, I hate all the Bianchis. Even Luca. What did he think was going to happen to her? Why didn't he protect her from their father?

"No one else needs to be hurt because of me," she adds softly.

"No one was hurt because of you." I know she feels that way about Luca, but so far, nothing has led us to believe that. If anything, he was hurt because of me. The Kings haven't gotten any closer to finding anything out. There's nothing but silence on the streets. But somewhere, someone has to know something.

She sighs. "Luca isn't the first."

Frowning, I ask. "What does that mean?"

"Nite."

"What about him?" I ask, stepping into her.

Her silvery-blue eyes meet mine. "He can't speak ... because of me. What happened to him is my fault."

"What happened to him, Mia?" I demand. The Kings don't know the specifics regarding Nite's refusal to talk. We were told he chose to take a vow of silence.

She bows her head, crosses her arms around her chest, and closes her eyes. She's closed off. I won't be getting any more information out of her about it at the moment.

I'm all this woman has. I'm not known as Bones for nothing. I own a fucking Kingdom. I've dug holes to bury bodies in the desert. I've ended so many lives, and now I have a chance to save one. Deciding what I must do, I remove my cell out of my pocket and dial a number I know can help.

"Well, well, well," she greets through a yawn. Of course, I woke her up. "It's the infamous Bones calling me. What can I do for you this early in the day?" She laughs, adding, "You better be calling to tell me you're on your way over."

"Not that kind of call," I say, taking a quick look at Mia, and she's staring at her bare feet. "I want to give you a story. An exclusive story." The Kings have had shit written about us for years now. We were too young to run an empire. Then it was our ruthlessness to knock anyone down who got in our way. Then it went to our relationships. Who we were fucking. Grave has been arrested multiple times in the past for his drug and alcohol use. That always got him front and center. But I've managed to stay clear. I'm never seen out with a woman, and I keep my nose clean and my mind on work.

"I'm listening," she says, shifting in bed.

"I'm going to be at Winstons tonight with the Kings. I'll arrive at eight thirty. Be ready."

She gives a rough laugh. "I know some are obsessed with you, Bones, but I don't think where you're eating will make headlines."

I smile. "It will. I'll be arriving with someone. A special someone."

"Oh?" I have her interest. "Who is she to you?"

I look over to see Mia standing in front of the shower, the towel wrapped around her still wet body and clothes underneath. She looks terrified with her wide eyes and trembling lips. "You are to make assumptions," I answer.

There's a long pause before she asks. "Her name?"

"Not giving it," I state. No one knows this woman even exists, and I've made those who do sign an NDA. If I give a name, then the Bianchis will know it's a setup. We need it to look like she's got me falling for her. That I'm taking her out for a nice dinner, not that we're playing them.

She huffs at my unwillingness to give her any information. "Is there anything specific you want me to add to the story?"

Mia's big eyes meet mine, and I smile. "Run with it." I hang up.

"What was that for?" Mia asks, her shoulders shivering.

"That was a reporter. She'll take pictures and make up all kinds of shit. We'll be all over the front-page news and social media by tomorrow."

"And?" she asks, biting her bottom lip nervously.

"And it will get back to your father. He'll see us as the happy couple."

She shakes her head softly, her wet hair sticking to her cheeks. "Dillan, you don't have to—"

"It's done, Mia." I interrupt whatever she was about to say.

Accepting my refusal to let this go, she asks, "What do we say when he asks why I came to Vegas in the first place? He has to know my brothers found me in California."

"We say it was Luca." I walk over to her, closing the small distance. Reaching out, I take a piece of wet hair and twist it around my finger while I stare down at her. "You were distraught over what happened to your brother, and I consoled you." We don't have to lie about that part. Especially since we think it was the Bianchis who hurt Luca to draw her here. We'll let them think they have that win.

"You really think that will work?"

"Absolutely." Her father won't care how she ended up in my arms as long as she stays there.

I release her hair and pull my phone out once more to send a text. "Go to bed and get some rest. You're going to have a busy day."

"Why?" she asks, her dark brows pulling together.

"You have a girls' day planned."

Her face lights up, and her lips part. "What ...?" But then it falls again. "I don't have any money. My brothers took that cash you gave me."

"Don't worry about that."

AN HOUR LATER, I'M EXITING THE PRIVATE ELEVATOR ON THE thirteenth floor at Kingdom in tower one and walking into our conference room to see Nite already waiting on me. I had messaged him after my conversation with Mia and told him to meet me here ASAP. Nigel let him in.

Setting my cell on the table, I unbutton my shirt and toss it onto the black surface as well. He stares at me with an arch of his brow. I wonder if he's thinking what I was thinking when Luca stormed into my office and started to undress. I undo my belt, then unzip my dress slacks and throw them over the back of a chair. Holding my arms out wide, I spin around in a circle, only dressed in my black boxer briefs. He's been here enough to know that we've got jammers in place for electronic devices, but I need him to understand that it's just us. And nothing is being recorded.

Dropping my arms to my side, I glare at him. "Why does Mia think that she's responsible for your vow of silence?" I demand.

He runs a hand down his face, letting out a long breath. Then he, too, stands and starts to undress down to his boxers. He spins around, showing me he's not wired, and falls back into his seat. I stay standing.

"It was all a lie," he says hoarsely.

Nite hardly ever talks. Everyone thinks he's a mute, but the Kings and I know the truth—he chooses to stay silent. "What exactly?"

"Rossi—John's rival—wanted intel on the Bianchis. He kidnapped me; thought I would talk. And when I wouldn't, they cut out my tongue." My eyes widen. "At the time, we thought it was regarding Mia, but it was just a ploy. When they realized I was no use to them, they dropped me off on Luca's doorstep. Along with my tongue. Thankfully, Luca rushed me to the hospital, and they were able to reattach it. But John saw an opportunity, and I decided to go along with pretending to be unable to talk."

I run a hand through my hair, trying to process and make sense of all of what he just said. "I don't understand. Why did you think it was about Mia? How did he know about her?" I thought she was some big secret. Granted, Rossi is dead now. The Kings helped Nite and Luca bury him in the desert.

"Rossi and John were friends way back in the day, before they were rivals. Back when Mia was born. We thought he was going to use her against the Bianchis. Since he knew John wanted to keep her a secret."

"And?"

"We just recently found out that it had nothing to do with her and everything to do with Haven."

"Luca's wife. Why would they care about her? They weren't married back then?" If this is true, then this happened back when we were in college. We were seniors when Nite went MIA for a few weeks. When he returned, he never spoke in public again.

"That's not my story to tell," he states, crossing his arms over his chest, and I know I'm not getting anything else out of him.

"You need to speak to Mia," I tell him.

He shakes his head. "I've gone this long without speaking. I'm not going to start now."

I fist my hands. "She deserves to know the truth."

Leaning forward, he places his forearms on the table. "There are a lot of things in this world that Mia deserves, but that doesn't mean she's going to get them."

TWENTY
MIA

AFTER DILLAN MADE his phone call to a reporter this morning, I got undressed and crawled into his bed, finally able to get some sleep. But it was just one big nightmare. The video played over and over in my head. It was me. Even though it never showed my face, I knew the moment they dragged me into the room.

I hate that I don't remember it. I knew Matteo had drugged me at some point because time was missing. But I never imagined that was what had happened. I woke up trying to remember and hoping I could piece together other parts that were gone, but no such luck.

Matteo wanted to scare me, and it worked. After he hung up, he sent me a voice text—said that would be my life. That next time, he'd just give me away for free if I didn't do what needed to be done. I've only been in Vegas for ten days, but I'm not moving fast enough for them.

Then Dillan got this crazy idea about giving my father what he wanted? Doesn't he understand it won't be enough? Give my father an inch, and he'll take a mile. He'll force his way until there's no stopping it.

"I'm so excited about dinner tonight," Jasmine states, bringing me out of my head. She picked the girls and I up thirty minutes ago to go shopping.

I sit in the passenger seat of her SUV while April and Alexa sit in the back. "Dead to Me" by Melanie Martinez is interrupted, and a female's voice takes over. "You have a new message from Big Daddy Dick." The voice goes on to read the text out loud. "Quit fucking ignoring me, woman! I'm going to give you until midnight, and if you have not responded to me by then, I will show up at your house, knock down your door, and tie you to your bed. I'll fuck that sweet cunt in ways you didn't even know were possible while my belt is wrapped around your neck. Then when I've had enough of that pussy, I'll move on to that smart-ass mouth of yours because we both know how much you love choking on my cock. Lastly, I will bend you over my knee with your hands tied behind your back and spank your ass until it's black and blue before I pin you to the floor and fuck it as well. You won't be able to walk for a week, let alone sit down. And that's a goddamn promise!"

A silence follows before Emilee begins to whistle. "Damn. Maybe you should get some lingerie for him while we're shopping today. Give him something to rip off before he has his way with you."

"A restraining order sounds more appropriate," April jokes with a laugh.

Jasmine just smiles, reaching over and presses ignore to the text, and the music once again fills the car.

"Are you going to respond to that?" I ask wide-eyed.

"Nope." She gives me a quick glance and winks. "A man is only as good as his word."

She pulls into a parking lot for what looks like a massive concrete building.

"Where are we?" I ask, looking around. Not many cars are here. I thought we were going shopping? Although I figured it'd be some-where secluded, so the public doesn't see me. This doesn't look like a shopping center of any kind. Honestly, I was expecting to be somewhere that Dillan paid them to close down just for us. He's extreme like that.

"This is the warehouse," Jasmine answers as we all exit the SUV and walk inside. Rows and rows of clothing span the large space. "It's where they keep all the Queens clothing."

"Huh?" *What's a Queen?*

"They have everything—Gucci, Fendi, Armani ... Any brand you want," she adds.

"I think you'd look gorgeous in anything white," Emilee adds.

"No." Jasmine grabs my shoulder and spins me to face her. "Is your skin always this color, or have you been tanning?"

I haven't got to spend much time outside. "Natural."

She snorts. "Lucky."

"Is your hair always this dark, or do you dye it?" She runs her hand through it.

I had fallen asleep with it wet after I sat in the cold shower, so it's wavy right now. "Natural." I've never colored my hair before, not because I didn't want to, but because I was never given the opportunity to have it done.

"Hello, ladies," a woman greets us.

"Hello, Georgia." Emilee smiles at her.

"You must be Mia." She turns toward me.

"Yes, ma'am."

"Come on. I just had a shipment come in. I was told to make sure you ladies had something that had never been worn."

"All of us?" Jasmine asks.

"Yes, ma'am."

We walk through a set of double doors into the back. Ten racks line a wall to our right.

"May I make a suggestion?" The lady they called Georgia looks at me.

"Yes, please."

"I think this would be absolutely stunning on you." She removes the hanger that has a garment bag attached to it. It reads Oscar De La

Renta in white letters. She unzips the bag and pulls out the material to the dress, and the girls gasp.

"Yes. That is exactly the color I was thinking for her," Jasmine squeals.

BONES

I WALK INTO my house and head straight to the master suite. Coming here so much feels weird. I think I've been here more in the past week than I have since I bought it.

I haven't wanted Mia up at Kingdom. Although it would be more convenient for me, there are too many eyes and too many people running their mouths. I kept her hidden because I wanted to keep Mr. Bianchi guessing. Now it's time to show her to the world.

Entering the bedroom, I go straight to her walk-in closet. Stepping in, I pause at what I see. Mia stands in the center with her back to me. Her hair is over her shoulder. The champagne-colored dress dips low down her back where the satin material gathers at her ass, giving it a wrinkling effect before falling down her legs.

My dick is hard, and my hands are fisted. I shouldn't want her the way I do. She's all I ever think about. I knew it'd be this way. My brother was right. I've never let my dick control me before, but it does with her. I crave her taste when I wake up in the morning.

She lifts her arms and tries to fasten a necklace.

I clear my throat. "Let me."

She jumps at the sound of my voice but doesn't turn to face me.

I step up to her, grab the chain, and fasten it. My fingers touch her skin, and I can't help myself. I run them down over her spine, making her shiver.

She spins around to face me, and my eyes sweep over the V-cut dress. Her boobs are smaller than most the women I've been with in the past. But I'm obsessed with hers. I love that in a world full of fake, she's real. No piercings, no tattoos—her skin is flawless. My eyes travel up and over her fragile neck to her face. Big silvery-blue eyes stare up at me, filled with apprehension.

She thinks I'm crazy!

That what I'm doing is insane. But maybe I'm not doing it for her father. Maybe I'm being selfish and doing it for myself? Maybe I want to be the one to show her off. She's my trophy. Something only I have ever had. No one else has ever touched her, kissed her, or fucked her.

Her eyes are outlined with black liner on top and bottom, making them even more prominent. Her lips are a nude color, and her lashes look like they've been dipped in ink. She bites her bottom lip nervously. "The lady said this is a good color," she says in a soft voice. If I didn't already know she was nervous, her voice would have given her away.

I take a step back and look over it. It's skintight until you get to her hips. It's got two slits in it, leaving a small piece down the center. I reach down, grabbing the soft material in my hand and pull it to the side to see she's wearing a matching-colored thong. I imagine ripping it off, turning her around, and bending her over the island to fuck her right here and now. "It looks perfect on you." I let go of it.

She blushes and looks away. I cup her face, her eyes coming back to mine. "Dillan." My name is breathless on her lips, and I regret that I set up a fucking dinner tonight. I'd much rather stay here, alone, in bed with her.

Her hands go to my waist, and her lips part. I lower mine to hers, and she opens up for me, letting me taste her.

Fuck, she's intoxicating. Is this what addiction felt like for Grave? If so, I now know why he could never stop. My free hand slides into her curled hair, and I tilt her head back.

I force myself to pull away, and her eyes flutter open. "Later," I promise and kiss her forehead. Then I turn around and leave her in the closet to head for a shower. I need a cold one.

TWENTY-ONE

MIA

I SIT IN the passenger seat of Dillan's car while he drives us to the restaurant. My heart hammers in my chest. I don't know why I'm so nervous. It's just a dinner with friends. Women do this all the time. I've never been around all the Kings at the same time and the girls. Not in this type of situation.

Dillan reaches over and slides his hand between one of the slits in my dress and grabs my thigh.

My pussy clenches. It's amazing what your body can crave once it gets a taste. I always knew I was missing out on not only human interaction but just the longing for a touch. The sex is great but put that to the side. Just the way he touches me here and kisses me there. It makes me a puddle of water at his feet.

Now I understand why women do stupid shit for a man who they could have no future with.

"You okay?" he asks.

"Yeah," I answer and realize that my legs are bouncing, and he can feel it. "Just a little nervous." I can't lie to him.

"Don't be. Everyone is going to love you." He looks over and smiles at me—a full, white toothy smile that shows off two dimples and makes his eyes light up from the lights on the dash.

I feel wet between my legs and pray that the thin cotton thong I wear is thick enough to keep the silk dress from showing how much he affects me.

He brings the car to a stop in front of our destination and removes his hand from my thigh. My skin is now cold. "Wait for me," he orders and then pushes his door open.

"Good evening, Bones." I hear a man greet him who stands on the driver's side of the car.

"Tony." Dillan acknowledges him. "Congratulations on the baby. How is he and the wife doing?"

I smile at his question. He sounds so "normal." You'd never guess he's a multibillionaire who runs with the Mafia and kills people.

"She's doing great. So is he. Thank you for the gift."

"Of course," he says, and I watch him walk around the back of his car. I take in a deep breath and run my sweaty hands down my bare thighs before adjusting my dress. I'd hate to make front-page news because I showed my pussy off to the world.

Dillan opens my door and holds out his hand. "Gorgeous."

I have to remind myself that this is just an act. I can't feel anything for this notorious man, but it's hard. Reaching out, I take his hand and allow him to help me out of his car. It sits low to the ground, so it's a little harder to get out with this dress. It is beautiful, though—with its champagne-colored silk, double thigh-high slits, and deep V-neckline with spaghetti straps, I'm practically naked. I didn't even try it on at the warehouse. All the girls agreed that this was the one, and I couldn't wait to put it on for Dillan as if I'm his prize to show off. I've lowered myself to an object for a man just so I can see the fire in his eyes when they run over my body.

Making my way to my feet, he shuts my door, and I watch the guy he was talking to get in and drive off with it. He cups my face, and my eyes rise to his, and that look that I've come to crave is there. As bad as I wanted to go out tonight like a normal couple would go to dinner with friends, I also wanted him to rip this dress off me and take me to bed.

Lowering his lips to my ear, he whispers, "You look every bit of a queen tonight, Mia."

Pulling back, he leans down and kisses me. My hands grab his suit jacket as his hands slide into my hair. He tilts my head back, giving him complete access to my mouth.

He pulls away and then begins walking us toward the double doors that one man holds open on each side.

It's a long and narrow hallway to an elevator. A man pushes the button, and Dillan nods at him, mumbling a thank-you. It opens, and we step inside, where Dillan pushes the twentieth floor. We ride up in silence. My heart hammers in my chest, and I hope he can't tell my hand is sweaty in his.

When the elevator stops, the door slides open, and we step into the restaurant as hushed voices hit our ears. It's dimly lit, and a single long-stem candle sits in the middle of each table. The place reminds me of a fishbowl with nothing but glass all the way around the restaurant, showcasing the city lit up at night.

"Good evening, Bones," the lady standing behind a hostess station greets us.

"Evening, Judy."

He seems to know everyone, but I'd expect nothing less from a King. It's just weird that everyone calls him Bones and not his real name. I wonder if he hates it that I call him Dillan.

The woman eyes me up and down and then looks back at him. Maybe it's just me, but she seems to have a questioning look in her dark eyes. Almost as if asking him why he's here with me. Or maybe that's just my insecurities getting the best of me.

"Has the rest of our party arrived?" he asks.

She nods, smiling. "They have. Follow me." Turning, she walks off, and we follow her.

Dillan leans down and whispers in my ear, "Breathe, beautiful."

The way he calls me beautiful does not help my breathing. It makes it accelerate. My pulse is racing, and I have to remind my feet to walk in these six-inch black Christian Louboutins so I don't trip and fall flat on my face. It makes me hate my family even more. How something so simple should never feel this way.

She ushers us to a round table right next to the window where everyone already sits.

"Damn, girl. I knew that dress would be fire." Emilee whistles, standing from her chair, and my cheeks redden as she walks around to hug me.

I pull my hand from his just in time to embrace her.

"It'll look even better on the floor later," Jasmine states, and the girls laugh.

Haven stands and walks around to hug me as well. "Anything new with Luca?" I ask her softly.

She pulls away, shaking her head. "No." Her fingers play with my hair, and I frown.

"I hate that I haven't gotten to see him yet," I admit.

She gives me a soft smile. "I know, but after tonight, it'll be different."

I nod, knowing she's right. I just have to get through dinner, and then I can see him tomorrow.

Haven returns to her seat, and Dillan pulls out a chair, gesturing for me to sit down. I slowly lower myself to the white leather, trying to position my dress properly and cross one leg over the other. The double-slit up the front isn't the most convenient. "Thank you," I say softly.

He takes the seat next to me. "Mia, you've met the ladies, but you haven't had the chance to meet Titan, Grave, and Cross." He points each one out.

I nod at each one, making eye contact even though I want to crawl under the table and hide until this dinner is over. "It's a pleasure to meet you all."

Titan smiles at me while Cross nods. Grave just glares at me, and I swallow nervously. This is going to go exactly how I imagined—

terrible. I don't miss the fact that Nite isn't here. Wonder where he's at tonight. Maybe he's with Luca since Haven is here with us.

Dillan slides his hand under the table and once again slips his fingers between my crossed legs, resting them on my thigh. I take in a deep breath, deciding that tonight will be my first night to willingly drink alcohol.

BONES

I CAN FEEL how tense she is. My hand rests between her legs on her thigh. The cool satin has fallen to the side, covering my hand. If I wanted to, I could slide my hand up between her legs to her pussy. Finger-fuck her right here at the table and then lick my fingers clean as if she's my main course. But I won't. If she were any other woman, I would, but Mia isn't just any other woman. She'd probably jump up from the table. Right now, she's a timid cat, ready to run and hide at any given second.

I'll fix that. It'll just take time.

She's sipping on a glass of champagne. I ordered it for her. I was watching her very closely and could tell she was lost when she stared at the menu for a few minutes, trying to decide what to drink.

She brings the glass to her lips when my brother speaks. "So, Mia, have you been to see Luca?"

I narrow my eyes on Grave. He knows she's not allowed up there.

"I—"

"Not yet," I interrupt her.

Mia lifts the drink to her lips again, taking a bigger sip this time.

He leans back in his chair, and April taps his shoulder. "Grave—"

"I just figured you would want to see him since you're the reason he's there." He cuts off April.

Mia chokes on her drink.

"Grave!" April snaps at him.

"That's enough," I growl at him, sitting up straighter and pulling my hand from her thigh.

"What?" He arches a brow at me. "Was that supposed to be a secret?"

"What does he mean?" Haven looks at me, and I sigh. "Bones?" she snaps, her eyes going to Mia, who is finishing her drink. She's going to be drunk if she's not already. I know the girl never drinks. "What is he talking about?"

Jasmine hangs her head, and so does Emilee. As far as the women go, I've only told Jasmine, so I'm guessing Titan has filled his wife in on the situation. April pulls her hand from Grave and slams her napkin down on the table, getting to her feet and storming away. Grave gives Mia a smirk before he gets up and follows his fiancée.

"Someone better start explaining what he meant," Haven orders.

Mia takes in a shaky breath. "I—"

"This isn't the place," I say before she can tell Haven what's going on. I'm not sure if we have eyes on us right now. The last thing we need is all of us fighting all over social media tomorrow with a headline about Luca being shot and it being his sister's fault.

"Not the place?" Haven gasps. "My husband is in a coma, and Grave is blaming Mia." She looks over at her sister-in-law. "Tell me, Mia," she demands. "What the hell did he mean?"

She licks her lips. "He—I." Mia clears her throat. "Matteo and the twins..."

"That's enough," I bark, making her jump. "We will not discuss this here."

Silence falls over our table, and Haven glares at Mia, expecting her to finish, but Mia's watery eyes are on her empty champagne flute. After a few seconds, Haven stands and storms off.

"Haven?" Mia jumps to her feet.

"Don't." I stand, grabbing Mia's arm to keep her from running after Haven.

She spins around to face me, her eyes swimming in tears. "She deserves to know."

"I disagree." Titan is the one who speaks. "Her knowing won't change what happened. It'll just have her upset at you over a situation you have no control over."

"But I did. That's the problem," she whispers. "I could have prevented this."

"Mia."

"I need a minute." She rips her arm from my hold and grabs her dress, picking it up off the floor, and I watch her enter the bathroom on the other side of the restaurant.

"Will you...?"

"Yeah." Jasmine and Emilee are already up and going after her before I can finish my request.

"Well, this is a disaster," Cross states, picking up his scotch and throwing it back.

"I'll be back," I announce and start walking off.

Titan stands as well. "Bones, don't," he rushes out, but I'm already walking toward the elevator.

Grave and April both have their backs to me as they wait on it.

"Why would you do that?" I hear her ask my brother when I approach them.

"It needed to be said. Haven deserves to know," he answers her as the door slides open. "She's using him. Mia has him fooled—"

I come up behind him and shove his back, pushing him into the waiting elevator, cutting off whatever bullshit he was about to say about me.

"Bones," April squeals, reaching out for me, but Titan had followed me and grabs her while the door closes with Grave and me inside before she can enter.

"What the fuck is wrong with you?" I get in his face.

He fixes his suit jacket that I managed to knock off his shoulder. "You think I'm going to sit back and let her ruin our lives? What we've worked so hard for?"

"She didn't do this," I shout, fisting my hands and trying not to knock his ass out.

"Luca could die." He presses his hands into my chest, pushing me back, and I stretch my neck. It's been a while since my brother and I have physically fought, and I really don't want to hit him. "Because of her. Don't you understand that?" He shoves me again, knocking me into the wall. "And then who do you think they'll come after? Huh?"

"Jesus, is that what this is about?" I snap at him. "I'm an adult, Grave. I don't need you to look out for me."

"I finally have a life." He points at his chest. "I finally have a reason to live. I love April with all I have, but I can't lose you, Bones." Shaking his head, he drops his eyes to the floor. "I can't ..."

"Hey." I grip his face and force his eyes on mine. "Nothing is going to happen to me. I promise. But I have to do what I need to do to save her. Please understand that."

Grave has always felt things more than anyone I know. That was why he was an addict. He always said it was to feel alive, but I think it was to numb everything. To forget our mother died when we were young and the fact that our father acted like he didn't exist. Grave always had a death wish. That's how he got his nickname. The drugs were going to help him live up to it. He's clean now, and I'm just realizing how it's affected him. How much he worries about losing what he's finally come to realize he has.

"Even if it means ruining all of us?" he asks. "Because that's what they will do the first chance they get."

"It won't come to that." I'll do whatever I have to do to make sure she's taken care of without the Bianchis touching the Kings and their queens. Even if that means surrendering myself to them. "I—"

"You can't promise that, Dillan," he interrupts me. "And even if you believe it, I don't." He steps back, and my arms fall to my sides again. "You need to let her go again. Ship her off."

"I can't do that," I say honestly.

He stares at me, his blue eyes hardening and his jaw sharpening. "You've fucked her."

It wasn't a question, so I don't respond to it.

Throwing his head back, he gives a rough laugh. "Can't fucking

176

believe it." His eyes meet mine again, and he pushes a finger into my chest. "Explain to me again how she's not using you."

"She's not."

"Bullshit!" he screams.

The door slides open just as the identical elevator beside us dings. April comes running into ours the next second. Titan comes into view, standing right outside of it.

"Grave." She breathes his name.

"Let's go home." He drapes his arm over her shoulders and exits the elevator.

Titan steps onto mine, and the door closes once again. He presses the button for the restaurant. "Not going to lie. I expected him to be knocked out on the floor. Thanks for saving me from having to deal with a distraught April."

I run a hand through my hair. "Fuck," I hiss.

"Put her first," he speaks.

I look over at him. "The Kings—"

"We're fine, Bones. We can handle ourselves. Do what you have to do."

I flinch at his words. Luca told me those same words, and I've already failed him. "It's not that simple." Titan makes it sound so easy, but I feel like I'm being pulled in a hundred different directions. I've never been this confused about what actions to take or how to handle something. I'm always in control. Mia has thrown everything off. I know I need to protect her, and I will. I'm just not sure how I can.

"It is," he says simply.

"How so?" I demand.

"No one is on her side. No one has ever put her first. Not even Luca. And fuck him for expecting you to take her on in the first place. All she has is you." He sighs. "I would put my wife first no matter what."

"That's different. She's your wife."

"Isn't Mia going to be yours?"

My eyes snap to his.

"Isn't that why we're here? To get John's attention and show him how much you love his daughter. And you don't half-ass anything, Bones."

He's right. The elevator comes to a stop, and we make our way back to the table. I see Mia sitting there talking to Emilee and Jasmine.

"Dillan." She stands when she sees me. "Where did everyone go?" she asks, referring to Grave and April.

"They left."

"What?" Her eyes widen. "And Haven?"

"She's gone too," Cross answers. "While you girls were in the bathroom, she came back and got her purse. Left without a word."

"I have to go find her." Mia goes to walk off.

I keep her in place. "No. We'll talk to her tomorrow."

"Dillan ..."

"I promise. Okay? Tomorrow."

Licking her lips, she finally gives me a nod, and I pull out her chair.

TWENTY-TWO

MIA

DINNER WENT BY slowly. I didn't say much. What was there to talk about? Everyone seemed tense. Even Titan kept staring at Dillan. And he stared back like they had some silent conversation going on.

It was awkward. And I just got drunk. After three glasses of champagne, Dillan had to help me to the elevator. To hell with whatever pictures and headlines are plastered all over the internet of me come tomorrow. It won't matter. None of it will.

Luca will hate me if he ever wakes up, and my sister-in-law already hates me. I should have never stayed in that beach house when I woke up after he drugged me. I should have run as far and as fast as I could while I had the chance. Then my brothers wouldn't have found me, and I wouldn't have gotten the only person in my family who actually cares about me shot.

"Let's go out," Jasmine announces as we step off the elevator on the first floor.

"I don't think ..."

"Come on." Jasmine sticks her bottom lip out at Dillan as we make our way down the narrow hallway to stand outside. "It's one night. Alexa and I need this before the clubs open and we're busy every night. Let's go out, have some drinks, and dance."

"You have to be home by midnight," Emilee reminds her with a laugh.

"Oh, yes." She smiles. "I have plans later." Jasmine refers to her Big Daddy Dick text that she received while on our way to the warehouse earlier today.

Bones looks over at me, and I nod. I've never gotten to go out before, so why not? My night is already fucked. It can't get worse. "Okay. We'll follow you guys," he says as the valet brings his car to a stop.

Opening up my door, Dillan takes my hand and helps me inside. I fall onto my ass and push my bare back up against the black leather seat and close my eyes.

"Hey." I feel a hand on my thigh, and I jump, my eyes springing open. Dillan is leaning across the center console, one hand on my thigh, the other cupping my face. *When did he get in the car?*

"We don't have to go out," he tells me.

"I want to." I want to forget about this night, the fight, and the fact that I have fucked up everything. "I'm fine. Promise." *Lie.*

But he seems to buy it because he pulls away and drives off. I lean my head back against the headrest again and close my eyes, feeling the way my head spins and noticing that my tongue is heavy.

DILLAN PULLS HIS CAR INTO A PARKING SPOT NEXT TO A RED Maserati, and I watch Titan get out before opening the passenger side door for Emilee. Jasmine pulls up next and gets out of a white BMW i8.

Dillan takes my hand, and we walk across the packed parking lot. Coming around a building, I see a long line of people waiting to get in. "Is it always this busy?" I ask.

"Oh, yeah." Jasmine is the one who answers me, tucking a piece of her red hair behind her ear.

I try to keep up behind Dillan while passing everyone standing in line and up a set of stairs.

"Kings." A man with a clipboard smiles at us. "Wasn't expecting you all tonight."

"Last-minute decision," Cross informs him.

"I know how that is." The guy writes something down and then opens the doors for us. "Give us ten, and Damian will have your usual table ready."

We enter the building, and the sound of loud bass hits my ears. The floor under my heels vibrates, and lights flash, making it hard to focus on anything. "Do you come here a lot?" I yell in Dillan's ear.

He shakes his head and bends down to speak into mine. "Cross and Grave used to."

I've never seen so many people in one place before. I've watched TV shows and movies where people are out dancing at clubs, but this one is three stories tall. A bar lines either wall to our left and right with a dance floor in the middle. Stairs are straight ahead that lead up to a loft area. Looking up, I see people looking over down to the first floor.

Dillan pulls me through the mass of people while Cross and Alexa lead us over to the bar at the back. He leans down and asks, "What would you like?"

Pulling back, I meet his eyes. The moment I got my first look at him in the limo, I thought he was gorgeous for a man. Evil but beautiful, nonetheless. He always has this look on his face like he hates the world. Or maybe it's just me and the position I've put him in. But right now, with all the flashing neon lights, they glow the prettiest color of blue I've ever seen. I guess that could be the alcohol talking. Isn't there a saying about how alcohol makes you find someone attractive who you normally wouldn't? Even so, that can't be what this is because I already find him that way.

"Surprise me," I say, licking my numbing lips, and his eyes drop to the action.

Reaching up, he cups my face, his thumb running over them before his eyes meet mine again. My thighs tighten, and my lips part. An open invitation that I want his on mine.

But he pulls away and faces the bar, ordering some drinks. My shoulders fall.

Of course, he's not going to kiss me in public. This is a fake relationship. It's not real. Not what he's trying to convince the world of anyway. Yeah, we've had sex, but it's not like he's going to shove my dress up, bend me over the bar, and fuck me for all to see.

He's motherfucking Dillan Reed—Bones—a King. Multibillionaire. He's probably got at least a hundred women right now blowing up his phone, begging to fuck him. Acting like he's interested in me while out in public would ruin his playboy reputation.

Turning around, he hands me a drink. I bring the straw to my lips and take a sip. My eyes fall closed, and I moan when the fruity liquid slides down the back of my throat. Damn, that's good. Is this alcohol?

Opening them up, I freeze, my lips still around the straw when I see him watching me.

I pull the drink back and nod once. "It's good." I play it off.

Stepping into me, he removes the drink from my hand and places it on the bar. "I said I liked it," I yell over the music, thinking he didn't hear me the first time.

His hand falls to my neck, and I swallow, my skin breaking out in goose bumps. Lowering his head, he whispers in my ear, sending a chill down my spine. "Dance with me."

Without waiting for an answer, he pulls away and grabs my hand, dragging me out to the dance floor. People part for us like he's fucking Moses, and the men nod their heads at him as if they know him personally.

"Want It" by SoMo starts to play. I nervously look around, but he cups my cheek.

"Look at me."

"I've never danced before," I admit. My heart races with nervousness even though I want him to pull me in close to his body and run his hands all over me, making my skin heat. Fuck, I'm horny and drunk.

"First time for everything." He repeats the same thing I said to him when he told me sex would hurt.

When he pulls me into him, I melt. His hands grip my body, moving my hips to the music. His eyes are on mine so intently that it makes me wonder what he's thinking.

"I want you to fuck me," I say, wanting him to know what's on my mind. Wrapping my arms around his neck, I pull him to me. Needing to be as close as possible while others run into us.

He groans, lowering his lips close to mine but not close enough to touch. Once again, he's refusing to kiss me in public. "Mia..."

Moving my head to the side, I run my tongue up the side of his neck to his ear and add, "How you like it."

His hands grip my hips painfully, and I close my eyes, imagining him being inside me and doing that. Bruising me. Marking me.

One of his hands slides up my bare back and grips my hair, yanking my face from his neck, forcing me to look up at him in the flashing lights. "You don't know what you're talking about."

"Kink," I say, and he arches a brow at the word. "That's what you like, right?" I pull my hands from around his neck and slide them down the sides of his button-up, feeling his taut muscles. They make my mouth water.

Maybe I'm naïve, or maybe I'm one of those dumb girls who will do whatever to please a man, but I want more. Maybe it's for me. I want Dillan Reed to fuck me, to own me. To consume me. I need him to take my mind off everything else in my fucked-up life and teach me something new. Show me what it's like to be with a King.

BONES

SHE STARES UP at me, her eyes heavy from the alcohol. When

she said she wanted me to fuck her how I liked it, I thought she had lost her mind. I know she didn't have any sexual partners before me, but how could she think I haven't enjoyed fucking her? Then she mentioned Kink, and it made sense. She means she wants me to dominate her.

I can't say that I haven't thought about it. That's how I've always been with women in the past. But they were all a means to an end sort of situation. "You sure?" I ask.

She nods, her eyes on my lips, hands gripping my hips. I'm so fucking hard, and she knows it. I can feel her body rocking against my dick, trying to tease me. She doesn't even know the meaning of that word, but I'll teach her.

She wants something different tonight, so I'll give it to her. "Come on." I pull her off the dance floor with one hand while pulling my cell out with the other. I check the availability for The Palace and then put it back in my pocket. "We're out," I tell the guys.

"Leaving already?" Jasmine whines, looking at Mia. She's too busy downing what was left of the drink Emilee handed her.

"Yep. We're going to Kingdom."

Titan smiles, knowing exactly what I'm about to do. We've shared the room before. "Have fun." He winks at Mia, making her brows crease from her confusion at his words.

I lead her out of the club and to my car, opening my passenger door for her. She stays quiet as we drive through town and pull into the private garage the Kings share at Kingdom.

Helping her out of the car, we make our way to the private entrance. "What are we doing here?" she asks.

"You'll see," I say vaguely.

Nigel stands in the corner behind a desk. "Bones, everything okay?" he asks.

I nod at him. "Yes. We'll be staying here tonight."

Grabbing a key card from my wallet, I scan it. The doors to the elevator open, and we step inside. Pressing the sixteenth floor, I grab her arm the moment the door closes and spin her around to face me. "It's not too late to change your mind," I whisper, cupping her face.

She gives me a drunken smile and then presses her lips gently to mine, letting me know she's ready.

The elevator dings, and we walk down a hallway to a door that reads *The Palace—every Queen needs a palace* written in rose gold. I press the code to unlock the door, open it up for her, and usher her inside.

TWENTY-THREE
MIA

WITH HIS HAND on my lower back, he guides me into the dimly lit room. It has a large foyer with a single purple light shining down on us. It reminds me of the club, just without the flashing motion.

Walking down a hallway into an open room, my eyes quickly scan the area. It looks like Kink. Just a smaller version of it. There are no separate rooms or windows for people to watch. Just us—me and him.

"What is this place?" I ask, walking over to what looks like a bench. "Is this Kink too?"

"No," he answers, coming up behind me. He reaches around my waist, his hands sliding into the slit of my dress, and my breath catches as his fingers crawl along my skin to enter my thong. My head falls back against his shoulder. "This is The Palace. Our Queens use it."

"Queens?" I whisper, my hips bucking against his hand, silently begging him for more.

His free hand reaches up to wrap around my throat, and wetness pools between my legs. "Kingdom has an escort service. They are our Queens."

I close my eyes and take in a deep breath. "Dillan." My hand finds his, and I grip his wrist. "I need more. Please."

He kisses the side of my face and then pulls both of his hands away, leaving my skin cold. "Do you trust me?" he asks softly.

"Yes," I answer without hesitation. Because I do. With my life.

"Turn around."

A shiver runs up my spine at the sound of his command. His voice is so cold—like it was that first night in the limo. It does something to me that I can't deny. It turns me on. Doing as I'm told, I turn around to face him. He reaches up and runs his thumb over my lips. I part them, and he pushes it into my mouth. I suck on it, and he lets out a growl.

Pulling away, he hooks his fingers into either strap of my dress and pushes the material down my body. I stand still, letting it fall on my heels. Taking my hand, he pulls me forward to step out of it, and my body pushes into his. I can feel how hard he is, making my heart race. We've had sex at least ten times since that first night a week ago, and it doesn't hurt anymore. Sore, yes, but it's not painful. It's turned into a dull ache, a need that only he can fulfill.

He pushes his hands into my thong, and it too falls down my shaky legs. "You will leave your heels on," he informs me.

I nod. "Okay." I'd agree to just about anything right now.

Grabbing my hand, he leads me over to the large bed that sits in the middle of the room. "Crawl onto the bed, facing the footboard." He slaps my ass at the command, and I yelp at the sting it leaves.

He goes to the end of the bed while I sit on my knees, facing him. There's a tall wooden-looking footboard that has three holes in it. He unlocks it, pulling it up. "Come here." He gestures with his free hand to move forward.

Swallowing nervously, I scoot closer to him. "A hand through each hole. Your head through the middle."

My heart races, and I pause for a second, my eyes meeting his stare. He arches a brow as if to ask if I have the balls to do as he says or am I going to back out. Taking a deep breath, I bend over, placing my arms through the holes on either side of the one for my neck. He reaches up and brushes the hair off my back to hang off the side of my face before closing the top half down, and I look over to see him lock it in place.

I shift on my knees to try and ease the ache between my legs.

Without saying anything, he walks out of sight, and I try to follow him, but the way I'm bent over, I'm forced to stare at the floor. The back of my head hits the footboard, making it impossible to lift my head all the way up.

I can't hear anything over my heavy breathing and blood rushing in my ears. I try to pull my arm free, but the holes are too small. He's got me secured, and I shift on my knees, whimpering.

"I haven't even started yet, gorgeous," I close my eyes as I feel my pussy clench. Goddamn. Just his voice makes me want to come.

The bed dips behind me, and I go to close my legs, but he slaps the inside of my thigh. "Keep them wide open."

"Dillan." His name is breathless. My head hangs over, and my hair covers most of my face. "Please."

He doesn't say anything. Instead, I feel something wrap around my right ankle. Then he spreads my legs farther apart, making my ass lower a little and my back arch more. I bite my bottom lip to keep from crying out as he stretches my body to the point it's painful. Something wraps around my other ankle, and I am no longer able to move my legs. I'm completely immobile.

My breath hitches when I feel his fingers run over my pussy, smearing the wetness before shoving a finger into me. I try to push my body back against him, but I can't. I fist my hands in frustration.

He chuckles at my impatience. "So greedy. I like it."

"Please?" I beg, fighting against the footboard.

"You're so wet, Mia." His fingers enter me again, and I whimper when he starts fucking me with them. But they're gone too soon.

"Dillan," I growl. I didn't know he was going to torture me.

"Yes, gorgeous?" I can hear the laughter in his tone.

"Fuck me," I demand breathlessly, not caring how desperate I sound or how my body is spread wide open for him to see.

BONES

I GET UP off the bed and shrug off my suit jacket, then rip my tie from my button-up. I take my time undoing my cuff links, my eyes devouring her secured to the bed. She's naked except for her heels. I placed her ankles in leather cuffs secured by straps connected on either side of the bed, keeping her legs wide open for me.

Whimpers and moans of frustration come from her perfect lips while she fights the position I put her in. I've always needed control in and out of the bedroom. And she is handing her body over to me however I want it. Only an idiot would pass that up.

My button-up falls from my shoulders, and I crawl back onto the bed. I lie on my back and slide my head between her legs so her pussy is right in front of my face. She's soaked and begging for me to take it. I wrap my arms around her thighs and pull her down onto my face. The sound of her crying out at the new position only makes me smile.

I lick her cunt. I feel her body tense as I suck her swollen clit into my mouth. The sound that she makes has me growling. My cock is straining against my slacks. But right now is about her.

"Oh, God..." She's gasping.

I don't slow down. I've been soft with her. Some would even call it making love. But I haven't had the chance to really fuck her. Make her mine. Use her. This is that chance.

Removing my arms from around her thighs, I slide my fingers into her while my mouth continues to fuck her.

She's rocking against my mouth, her body tensing. The sound of her calling out my name penetrates my ears, and I can feel how close she is.

I don't let up or stop. No, I get more forceful until she comes all over my face.

Pulling out from underneath her, I sit up and turn to look at her while I lick my wet lips. She's shaking, body covered in sweat, and I can hear her trying to catch her breath.

I get up off the bed and go stand in front of her. "My turn, beautiful." Reaching down, I unzip my slacks and pull out my hard dick. Her head hangs over the footboard, hair so long it almost hits the floor.

Reaching down, I gather it all in my hands and hold it at the base of her neck, lifting it at the same time. "Open up for me, Mia. It's time I fuck those pretty lips." She hasn't given me a blow job yet.

I run the head of my cock along her parted lips, and she looks up at me through watery lashes. "That's it." I smile down at her. "Open wide." I shove my hips forward, and she tries to pull away. I know her mouth has never been fucked before, so I'll try to be as gentle as I can, but I'm not about to promise her anything.

Pushing it in farther, she gags, and I pull out. She coughs, so I shove two fingers into her mouth, and fresh tears run down her face. I decide just how far I will be able to go and remove my fingers from her mouth to give her a second to catch her breath. "Breathe through your nose, Mia," I tell her.

Grabbing my dick again, I slide it back into her waiting mouth, and instead of letting go, I grip the base tightly and start to fuck her. Closing my eyes, I throw my head back and slide my hand up and down my shaft and my piercings while I slam my cock into her mouth.

She gags, but I ignore it. It feels too good. I'm too close to coming. My body stiffens, and I pull out just in time to stroke it, coming all over her beautiful face.

TWENTY-FOUR
MIA

I LIE NAKED in bed next to Dillan. We just finished up in the shower at The Palace. My body still shakes, and it hurts to swallow. But I can't stop smiling. I feel stupid. Is being used supposed to feel this good?

He slides his hand over my waist and turns his body into my side. "How do you feel?" he asks, propping himself on his forearm to look down at me.

I look up, meeting his stare. "Great."

His eyes search mine, but there isn't a hint of happiness, and my smile falters. "How-How do you feel?" I stumble over my words.

He doesn't answer. Instead, his hand moves up my body, where he wraps his fingers around my throat. I arch my neck and swallow against it, making me wince. His blue eyes are hard, and my heart starts to race again.

"I hurt you," he says softly.

"I'm fine," I whisper. "Promise."

I sit up, and his hand falls from my neck. I get up and straddle his naked body. His hands go to my bare hips. I look down at his chest. He has a tattoo of a skull with a tilted crown on it, among many others. I run my fingers over it. "How did you get the name Bones?" I wonder.

Reaching up, he twirls a few strands of my hair around his finger. "There was a kid who kept picking on my brother. I sat back and watched a couple of times but didn't want to intervene. I figured it would just make it worse on him. Then school was over one day, and I watched the kid shove my brother's face into the wall and break his nose. I pulled him off of Grave and broke twenty of his bones with my bare hands. I got suspended." He shrugs. "But when I returned to school, everyone called me Bones. It just stuck."

"How old were you?" I ask.

"Uh..." His eyes drop to my breasts before returning to mine. "Middle school."

My eyes widen. "You were so young."

He nods. "We were taught how to fight at a young age."

"Like my brothers," I whisper, and his eyes soften. "Do you ever wish your life was different?"

He doesn't answer, but his hand falls from my hair.

My eyes drop to the tattoo around his neck, unable to meet his eyes. He sits up, his hands going to cup both sides of my face. He gently kisses my forehead.

"Mia—"

His ringing cell interrupts him. He taps my thigh, and I crawl off him. Lying down on my back, I watch him get out of bed and go over to where his slacks lie on the floor, and he removes his cell from the pocket. "Hello?" He runs a hand through his dark hair. "Yeah. I can be there in thirty minutes." He hangs up and walks over to where my dress and underwear are on the floor.

He walks back to me and leans in, gently kissing my lips before dropping them on my chest. "Get dressed. We have to go."

"Where are we going?" I sit up.

"I'm taking you back to the house to drop you off," he says before entering the bathroom, and I know that's all he's going to tell me.

BONES

THE FOLLOWING MORNING, I sit down at my desk just as my cell goes off.

"Hello?" I answer when I see who it is.

"Mia Rosa Bianchi," Marsha Wells says in greeting.

I sit back in my chair. Damn, even I'm surprised at how fast she found that out. "Someone really did her homework."

"Not quite." She snorts. "As much as I'd love to take credit, it was an anonymous tip."

"Anonymous tip," I repeat, not liking the way those words sound.

"Yep. I took two photos of you guys together the moment you arrived and posted them. Only took an hour for someone to contact me."

"I see."

"I feel like you're holding an even bigger story from me."

"I don't know what you're talking about."

"Well, the same anonymous caller also informed me that Luca is in the hospital for a gunshot wound."

My teeth grind. "Can't believe every source ..."

"True. But I just so happened to have someone follow Haven after she ran out of the restaurant. Care to explain why she went straight to the hospital? I was told that Oliver Nite was also seen there."

I don't say anything to that.

She laughs at my silence. "I'll give you twenty-four hours to give me a better story, Bones, or I'm going to plaster Luca's all over the internet."

My hand grips the cell.

"She's pretty." She goes on. "Exactly what I'd expect a Mafia princess to look like."

I don't like the way she talks about Mia, as if she's threatening her. "Marsha—"

"And I'm guessing there's a reason no one knows she exists. Once

I tell the world of her existence and that Luca is in a coma, she'll have a big target on her head. Wouldn't that be a shame if anything happened to her." *Click.*

"Goddammit." I throw my phone just as the door opens. Titan enters, jumping back to avoid being hit by it flying across the room.

He bends down to pick it up off the rug. "You have a visitor," he announces.

"I'm busy," I growl.

"Bones?" Haven says softly, entering behind him.

I shake my head. "I don't have time ..."

"I'm coming to apologize."

"I don't need it." I point at the door. "Leave."

"Bones, please?" Tears fill her eyes.

Running my hands through my hair, I sigh. "I don't ..."

"Jasmine came by the hospital earlier this morning. She filled me in on everything regarding Mia. Why didn't you ...?"

"She didn't want you to know. Thought you would blame her."

"I ..."

"Which you did. So you just proved her right," I point out.

Her bottom lip starts to quiver. I don't have time for this shit today.

"I need you to kill John Bianchi."

Titan snorts.

"Don't you think I'd do that if it was an option?" I growl.

"It has to be." She goes on. "It's our only option."

"No, it's not," I snap. "We've been in bed with the Mafia all of our lives, Haven. If we kill him, then it puts a target on our heads. All of our allies will turn on us." I shake my head.

"Please?"

"No, I won't put the rest of the Kings in danger." And I find it odd that John hasn't shown up. I mean, his eldest son is in the ICU because he was shot, and his father is nowhere to be seen? Something just isn't right about this. John Bianchi is a sadistic prick, but Luca runs everything here in Vegas for his father. I know that Nite has taken over the operation for the time being, but still, John should have made himself known here by now.

"Luca would do anything to save Mia."

"He fucking left her!" I shout. "I've known him my entire life. I've seen him on pretty much a day-to-day basis for the past ten years, and he's never once mentioned her." He even had the chance to come clean when I saw her, and he chose to keep her a secret.

"He was the one who sent her away." She sniffs.

I snort. "That makes even less sense."

"To save her," Haven adds.

"What good that did for her," I argue.

"They won't stop until Luca is dead. They know he's the only one who cares about her."

I do, but I keep that to myself. Too much already going on to add fuel to this fire. If Haven knew how I felt, then she'd use it against me. Make me feel guilty even more than I already do.

"I'm pregnant." She starts crying.

I slam my elbows on my desk and run my hands through my hair. *Well, this is going to be another shit day.*

"Fuck," Titan whispers, turning to face the floor-to-ceiling windows overlooking the Strip.

Silence fills the room as she sits down on the couch over by Titan and the window. My door quietly opens, and I look over to see Mia enter the room. She comes to a stop when she notices Haven sitting with her eyes looking down at her hands in her lap.

Taking in a deep breath, Haven speaks softly, "We've been trying to get pregnant, and I was late. I just felt it. I knew I was. I couldn't wait until he got home, so I ran and got a test. I went up to Glass. I used the restroom first because I wanted to have the test to show him. When I came up the stairs, he was lying in the hallway. The back door hadn't even been latched yet." Her watery amber eyes meet mine. "I need you to find Luca's brothers and John. I need you guys to kill them."

"We can't do that. I'm sorry, but this changes nothing." Titan is the one who speaks.

"It changes everything!" she screams, jumping to her feet and turning to face him. "I need you to kill them to save my family. To save Mia, Luca, and our baby." She cups her mouth to silence a sob, and Mia walks up behind her, placing a hand on her shoulder. Haven spins around and immediately opens her arms while Mia embraces her. They both cry.

I stand from my seat and walk over to Titan.

"What do you want to do?" he asks me.

"Call a meeting in fifteen. Get everyone there. Including Haven, but give me a minute with Mia."

He nods and walks over to the girls. He pulls them apart. "Come on, let's go get you a water."

Mia wipes her eyes, then rubs her hands on her jeans.

I pick up my phone off the desk where Titan had set it and call back the last number.

"Yes?" she draws out the word.

"I have a better story. But I need you to give me until Friday."

She takes a few seconds to respond before saying, "It better be good." Then she hangs up.

"What are you doing?" Mia asks me.

"What needs to be done." Then I grab her hand and pull her from my office.

TWENTY-FIVE
MIA

ILLAN DRAGS ME down the hallway to a set of glass double doors and pushes me inside. It's got a long, black table with a skull carved out of it along with Kingdom at each end. He pulls out the chair at the head of the table and ushers me into it.

"What are we doing in here?" I ask.

"Having a meeting. The others will be here any second," he answers, checking his watch.

I look up as the door opens and the rest of the Kings enter. It's the first time I've seen Grave since dinner last night. I hate how much it bothers me that he doesn't like me. As if I have to prove myself to be in his circle. The sad part is that I want to.

"What's going on?" Cross asks, entering behind Titan.

Dillan waits for everyone to get in and settled. Haven sits next to me, holding on tight to a water bottle. Dillan grips the back of the chair I sit in and leans over it. "I just spoke to Marsha. My plan last night backfired."

"How so?" Grave asks. Sitting up straighter, he has his attention on his brother.

"How bad?" Cross inquires.

"Pretty fucking bad," he answers, pushing off the chair. I look over my shoulder to see him crossing his arms over his chest. "An anonymous caller informed her of who Mia was."

Titan frowns. "How is that bad? We wanted her name out there."

Dillan goes on to add, "True, but this caller also mentioned that Luca was in the hospital due to a gunshot wound."

Titan snorts. "We've got NDAs all over that place. She's reaching ..."

"She had someone follow Haven last night when she stormed out of the restaurant. They are aware that she went straight to see him, and that Nite was there."

Haven lowers her face, letting out a sigh, feeling bad for her reaction last night.

"Fuck." Grave slams his fisted hands down on the black surface of the large table.

"So the question is, who the fuck is this anonymous caller?" Cross demands.

"Has to be one of the Bianchi boys," Grave assumes.

"No," Dillan argues. "They said *a* gunshot wound. Not wounds. Whoever called in doesn't know the truth. Just a part of it."

"Well, that makes sense, considering we're not even sure it was one of the Bianchis." Cross shrugs.

"We've had tight security on Luca. He hasn't had any visitors other than those in this room." Titan is the one who speaks. "Besides Nite, and we all know he's not speaking to anyone."

Everyone looks at me, and I stiffen. "What? I didn't say anything."

"Who else knows you exist?" Grave arches a brow, sitting back in his seat.

"No one," I rush out.

"Bullshit."

"Grave," Dillan snaps at him.

"What about the auction?" Titan offers. "You said you bought her in New York. There had to be people there who saw her."

Dillan shakes his head again. "No one there would say a word. It's too tight-lipped. Everything was anonymous. If someone recognized me and decided to speak, they would be killed. They wouldn't risk their lives for her name."

"There was that one guy," I say, and everyone looks at me once again.

"Who?" Dillan growls.

"He was there. In that house you took me to afterward." I vaguely remember a guy in that room that Dillan dragged me into.

"Where the hell did you take her?" Grave snaps at him.

He sighs. "That was Tristan Decker, and he wouldn't say a word to anyone."

"So now what?" Cross asks, everyone obviously agreeing with him because no one argued the fact that this Tristan guy might be the anonymous caller.

"She thinks I'm hiding a better story," Dillan answers.

"There's nothing else to tell." Grave tosses back his energy drink in one gulp. "We could move Luca—"

"Too risky." Dillan shakes his head, not even allowing his brother to finish that sentence. "She gave me twenty-four hours before she went public with the story. I told her I had a better one but to give me until Friday. She agreed."

Silence falls over the room, and I feel the temperature change. I rub my sweaty hands on my jeans and bite my bottom lip.

Grave is the one who breaks it. "What the fuck are you going to give her, Dillan?" He growls his first name, and I watch his body stiffen. I have a feeling they don't call each other by their given names often.

"Friday night ..." He looks at me, and I hold my breath. "Mia and I will announce our engagement."

BONES

"ARE YOU FUCKING insane?" Grave shouts, jumping to his feet.

I ignore him, keeping my attention on Mia. She looks terrified right now. Eyes wide, bottom lip trembling, shoulders shaking. "No, Dillan. We don't have to do this," she whispers.

Grave snorts, still convinced she's playing me.

"I think it's a great idea." Titan nods his head.

"Of course, you would," Grave growls at him.

"The anonymous caller outing Luca's health jeopardizes everyone a lot more than an engagement. She needed a better story. This is better. Bigger," Titan explains.

Grave gives a rough laugh. "A better story would be that you and Bones both fuck your wife."

Haven bows her head, and Mia's wide eyes go to Grave. He notices and smirks. "Oh, your soon-to-be *fiancé* hasn't told you that?" She looks back at me, and my teeth clench. "Yeah," Grave goes on, and her eyes swing back to his. "Bones started fucking Emilee in high school and throughout college ..."

"Grave," Titan warns.

That doesn't stop him. "Then she ran back here because she was in trouble and started spreading her legs for Titan, who was nice enough to share her with Bones—"

"That's enough!" Titan shouts, getting to his feet.

"You know what." Grave throws his hands up. "You all do what-ever the fuck you want, but leave me out of it. I'm not losing what I've worked my ass off for because of pussy, and I'm sure as hell not dying for someone who doesn't give a fuck about us." He turns around and walks out, shoving the glass double doors open so hard I'm surprised they don't shatter.

"I'll do whatever you want me to do, but are you sure this plan will work?" Cross asks me, ignoring Grave's outburst. He looks over at Mia, who is now staring at the table, and adds, "The last one didn't go so well."

"Yeah." At this point, it has to. This was always going to be the next step after we announced her to the world. It's just happening sooner than I wanted.

"I'm going to go to the hospital," Haven finally announces, standing. She's ready to get the fuck out of here.

"I'll go with you." Mia stands and starts to walk toward the door, and I grab her arm.

"She'll be right there," I tell Haven, and she exits. "Mia—" I stop myself, not sure if we should talk about our fake engagement coming up or the fact that I've fucked my best friend's wife. I haven't slept with Emilee since she and Titan got married. She belongs to him now. But what Grave said was true. I can't deny that.

Mia chooses for me. "I don't have a choice, right?" She arches a brow in challenge, and I clench my teeth. "I've never had the option before. Why would I think I'd get one now?"

"I'm protecting you," I growl.

"No." She jerks her hand from my hold. "You're giving my father what he wants." Pushing her chest into mine, she bares her teeth. "I never thought you'd be the type of King that bowed to anyone. Guess I was wrong." Then she storms out of the room.

Running a hand through my hair, I make my way back to my office, ignoring Titan and Cross, who still sit in their seats staring at me. Of course, Titan storms into my office once I sit at my desk. "You're letting her go to the hospital?"

I bow my head. I just want one fucking day to myself. Just one. "Yes." I sigh.

"Why?" he wonders. "Marsha—"

"She posted two pictures of us last night trying to get a hit on who Mia was. She got it. She may not have run the story I wanted her to this morning, but Mia's face is out there." Just as I say it, my cell dings, and I pick it up to see it's a text from Lola—a woman I used to fuck in New York until she got too clingy and wanted me to meet her parents. I cut it off immediately after that. I glance at it.

Lola: Hey babe, I'm in Vegas ...

I don't bother to read the rest. "If she wants to go see Luca, I'm not going to stop her. Plus, Nite is up there." We have security all over that private wing where I had Luca moved. His life and Haven's life are in as much danger as Mia's.

"Don't let Grave get to you," he adds softly. "He's going through a lot."

"Yeah, I know." He and April may seem to be doing well, but who knows how much they are still hurting. I don't expect what they went through to go away overnight. "I'll go talk to him." I stand.

Titan looks down at his phone. "He messaged me after he left the conference room. It said heading out for a few hours," he states. "I told him to take the day off, but he said he'd be back."

I frown. "Where did he go?"

Titan runs a hand down his face. "He needed to go to a meeting."

I nod and sit back down, understanding why my brother is lashing out the way he is right now. He's an addict. Every day, he wakes up and has to remind himself that he wants to be better than he was. For himself, for April, for their future kids. And some days, you need a little more help than others.

I hate to think that my life choices are contributing to that.

Titan plops down in the seat across from my desk. "So about this engagement ..."

"Maybe Grave is right." I sigh. "Maybe there is a better way to buy the time I need other than putting Mia through this." As much as I want to protect her, my plan isn't to make her life worse. And at this point, I'm not sure what her father is up to.

"I just want to remind you that I think a wedding is your best bet."

I nod. "So you've said."

TWENTY-SIX

MIA

I SIT IN Haven's passenger seat, staring out the window while she drives us to the hospital. I finally get to see my brother, and my mind is on Dillan.

It's not like I ever thought I'd get the chance to marry the man of my dreams. You can't meet someone when you're locked away in a house all your life.

"If it means anything, Bones wouldn't do something unless he thought it was right," Haven speaks, breaking the silence.

"All of a sudden, you're on his side?" I ask, not caring to look her way.

She sighs heavily. "I don't want anyone else to get hurt. Bones can protect you."

"He can't save me," I say softly. My chest tightens, knowing how true that is. My brothers know where I am, and they've put Luca in the hospital. They cut off my lifeline. Dillan may think he has the upper hand, but he doesn't. And even if he does, he won't for long.

"It's not like you have to actually marry him," Haven goes on. "Just make it look like it's believable. Put on a show." She laughs. "The Kings are good at those."

I stay silent for the rest of our way to the hospital. Parking, we walk inside and take the elevator up to the tenth floor. The door opens, and I see Nite standing up against a wall by a door. He's staring down at his cell, typing away.

I used to think I was in love with him. Nite was the only man around my age who knew I existed, who wasn't blood-related. Even though my parents did adopt him when we were younger. But I'm the reason he is the way he is. This is why I knew he would never find me attractive. Men like him and the Kings don't fall for girls like me. I say girl because they prefer women. And I'm not that. I have no life experience or education. If I manage to survive this, I'll just be sold off again. It's all about how much my last name can bring in.

"Any news?" Haven asks him.

Looking up, he shakes his head, and I feel my chest tighten. I did that to him. Made him a mute. Not very many people know, but I'm the reason he has no voice.

I follow Haven to the door, and she pushes it open for me to enter. His room is large, with a sitting area over by a window that overlooks Vegas. We're high enough up that we can see the Strip from here. The four towers that say Kingdom across the top stand out. Almost like it's laughing at me. A reminder that my life is a joke.

It's not the fact that Dillan is actually pretending to love me. It's that he's going to let my father think he's won. That's a hard pill to swallow when you've been choking on it for years.

"Hey, babe," Haven says, walking over to the bed. "Guess who came to see you?"

My eyes finally look at my brother, and my stomach drops. He's got tubes and wires everywhere. One is down his throat. His skin looks ashy. The room gives off a cold chill that makes me shiver.

I come to a stop, refusing to come any closer.

"It's okay," Haven notices. "They say he may not be awake, but he can hear us." She gives me a small smile. "I'm sure he'd love to know you're here."

I shake my head and swallow the lump in my throat. "No—"

"Mia." Walking over to me, she takes my hand. "I'm sorry for blaming you, but this is not your fault. Do not blame yourself."

"But it is." I sniff. "And I'm so sorry."

"It's not. None of it is. We know that, and he knows that."

If he ever wakes up, he'll hate me. She doesn't know that he wanted me to stay away. That when I called him, he told me not to contact him. All I can do is prove I'm sorry, and I haven't figured out how yet.

BONES

I PARK MY car in front of the house, not pulling into the garage around back because I won't be here long. It's a little after two in the morning, and I need to be up at Glass by four to close it down. Entering the house, I stop and listen. It's silent. Either Mia's asleep or she decided to stay at the hospital tonight. I haven't heard from her since they left Kingdom earlier today, and I hate how much that's driving me crazy. I've never waited around for a woman to call me. Or cared to wonder where they were. I've always been the one too busy to text or call back. The closest thing I've ever had to a relationship was my high school and college years with Emilee. We were never a couple, but we had an understanding that we were exclusive. She gave me what I needed in the bedroom without the clingy girlfriend bullshit. She didn't expect me to love her, and I didn't feel the need to pretend I did.

Making my way to the bedroom, I open the door to see she's in bed. Nite had texted me earlier that they plan on keeping Luca in his coma a little longer.

My cell rings, and I look down to see it's April. "Hello?"

"Bones," she whispers my name. "I hope I didn't wake you."

"No. You're fine. Everything okay?" As I ask the question, I'm already walking toward the front doors of my house and stepping outside on my porch to look over at theirs. I see several lights inside the house are on. I frown. She's always up early because of the flower shop she owns, so for her to be up this late is odd.

"It's Grave." She sighs. "I tried calling Titan, but he didn't answer. Then I saw your car parked out front."

I'm running down the stone steps before she even finishes her sentence.

There's a long pause before she asks. "Can you come over?"

"I'm already on my way. What's wrong?" I question, my heart racing, thinking the worst. My first thought is that he's relapsed—swallowed too many pills. He's facedown in his own vomit, and he's too heavy for her to move.

"I-I don't know." April sniffs. "He won't talk to me. I tried calling Titan," she repeats. "I'm sorry." She begins to cry.

"Don't apologize. I'm on my way." Hanging up, I start to run across the cul-de-sac over to their house. Titan and Grave have gotten really close this year. More than they were before. Titan's the one who dropped him off at rehab. I hate that Grave felt he couldn't talk to me like he could Titan, but I didn't care who my little brother spoke to as long as he sought help when he needed it.

I'm breaking a sweat by the time I run up their steps, and she meets me at the door. I notice her bloodshot eyes and runny nose. Her makeup is smeared in places and completely rubbed off in others. She's holding a wad of tissues in her hand. Her purple hair is up in a messy bun, but pieces fall out of it around her face. She grabs her black silk robe and wraps it around herself to cover up her white spaghetti strap shirt and matching cotton shorts.

"Where is he?" I ask, sucking in a breath.

"Kitchen," she whispers.

I practically run down the hallway and rush into the kitchen, coming to a stop. He sits at the table, facing the five rectangular floor-to-ceiling windows that overlook the cul-de-sac. The curtains are open so you can see our private clubhouse in the middle.

My eyes quickly sweep over his profile view, checking for blood or any sign of injuries, but I see none. He's wearing a black T-shirt, showing off the tattoo of April on his arm that he had Cross do. He has his ripped jeans on, and he still has his combat boots on. He sits motionless, one hand holding a glass of scotch, the other holding the open bottle.

"Kyle?" I say his name, sitting down to his right at the head of the table. He doesn't acknowledge my presence, and I wonder if he's already high on something. "Grave. What's wrong?" I ask, needing him to speak to me. "We can't help you if you don't tell us what's wrong."

He blinks, lowering his blue eyes to the table. "Do you ever test yourself?" he asks, his voice low and rough, making me frown at his question. Before I can answer, he snorts. "Stupid question. You don't have any limits."

"That's not true." I reach out my hand to his, but he jerks away, so I pull back and link mine together on the table.

His knuckles whiten, gripping the glass and bottle tighter as if I'm going to take them away from him.

"I'm not an alcoholic." He gives a rough laugh. "Spoken like a true alcoholic, huh?" Lifting the glass, he brings it to his face, and he stares at it like it holds the answer to all his problems. "I mean, I never *needed* a drink. I liked a drink. There's a difference. I needed the pills, cocaine ..." He swallows, setting the glass back down but not letting go, and admits, "I miss it."

I hear something to my left and look to see April leaning up against the wall under the archway at the far end of the kitchen. She's behind him, where he can't see her. The look of pain in her eyes makes my chest ache.

"I hate feeling." He sniffs. "I was doing so good. Everything seemed better. But ... but I keep having the dreams. Nightmares." He corrects himself and drops his voice to a whisper. "About the baby."

I look back at April, and she's gripping her robe with one hand. The other is over her mouth as she begins to silently cry at his words.

"But it's not me. It's like an out-of-body experience." He frowns, confused by that thought. "I'm standing by watching April cry. And I can't help her. I can't talk to her. I—" He sniffs again. "I'm helpless. But I can feel pain. Her pain. It's unlike anything I've ever felt before. Crippling. And I realize it's not her crying. It's me. My chest is so heavy, I can't breathe." He lifts the glass once again, but this time, he slams it down on the table, making it rattle.

Looking over at April, she now has both hands over her mouth and nose as tears run down her face.

"It's unbearable. The thought of her feeling that." He shakes his head. "And then like a punch to the face, it's gone, and there's nothing. She's gone, and I'm watching me. The old me. I'm alone in a room, fucking high. I tell myself to stop. To move. To get up. But I can't. I watch myself snort a line while I scream not to do it. And I'm numb." He looks over at me for the first time, and his eyes swim in tears. It makes my breath catch. That I can't help him. That I can't save him from himself. "All the pain is gone," he says, looking away. "And for those few seconds, life is back to what it was—a black hole of nothing. Nothing exists. Not to me. There's only silence, and I realize just how much I miss it. But then." He swallows. "Then I wake up, covered in sweat, trying to catch my breath. I look over, and April's sleeping. She—" He clears his throat. "She looks so peaceful, and I tell myself that's why I have to stay strong. For her. Because she's so strong."

"Kyle—"

He throws the glass of scotch, and it shatters one of the windows, glass flying everywhere. I watch April's body shake as she slides down the wall, pulling her knees to her chest, still covering her mouth and nose while she sobs.

"I woke up today." He angrily wipes the tears from his face that have started to fall. "And for the first time in a while, I still wanted to get high. Seeing her wasn't enough. Because I'm fucking weak." He gives a rough laugh. "That's why I bought this bottle." He tosses it up, catching it with his right hand. His skull ring clanks against the glass.

"I thought one bottle won't hurt. That if I had a couple of glasses, maybe it would help me sleep. Knock me out and keep the night-mares away. It was like I was in the dream, watching myself stop at the liquor store and buy it." Holding it up, he scrunches up his face, and then he chucks it at another window, breaking it as well.

The sound of the glass shattering makes me flinch.

"That's another thing that makes me weak." Slamming his elbows on the table, he bows his head, gripping his hair.

"No, you're not," I tell him, clearing the knot in my throat. "You're the strongest person I know."

He snorts, his hands dropping. "I'm a bastard. What I said to Mia at dinner the other night—"

"Don't worry about it."

"What I said to her up at Kingdom—"

"Grave, it's okay. You've been through a lot."

"Stop making excuses for me," he shouts at me. "You would always cover for me when it came to Mom and Dad." He throws his arms out wide. His watery eyes now glaring at me. "There's no one left but you and me now. So just stop pretending that I'm not a fuckup."

Silence falls over the room, and I take in a shaky breath. "You're not—"

"I just thought making others feel pain would make me feel better." He interrupts me, softening his words. "I-I just want to feel nothing." He chokes out the words. "And April. She deserves better. For the first time since I met her, I thought of walking away from her on my way home from work tonight. Giving her a chance at some-thing better. What she deserves, but nothing—" He slams his fists down on the table. "Nothing short of death would make the pain of losing her go away. And that's another reason I'm so fucking weak." He lowers his voice. "It's like Dad always said—love makes a man weak."

I flinch at his choice of words. He paraphrased them, but it's exactly what our father meant. "He was wrong." I reach out for him, but he shoves my hands away and jumps to his feet, the chair scraping across the marble floor. "Grave—"

"That's what makes me a bastard." He shouts again while angry tears run down his face. "Because I wouldn't be strong enough to let her go." He takes in a deep breath, and we hear her sob.

He spins around, and his shoulders fall when he sees she's been listening. She gets to her shaky feet and runs to him, arms open, and wraps them around him. "Don't leave me. Please ... please don't leave me," she cries, clinging to him for dear life while his arms stay at his sides.

"I'm so sorry," he whispers, so much pain evident in three little words. Closing his eyes, he repeats. "I'm so sorry, April."

"No." She pulls away, placing her hands on either side of his face. "Don't. Don't you ever be sorry."

"It's my fault," he goes on, shoulders shaking.

"No—"

"If you hadn't met me, then you wouldn't know the pain I put you through. The baby..."

"No," she growls, getting angry with him for blaming himself for something he had no control over. "That's not true."

"I didn't take a drink," he tells her, shaking his head quickly.

"I know." She nods, sniffling, trying to pull herself together.

"I haven't done any drugs ..."

"I know, babe. I know."

He lowers his face, placing his forehead on hers. "I ... love you," he chokes out.

She lets out a sob before licking her lips. "I love you."

His legs give out, and he falls into the chair, and she goes with him, straddling his lap. He wraps his arms around her, softly rocking them back and forth.

"Grave!" I hear Titan call out, and the front door slam shut. "April!" He rushes into the kitchen to find us and comes to a stop.

I stand from the table and turn to face him. His wide eyes search mine and then my face. His look of concern turns to panic, and I realize I've been silently crying. "What happened?" he asks. "I'm sorry I missed your call." His eyes go to the broken windows. "What—?"

"It's okay," I tell him, pulling myself together. "Everyone's okay."

TWENTY-SEVEN

MIA

I OPEN MY heavy eyes to the dark room and sit up. "Dillan?" I call out, thinking I heard something. Picking up my cell, I see it's almost four in the morning.

Pushing the covers off, I get out of bed and enter the bathroom. I hear the shower running before I see it. Bones stands under the sprayer, his back to me. Both hands on the wall, head down. It's dark in here. He doesn't have any lights on, just the few under the countertops, giving the large room a soft glow.

Reaching up, I remove the Kingdom T-shirt I wear and slide the underwear down my legs before opening the glass shower door. His muscles tense as he lets the water run down over his inked body. I can hear his heavy breathing over the shower. I place my hand on his back, and he jumps, spinning around, and I take a step back.

He stares down at me, and I frown when I see his eyes are bloodshot. "Dillan—"

Reaching out, he cuts me off and pulls me to him. Without saying a word, he lowers his lips to mine and kisses me. Fervently. Taking my breath away.

His hands slide into my hair, and he tilts my head back, his mouth dominating mine. I want to be mad at him after what I found out today about him and Emilee, but I have no right to be. He had a life before me, and I can't change that. I think that's why I focused more on our upcoming fake engagement rather than what I really wanted to talk about.

Pulling away, I suck in a deep breath and open my eyes to look up at him. "You okay?" I ask softly, running my hands down his slick back, feeling how tense he is while the showerhead sprays it.

He doesn't answer, but he doesn't have to. I already know the answer, and it's no. Something is wrong. Instead, his eyes roam over my face and neck. They drop to my chest, and he licks his wet lips.

"Talk—"

His lips come down on mine again, cutting me off, and he spins us around, pushing my back to the wall. His hand drops to my thigh, and he lifts it up, wrapping it around his hip. Then he's sliding into me without any foreplay. It hurts, forcing me to cry out into his mouth.

I pull away from his lips to suck in a breath, and he buries his face into my neck, not caring. He starts to fuck me, hard and fast, shoving my back into the warm tiled wall as the water comes down over us. And I let him take whatever he needs from me. He's hurting. I can feel it in the way his fingers dig into my thigh. The way his breathing picks up and the fact that he refuses to look me in the eyes.

I wrap my arms around him and squeeze. "It's okay," I tell him, not sure what he needs, just knowing that I want him to know I can give it to him.

He doesn't let up. He slams into me harder, and my breath hitches. He drops his hand from my hair to my other thigh and lifts that as well, both of my feet now off the shower floor.

I wrap them around his narrow hips, hooking them together, trying to hang on to his wet and slippery body.

He grunts, his hands slapping on the wall above my head, and I tilt mine to the side to get fresh air because I'm choking on the water spraying on us from above.

This is nothing like the other times we've had sex. Even last night at The Palace felt intimate. This is a distraction for him.

I place both hands in his hair. "I'm here," I tell him breathlessly, and he pulls back the best he can with my legs wrapped around him, slamming into me. "Right here."

He's being so rough that it's painful, and tears start to sting my eyes, but I don't stop him. I have a feeling this man is never as vulnerable as he is right now. So I take it. Let him use me. It feels nice to be needed for once. To help someone rather than cause pain.

"Dillan—"

He reaches up and slaps his hand over my mouth, shutting me up, and I close my eyes, breathing heavily through my nose. He lets out a groan, slamming into me once again, and I feel his body stiffen against mine while his cock pulses inside me.

We stay this way for a few seconds while he tries to catch his breath, and then he pulls his head from my neck and drops his hand from my mouth. I suck in a deep breath, swallowing some water. He lowers my feet to the floor, and I whimper when he pulls out. He takes a stumbling step back, running his hands through his dark hair to push it back from his face. His eyes stay on the floor. Without saying a word to me, he turns and exits the shower. Grabbing the towel hanging on the hook, he wraps it around himself and exits the bathroom.

I turn off the water and get out myself. Grabbing the spare towel, I wrap it around me and rush out to find the bedroom empty. I see the door to his closet open, and I walk in to see him getting dressed, pulling up a pair of dark gray slacks. "Where are you going?" I ask, leaning against the doorframe.

"Work." His answer is clipped.

I frown. "It's almost four in the morning."

He doesn't say anything to that, just slides on a black button-up and starts buttoning it. Once done with that, he puts on socks and shoes. He turns to exit, but I stand, blocking it. "Talk to me," I urge.

"I'm late." That's all he says and shoulders past me. Then I hear the bedroom door open and slam shut.

I crawl into bed with wet hair and his cum dripping out of my pussy, worried that something has happened and I'll never know what it was because he's emotionally shut himself off to me.

I sit silently next to my brother's hospital bed. A quick look at the clock tells me it's almost midnight.

Haven sits up over on her cot and rubs her eyes, yawning. "Anything new?" she asks.

"No." I release his cold hand and set it down on his bed.

She runs a hand through her tangled hair. "I'm exhausted."

"Go home. Just for one night and get some rest," I tell her. She can't get much here. It's a nice setup, but it's still not home. They come in all hours of the night and day, checking on Luca and running tests. The machines constantly beep. She deserves to go home and get a good night's rest.

"I can't go home," she whispers. "Everything there reminds me of him being here."

"Come home with me," I offer, knowing that Dillan doesn't have any other rooms set up for company. I can put her in his office. The couch is really comfortable. All she needs is some blankets and a pillow. She'll have the entire second floor to herself.

"No." She shakes her head softly. "I don't want to bombard you and Bones."

I look down at my hands in my lap. "He hasn't come home in three days." The last time I saw him was in the closet. He got dressed and left without an explanation, and he hasn't returned since. Well, not that I've seen. I guess he could have been there while I was sleeping. He's avoiding me. I'm not sure what I did, but I hate the unknown.

"What?" Her head snaps up to look at me. "Is he staying at Kingdom?"

I shrug. "Don't know. Haven't heard from him." No phone call to get the fuck out of his house. Or text to tell me that our pretend relationship is over. Not a fucking thing. I'm on my own to figure it out myself.

"In three days?" she growls.

I nod my head and stand.

"What happened to you two getting engaged?" she reminds me.

"As far as I know, it's still on." I shrug, not too concerned about it. Something tells me it won't be happening. Not if he's as smart as he thinks he is. "Come stay with me. Just one night. You need a good night's rest."

She gets up and walks over to Luca's bed. Running her hand over his forehead, she gives a sad smile. "Yeah, that sounds good." Leaning down, she kisses his hair. "I'll be back tomorrow."

BONES

I WALK INTO my house and go straight to the kitchen. I stop at the fridge when I hear my phone going off. Pulling it out of my pocket, I see it's an incoming text.

> Lola: I've been calling you. I'm in town for a few more days. I want to see you.

I IGNORE IT. OPENING THE FRIDGE, THE LIGHT FLIPS ON. I LOOK up to see Haven standing there. Her red eyes let me know that she's been crying. Probably because Luca still hasn't woken up yet.

"What are you doing, Bones?" she growls.

"What are *you* doing, Haven?" I throw her own question back at her while grabbing a bottle of water out of the fridge.

"Why are you doing this?" She avoids my question like I dodged hers.

"Doing what?" I run a hand through my hair. I'm exhausted and not really in the mood to play games right now.

"Why are you shoving Mia away? You say you're going to announce an engagement and then ignore her?"

I walk past her. "I don't have time for this ..."

"Want to know what I think?"

"Nope." *Don't care.*

"I think you're falling in love with her."

I come to a stop and spin around to face her. "You don't know what you're talking about."

"You're a lot of things, Bones, but you suck at lying." She walks over to the table and falls down into a chair. "That's why you're avoiding her."

"I'm not avoiding her." Not a total lie.

I haven't wanted to see her since the night I went over to Grave and April's. Our father raised us to feel nothing. Grave never was that guy, but I was. And then when I saw his breakdown that night, I had an overwhelming feeling of rage and guilt. I felt like my hands were tied, and I was unable to help him. Then Mia walked into the shower, and I realized I needed her. While I was fucking her, all I could think about was that I understood why Grave stopped and bought that bottle of scotch on his way home. Mia is my drink of choice. My drug to numb the world. She knew I was hurting, and I just used her. And the worst part is that she let me.

"Why aren't you coming home?" Haven demands like she's the wife who waits around for a husband she never gets to see.

"Because I'm not able to." I slap my hand down on the table, making her jump. Lowering my voice, I add, "I'm working Kingdom during the day and Glass at night."

"There are three other Kings."

"Glass is not their responsibility," I argue.

"And the engagement?" she asks.

"What about it?" I sigh.

"Are you calling it off?"

I don't answer.

"So you're going to pretend to get engaged, and then what?" She goes on in my silence, "Break up with her in a week?"

I remain silent.

"Why won't you just tell her how you feel?"

"What do you want me to say, Haven?" I lift my arms out wide, and then they drop to my sides.

"Is this about your pride?" she wonders.

"No." I snort, falling down into a chair opposite her. My legs are too tired to stand anymore. "Truth." I sigh. "Because if I tell her how I feel, then she'll stay. And I won't be like him." I shake my head. "I won't be like her father and keep her prisoner." Once this shit with her family is handled, she and I will publicly announce that we've ended things. Then she will be free to go on and live her life how she wants.

"Jesus," she hisses. "Is that what you think love is? A life sentence."

I don't answer her. Instead, I take a drink of my water.

"Being in love"—she pauses—"is like knowing the sun will rise tomorrow." Looking at me, she sighs. "It's nothing like a prison, Dillan. Mia has never known what it feels like to have someone love her. Not like the kind of love I know she wants. And don't give me that shit where you say you don't know how to love." I open my mouth, but she continues, "Loving someone is putting them first."

I flinch at her words; how close they are to what my father used to tell my brother and me.

"And you've already done that with Mia. So don't be so hard on yourself, Bones." She gives me a kind smile. "Definitely don't ignore her. She's been ignored all her life."

Haven gets up and goes to walk out of the kitchen but stops.

"Hope you don't mind, but Mia set your study up for me to stay in tonight. So I hope you're not home to work. I'm tired."

"No," I tell her, and with that, I hear her walk up the stairs to go to bed.

Taking another drink, I decide to blow off some steam. I need to think and free my mind. So instead of going to bed, I make my way to the basement.

Flipping the light on, I look over the four batting cages as the lights buzz. Baseball was my dream. At one point, I thought it would be my life, but deep down, a part of me knew that would never happen. Then I got injured and was told I'd never play again. My dreams of going pro were over.

My father was thrilled because he wanted me at Kingdom as much as possible. Honestly, I'm surprised he even allowed me to attend college. To him, it wasn't needed. He had already established Kingdom to hand over to Grave and me, so why waste time with a degree?

Removing my shirt, I grab a bat that hangs on the wall and open up the cage. Stepping inside, I don't even bother with gloves or a helmet. I never do.

I walk along the inside of the cage to the far end and turn on the pitching machine. Then I make my way back to the front and take my stance, ready to knock the fuck out of them.

TWENTY-EIGHT

MIA

I WAKE UP to see I'm alone in bed, but I'm not surprised because Dillan is avoiding me. Getting up, I use the restroom and check my cell to see if he's called or texted. Nothing.

Sighing, I decide to make my way to the kitchen to grab a drink. I'm headed back to his bed when I see a door slightly open underneath the stairs that I haven't seen before.

I tiptoe over to it and softly pull it open the rest of the way. A set of black carpeted stairs lead down to what I'm guessing is a basement. I see the lights are on. Thinking I should go back to bed, I hear a cracking noise.

Shutting the door behind me, I walk down the stairs to an open room. And just as I suspected, it's a large open basement. It has black-painted walls and a gray epoxy floor with a high ceiling.

Dillan stands in what looks to be a rectangular cage that is made up of floor-to-ceiling netting. He holds a baseball bat in his hands while only dressed in a pair of jeans that sit low on his narrow hips.

A device at the other end shoots out a ball, and he swings at it. The crack noise follows as his bat makes contact with the ball, sending it flying across the cage.

He readjusts the bat, bends his knees, and another ball flies directly at him. Once again, he hits it, making a grunting sound.

I find a long bench against the wall underneath a rack of baseball bats and sit down.

He hasn't noticed me. But I'm easy to ignore.

Another ball shoots out and he swings, missing this one. He lets out a curse under his breath as if he's playing in a game and letting his team down.

The next ball is launched at him, and he swings, hitting it.

I watch the way his back muscles tighten in his stance. The way his jaw sharpens right before he swings. And the way his abs tense when he sucks in a breath.

The man is gorgeous. It's so unfair how attracted I am to him, knowing that he's just going to walk away from me once this is all over. That my time with him is limited, and who knows when that will be.

He hits one more and then stands to his full height. Dropping the bat to hang down by his side, he turns to exit the cage, and his eyes land on mine, making him pause.

I stay silent. What is there to say at this point? He's avoiding me, and I'm stalking him. Seems pretty obvious to me who is the one obsessed here.

He clears his throat and exits the cage. Walking over to me, he hangs the bat up and grabs a towel off a shelf, wiping his sweaty face.

"Do you come down here often?" I break the awkward silence.

"Not as much as I'd like." He surprises me by answering.

"It's nice," I say stupidly. It's exactly what I'd expect a King to have.

"We all have one," he adds.

"Batting cages?"

"Basements." He points over at a door in the corner of the far end. "There is a tunnel that runs from each house."

Of course, there is.

"Grave has a bowling alley. Cross has batting cages like me, and Titan has a shooting range."

I have a feeling none of them get used often. Dropping my head to avoid his stare, I, however, can't avoid the elephant in the room. "Why are you avoiding me?" I ask softly.

Feeling his hand grab my chin, he forces me to look up at him. "I'm not avoiding you."

"Then where have you been?" I hate that I care what he's been up to. That he's taken up my mind. Filling it with thoughts that he's been with someone else. A woman that he wasn't forced to have a fake relationship with. "I can leave if you want me to."

His dark brows pull down. "Why would I want that?"

"So you can come home," I answer. "I don't want you not to come home because I'm here."

Letting go of my chin, he grabs my hand and yanks me to stand. "Dillan—"

He cuts me off, his lips on mine. The kiss is tender, and it doesn't make the situation any better. Just makes me even more confused as to what we're doing. There's no reason to kiss me right now. No one to show off to. I'm overthinking it, and I know it. But I'm not a fuck 'em and leave 'em kind of woman. He has to know what he's putting me through.

He picks me up off the floor, and I wrap my legs around his waist, and he sits down on the bench. Pulling his mouth free of mine, he rips my shirt up and over my head. I undo his jeans and pull out his dick. He's as hard as I am wet.

Fuck, I should not be this attracted to this man. I shouldn't need him as much as I do.

His hand goes to my hair, pulling my lips back onto his. His other hand grips my ass, his hips rocking back and forth while my hands fall between our bodies.

"You're not leaving me," he growls, pulling away from my now swollen lips again.

"No?" I ask breathlessly.

225

"No." His hand drops between us, and he pushes my underwear to the side, sliding his cock into my pussy, making me whimper. "You're staying here. With me. Forever." His hands fall to my hips, and he moves my body, rocking them back and forth, fucking his dick. We've never done it like this before. But even though I'm on top, he's the one controlling me.

"Okay," I agree. My head falls back, giving his lips access to my neck. Being his prisoner sounds pretty good to me. "Just don't stop," I whimper.

"Never." He grabs my hands and shoves them behind my back, holding them hostage in one of his while the other comes up and wraps around my throat, taking away my air. I don't fight him, giving him whatever he wants. Dillan Reed can do whatever he wants with me, and I realize I'd beg him for it.

WE LIE IN HIS BED, HAVING JUST FINISHED ROUND TWO. I straddle his hips, my fingers tracing the scar on his arm. It's hard to see due to the ink, but once you find it, you can't miss it. "I saw the picture of you in the hospital with your arm in a cast," I say softly, filling the silence.

He's underneath me, one tatted arm under his head. The other rests on my hip, his fingers gently massaging my skin.

"What happened?" I ask when he doesn't acknowledge my previous statement.

He's quiet for a long second before he lets out a slow breath. "Broke my arm."

My eyes find his. That was obvious. "How?" I push to see just how much he'll open up to me. I've never had someone tell me about themselves before.

"Emilee wanted to go out that night. There was a concert for all ages at a club. The night didn't go how we planned," he answers vaguely.

I was wondering how to mention her, but he just did. So I turn the conversation to her. "She was in the pictures I saw."

He nods once. "She and Jasmine made us scrapbooks before we graduated college."

"You've always been close," I wonder, but he doesn't respond. I guess, technically, that wasn't a question. Taking in a shaky breath, I ask what I've been dying to know ever since Grave told me about them. "Do you love her?" Who knows when I'll see him again. Or when this will end. I want to know everything there is to know about Dillan Reed. And as far as I know, he could go back to avoiding me soon.

His brows pull together, his blue eyes searching mine. "She's married to Titan." As if that explains everything.

"We both know that sometimes marriage doesn't equal love," I state. The Mafia doesn't marry for love. They marry for power. Luca got lucky that he got to marry Haven. He had to fight for her, and at times, I didn't think my father was going to allow it.

He grabs my hips, picks me up, and places me on the bed beside him. I've pushed him too far. He's going to shut me out. More so than he already has. But he surprises me by lying down and turning onto his side so he can face me. His fingers gently run over my jawline as his eyes find mine. "I loved Emilee as much as I could at that time of my life." I'm about to say I don't understand when he goes on. "We started hooking up, then my mother passed away my senior year in high school. Emilee was there for me when I needed her."

For some reason, that word makes me more jealous than love. I want him to need me. I understand how lonely it can be to have no one.

"We had an understanding. It was strictly sex. She was never one of those women who needed more. And I'm that guy that wasn't going to give more."

My chest tightens at his words.

"I was selfish." His eyes drop to my neck, and his fingers feel my pulse racing. I'm hanging on every word he says. Wanting to know

227

the Dillan that the world doesn't get the privilege to know. "I knew how Titan felt about her, but I didn't care. I needed her too much to share her." His eyes meet mine. "I knew if she gave him the chance, he'd take her from me."

"So what happened?" I ask, licking my lips. "Between you and her?"

"Senior year of college, I was about to sign with the MLB, but I broke my arm, and that dream ended. I hated everything. Everyone. I shut her out. More than I had already been doing. Then me, Titan, and Cross all graduated and took over Kingdom. I never spoke to her again. She moved to Chicago after she graduated. I buried myself in the life I was forced to have. She ran from hers." He shrugs. "Then when she came back, Titan took his chance." He gives a soft smile as if he's truly happy for them.

"But you three have slept together since she's been back?" I add, remembering what Grave had said.

"We have," he agrees. "It doesn't mean she and Titan love each other any less. It just means that they were comfortable allowing me to join them. Sex is different than love, Mia. They're not the same."

The way he says it makes me feel stupid, like I should feel nothing for him just because I let him use my body. But I'm not sure I can separate the two. Not like he does. I feel something for Dillan, and I understand how idiotic that is. A King could never love a no one. My eyes drop to his tatted chest. "Do you still...?"

"No." He answers before I can even finish. "Not since they got married. And I won't. She's his wife. And I would never cross that line."

"Would you, if they asked you to?" I ask, unable to stop myself from looking up at him.

His blue eyes search mine, and I hold my breath, knowing what he's going to say. I shouldn't have even asked. Of course he would. Why not? What kind of man would turn that down? Definitely not a King. He's probably had multiple women at once. He's probably done things that I don't even know exist.

I turn my back to him and go to get out of the bed to take a shower, but he grabs my arm pulling me onto my back. "Dillan—"

He straddles my hips, pinning my arms down to the silk sheets by my head. "I'm here with you, Mia," he whispers, lowering his face to my neck. "I'm only fucking you, and you will only be fucking me."

I arch my back, my pussy still wet from the other two times he's fucked me tonight.

Letting go of one of my wrists, he lifts his hips, positioning himself between my legs, spreading them wide open. Making me cry out as we go for round three.

BONES

THE FOLLOWING MORNING, I walk into Kingdom feeling well rested even though I didn't get much sleep last night. I spent what little time I was home in bed with Mia.

My cell rings as the elevator doors open, and I dig it out of my back pocket to see it's Marsha. Sighing, I hit answer. "I said give me until Friday."

"You sorry son of a bitch!" she screams in my ear.

She's so loud that I pull it away from my ear. "Jesus—"

"You think you fucking own everyone!" She continues shouting. "You fucking piece of shit."

Click.

"Well." That was weird.

Pocketing my cell, I look up at the receptionist, and she smiles kindly at me. "They're in the conference room waiting on you, Bones."

I push the doors open and see everyone already in their seats, including my brother. His blue eyes are on the energy drink in his hands.

"I just had an interesting call. Can anyone tell me what it was about?" I ask, knowing someone in this room had something to do with it.

Grave sits back in his seat, his eyes meeting mine. "I did it."

"What exactly did you do?" I question.

"I've had a tail on Marsha." Opening up an envelope that sits in front of him, he tosses some papers in front of me. "I sent these to her this morning."

Spreading them apart, I look over the pictures of her straddling a man who lies on a bed. His hands are on her hips. The windows are open, showing her bare chest, and you can see the wedding ring on his left finger. Obviously, Marsha isn't married.

"What are we looking at exactly?" Titan asks, picking one up.

"That is James Knowles."

"James Knowles as in the DA, James Knowles?" Cross questions.

"Yep." Grave nods.

"He's not married to Marsha," Titan adds.

"Nope. They're having an affair." He looks up at me. "I want you to find what I have with April. But I want you to find it on your own and not be forced into it. If Mia is the one for you, then great. But fuck anyone who thinks they can tell a King what to do."

I fall into my seat.

"So you got her to back off?" Titan asks Grave.

"I told her if she released anything about Luca being in the hospital, I'd personally drop off these pictures of her and James to his wife. Then I'd make sure they were leaked online." He shrugs. "Not sure what she'll post now, but she won't be waiting for your engagement announcement this Friday."

"Thanks, Grave," I say, but a part of me is disappointed that I won't be announcing my engagement to Mia. I don't know how to feel about that.

TWENTY-NINE

MIA

NOW THAT MY picture has been online, I'm able to go out in public. Dillan doesn't want me out and about alone, so I called Jasmine today to see if she wanted to go to lunch. Thankfully, she swung by and picked me up from Dillan's to take me to Kingdom to eat with the girls.

We're walking out to her car when she looks at me over her shoulder. "Want to drive?"

My feet come to a stop. "Really?" I can't keep the excitement out of my voice.

"Of course." She dangles the keys to her SUV out in front of me.

All of a sudden, I'm nervous. Her car is expensive. I'd hate to crash it into the building. Then I'd owe her and the Kings. "I don't know."

"I promised you I'd teach you to drive."

I turn around to see Dillan walking out of their private entrance, coming down the steps dressed in a black button-up with the sleeves rolled up, showing off his tatted forearms and matching slacks. He looks so good in black.

"But—"

"Get in. I'll sit in the back," Jasmine tells me, and I swallow nervously. I can't say no to both of them.

I slide into the driver's seat while Jasmine crawls into the back, and Dillan sits to my right, closing the door. I feel sweat start to bead on my forehead.

"What's the first thing you do?" he asks me.

Uh ... "Start the car?"

"No." Jasmine scoots to the edge of her seat and pokes her head into the front space. "The first thing a woman does is lock her doors. The moment you shut your door, you lock them."

I look at Dillan, and he seems as confused as I am at her statement. "Lock the doors?" I question.

She nods once. "There is this thing called sex trafficking." Dillan stiffens at her response. "And it is very real. I've experienced it first-hand." Before I can ask her what she means exactly, she goes on, "I've also heard stories. It's not just the trafficking industry, but about women being taken in general." She licks her lips. "This one woman was in Oregon. The surveillance camera showed her walking out to her car from the store. When she got in, she turned around to place her purse in the back seat, and as she did, a guy opened her door and yanked her out. Another car pulled up next to it, and he threw her into the back and drove off with her." She holds up her pointer finger. "Another was of this woman in Texas. She was driving her boyfriend's lifted truck. The surveillance camera showed her entering the store. There was a truck parked three spaces over. A guy got out of the passenger seat and followed her inside while the guy who was driving got out and crawled under the truck. When the woman went to get back in the truck, the man underneath it slit her Achilles tendon, then crawled out from under the truck while the one who had followed her inside grabbed her, and they took off."

"Jesus," I gasp.

"They found her body three days later in a field. She had been sexually assaulted and murdered. Dental records had to confirm her identity."

I swallow, and Dillan's jaw sharpens.

"And never, I mean, never smell something that someone gives you," Jasmine goes on.

"Why would someone give me something to smell?" I ask wide-eyed.

"Like, I read where men and women hang out in parking lots pretending to sell flowers or having women smell perfume samples. Anyway, the point is that they were laced with some kind of concoction that made their victims pass out almost immediately. Then they would take the women."

I swallow nervously while staring at Dillan. He's looking out the windshield, jaw set in a hard line and his arms crossed over his chest.

"And don't ever let someone borrow your phone to call a loved one," she states. "It's a ploy. They come up to you and say 'oh hey, my phone died; may I use yours to call my husband, sister, mother' ... whatever. Only to call the person who is outside in a shady van. They get your cell and hack into your phone and track you down hours later while you're sleeping in your bed. I mean, some people would say that God tests you to see if you're kind. But these days, you can't afford to be nice. God's not testing you. I promise you. He's not sending an angel in disguise to see if you're worthy for a better after-life. Be a bitch. Tell them no and save yourself. I'll chance going to hell any day over being mutilated and left in a ditch."

"What the fuck, Jasmine?" Dillan barks. "Where did you read all of this shit?"

"The internet. Or on a show of real-life crimes. Don't you watch TV?" she asks but doesn't let him answer. "It's all over the news on any given day. Hell, I was followed around a Target once. I immediately found a manager and told him. He escorted me out." She begins to dig in her purse and pulls out what looks like metal bunny ears. "You need one of these." She places her two fingers through the holes and holds it up to Bones's tatted neck. "If a man puts his hands on you, you jam this into his jugular." She pretends to demonstrate on Bones. "All the way until your knuckles are in his fucking

233

throat. Then you rip that bitch out. When he falls to the ground, gasping for air, you stand over him and watch the motherfucker bleed to fucking death." She gives me a bright smile. "And once you know the devil has come to collect his sorry fucking soul, then you call the cops. A dead man can't sue you for attempted murder. It's your word against his. And he'll lie to save his own ass. I am always watching my surroundings. When I'm walking to my car in the daylight, I look at the cars I walk by to see their reflection behind me to make sure I'm not being followed. I always have a gun on me too. Just in case I feel like a bullet will do a better job. But you can't just walk around with one of those in your hands. Not like you can your keys."

I reach over and lock the door.

"That's it!" Dillan snaps, immediately unlocking it. "We're not practicing today." He gets out of the car, slamming the door and making me jump.

"What?" I gasp. "Dillan ..." But he can't hear me as he rounds the front of the car. He rips open the driver's side door and yanks me out.

"But you promised—"

"I lied." He interrupts me, pulling me around the car and placing me in the passenger seat of his vehicle that was just parked a few cars down from Jasmine's. He slams the car door shut.

What the fuck? I look up to see her mouth, "I'm sorry," before he gets into his driver's side seat.

BONES

I ENTER THE house, and she's following me. I can hear the heels of her shoes stomping on the marble floor.

"Dillan!" she demands.

I ignore her, entering the bedroom.

"We had a deal!" she yells.

"I lied." I start undoing the buttons on my shirt. I wasn't done with work for the day. Hell, it's barely noon, but my mood has soured enough that I'm not going back. I'll work from home the rest of the day.

She comes to stand before me, hands on her hips and lips thinned. "Then I'm breaking off this fake relationship."

I laugh at that.

She lets out a growl. "I'm serious."

And so am I. I've never thought about how dangerous the world is for a woman. Especially a woman like Mia Bianchi. Her name is out there now. We've gone public. Everyone knows she exists. Every enemy her father has makes her their favorite target. Every enemy I've ever had makes her an easy target. Fuck, I was so stupid.

"I'm serious!" she shouts. "The fake relationship is off, and I'm out of here." She turns for the closet, and I grab her upper arm, spinning her around.

Cupping her face, I drop my eyes to her chest. It's rising and falling quickly at her heavy breathing.

"I'm leaving." She lifts her chin.

"You're not going anywhere, Mia." My eyes meet hers. "You belong to me."

"Fuck you, Dillan!" She goes to turn from me.

I grab her upper arm, yanking her to me. Letting go of her, I lean down and grab her thighs, lifting her off the floor and slamming her ass onto the counter. My hands go to her hair, and I kiss her.

Her hands come up, and she shoves my face away. "Take that back," she demands.

I smirk. "Excuse me?"

Her eyes narrow on me. "I said take it back."

"No." I place my hands on either side of her face. "I won't take either one back. One, because I'm not letting you go anywhere. And two, because you do belong to me."

"I'm not your property," she snaps.

"You're right. You're not my property. You're going to be my wife." She swallows as I run my hand through her hair. I haven't told her that we no longer need to get engaged. A part of me still wants to go through with it. But it wouldn't be pretend anymore. "And that may not mean anything to you, but it means something to me." I go along with it.

Licking her lips, she whispers, "And what does that mean exactly?"

"That I'm going to protect you. That I'm going to make sure no one ever hurts you. That I'm going to spend the rest of my fucking life putting you first. And that includes not putting you in danger." My father was right—I'll put her before everything else, including myself.

"Everyone gets to drive, Dillan." She rolls her eyes like I'm the one being dramatic.

"I'll buy you a car and a chauffeur." One of those military-grade tanks. Problem solved.

"I want a normal life," she argues.

I hate to break it to her, but she'll never have one of those. Not as a Bianchi and definitely not as a Reed.

THIRTY

BONES

I 'M SITTING IN my office at Kingdom when my door flies
open. "Just because you're in business with me doesn't grant
you access to my office whenever you want," I inform Jasmine.

"Actually, that's exactly what it means." She plops down in front
of my desk, letting me know she's staying a while.

"You may go," I dismiss her.

"I think I'll stay." She gives me a bright and annoying smile

"Jasmine," I growl.

"You're being a dick. What's new?"

"And you're sticking your nose where it doesn't belong." Jasmine
never comes to visit me, so I know exactly what this has to do with.

"You know ... I've never considered you to be like your father"—
she shrugs—"but I see it more and more with Mia."

I fist my hands to keep from reaching across the desk and wrapping them around her neck until her eyes roll into the back of her
head. "Get out," I order through gritted teeth.

She stands and walks over to the wall. Pulling a picture off it, she
runs her fingers over the glass and smiles. "You all had other dreams."

Walking back over, she places it on my desk in front of me. "You wanted something more."

"Yeah, well, we don't always get what we want, do we?" I ask, arching a brow, and she ignores my question.

"I know you have feelings for her."

I snort.

"But trust me, you want someone who would choose to stay with you, not because they're forced."

My eyes meet hers.

"Don't be your father, Dillan. You have a chance to give someone what you never had. She needs your help, and she deserves to live a life, whether that is with you or not." With that, she exits my office.

I pick up the picture. It's of Cross, Titan, and me on our college baseball field. My brother, Grave, took the picture. He hated sports. Well, plus he'd never be able to pass the drug tests.

Leaning back in my seat, I sigh. "Fuck." Jasmine is right. And I hate that.

IT'S A LITTLE AFTER NOON WHEN MY DOOR OPENS, AND MY brother walks in. "Hey," I say, sitting back in my chair and giving him my full attention. He seems to be doing better. But I thought he was better before, and he obviously wasn't.

"How are things going?" I ask him.

He nods. "Good."

"The wedding?" I push. I haven't gotten to speak to him privately since that night at his house. After Titan arrived, we sent April and Grave to bed while we stayed behind and cleaned up the broken glass inside the kitchen. A crew was there the next morning to replace the windows.

"It's still on." He gives a soft laugh.

"That's not what I meant."

He sits down in the seat across from me. "Do you love her?" he asks.

I don't answer.

"I love you, Bones. As a brother, as a best friend, and as a father." He sighs. "You practically raised me. And if this is what you want, then I'll support you." He pauses, licking his lips. "But I want you to be happy. You deserve that." Looking down at his hands in his lap, he goes on, "I want you to find what I have with April."

I go to open my mouth when my cell starts to ring. Picking it up, I frown, seeing it's Haven. "Everything okay?" I ask in greeting, already jumping to my feet.

"He's awake." She sniffs. "Luca's awake, and he's asking for you and Mia."

THIRTY-ONE
BONES

MIA AND I rush into the hospital, her hand in mine. I ran out of Kingdom and went by my house to pick her up. I called her on my way, and she was already getting ready. Haven had called her too to tell her the good news.

I nod to the guard as we pass by him. I release her hand, open the door, and usher her in with my hand on the small of her back.

Luca sits up in his bed, his pale face instantly frowning at us. I figured he'd be pissed at me once he woke up and realized what I've been doing.

"Hey." Mia goes over to him, gently hugging him. "How are you feeling?"

"Give us a second," Luca tells her.

Her dark brows pull together. "Luca ... I don't think—"

"Give us a second!" he yells, making her jump.

She squares her shoulders and parts her lips, but before she can argue with him, my eyes meet hers. "It's okay." I'm trying to defuse a bad situation between them. He just woke up from a fucking coma. The last thing I need is a sibling feud.

She spins around, her dark hair slapping her in the face from the motion, and storms out of the room.

"You didn't have to yell at her," I tell him.

He turns his pissed-off attitude at me. "What the fuck are you doing, Bones?"

"What you asked," I say, dodging the real answer.

He reaches for his remote and turns up the volume on this TV. I look up at it and curse myself when I see a picture of Mia and me making out plastered on the screen.

"One of the heirs to Kingdom—Dillan Reed, known as Bones—has been spotted around Sin City with who we know as the Mafia Princes—Mia Bianchi. The two apparently have been living together in his home right outside of Vegas. The couple has been spotted out a lot lately, but it's clear that they've been together for quite some time. The two are not shy about their public affection. I see wedding bells in their near future ..."

So this is what Marsha ended up going with after Grave put a halt to the story she wanted to run? I'm not surprised. She probably knew that Luca wouldn't approve of what I was doing, and she was hoping to fuck me in the best way she could. Or she wants a target on Mia. Marsha had threatened that Mia's life could be in danger if the public knew who she was and that her brother was in a coma.

"This is not what I asked you to do," he snaps, clicking it off as if he's seen enough. "I told you to ship her off."

"I did that. She came back," I growl defensively.

He snorts. "You expect me to believe that she chose to come back here for you to parade her around like a fucking trophy?"

"No!" I shout. "She came back here because Haven told her you were shot."

His jaw sharpens, and his eyes slide to the door. "What was she doing talking to my wife?" he demands.

I let out a long breath and make my way over to the window that overlooks Vegas. I hate this city. I've always wanted out. I think that's why I bought a secluded beach house in Malibu and a log cabin in the mountains. I even have a penthouse in New York. I never get to use any of them, though, and never will.

"Bones?" he commands at my silence.

"Who shot you?" I ask, keeping my back to him.

"Doesn't fucking matter." He snorts.

"It does." I turn to face him, placing my hands in the pockets of my jeans. "Who shot you?"

He looks away from me, his jaw sharpening. He looks like shit. His color is yellowish. He's lost some weight, his cheeks hollowed, lips chapped. "I don't know." Lowering his dark eyes to his hands that sit on his lap, he sighs. "I didn't get a look at them."

I frown. "You sure?"

"Of course," he snaps. "Why would I lie about that?" His eyes meet mine.

"What if I told you it was your brothers?" I offer, seeing how he feels about that idea.

He gives a rough laugh that makes him flinch from pain. "No. They're stupid, but they don't have a death wish."

Leaning my back against the windowsill, I cross one ankle over the other. "I shipped Mia to my beach home in California. And three days before you were shot, she had visitors."

His brows pull together. "Who? Who did you tell she was there?"

"Not a soul." I shake my head. Well, technically, that's not true. Nigel knew she was there because he went with me, but he knows all of the Kings' secrets. He would never tell. "But that didn't keep your brothers from finding her."

"Wait." He holds up a hand. "My brothers found her in California?" I nod. "What does that have to do with why she's here now?"

"They roughed her up—"

"Fuck!"

"And told her to return to me. Make me fall in love with her and marry her."

He stares at me for a long second. His eyes are full of confusion, then he laughs. "Ow." He places his hand on his stomach. "Don't make me laugh, Bones."

"Does it look like I'm joking?" I arch a brow.

He sits up straighter. "You can't be serious ..."

"Three days later, she called your phone, and Haven answered. Told her that you had just been shot. Haven sent her the jet, and Mia showed up while you were in surgery."

"I don't ..."

"We all think that they hurt you to bring her back when she didn't move fast enough for them."

He lays his head back on his pillow and lets out a long breath.

"That night in my office, you told me that your father wanted me with her. Why?" I demand.

"He wants Kingdom," Luca says simply. "He always has. Says that your father left him out of his share."

I nod, turning to face the window again. I already knew that, but I wanted to hear it again. Make sure that I'm not losing my mind or going crazy. Because that sounds fucking insane. "He just thinks that's some pussy will make me hand over my life?"

"Hey!" he snaps from behind me. "That's my sister."

"Watch it, Luca. You sound like you actually care about her," I say dryly.

"You son of a bitch!" he snaps.

I turn around to see him trying to get out of bed, but he's connected to too many machines. And he's too weak. He may be awake, but he won't be himself for a while.

The door opens, and Mia comes running into the room. "What is going on?"

"Stay the fuck away from him, Mia," he growls, still trying to get out of the bed.

"Luca—"

"Where is Nite?" he demands, interrupting his sister. "I want him here. Now!"

"I'll call him for you." I pull out my cell and bring up his number.

"No, Dillan ..."

He picks up the call but doesn't speak. "Hey, I need you to come and pick up Mia. She's at the hospital. Luca is awake and wants you to take care of it." My hard eyes meet her large ones. I hate the way my chest tightens at the thought of having to walk away—hand her over like she doesn't mean a damn thing to me. But I've always been that guy who does whatever must be done. And I have to let her go for her sake. She'll be safer away from here, away from me. "She's your problem now." I hang up. "He's on his way," I say and pocket my cell, exiting the room.

MIA

"What the fuck did you say?" I demand, looking at my brother.

He's bent over, sweat covering his forehead, and he's holding his stomach. He looks up at me through his lashes, sucking in a deep breath. All he's done is yell at me, and he looks like he's run a marathon. "It's for the best," he says vaguely.

"Luca—"

"Nite can take you somewhere." He interrupts me. "Anywhere is better than here." Mumbling, he lowers his voice to talk to himself. "Should have known Nite was a better choice from the beginning."

"Lu—"

"He'll stay there with you." He interrupts me again. Glaring, he adds, "Do you think you can keep your hands to yourself with him?"

My mouth falls open at his question.

"If you have the urge, remember he is your adopted brother."

Why am I being judged for what they have done all of their lives? Am I supposed to stay a virgin forever? Am I not supposed to be happy? Find someone to fall in love with? I'm not suggesting Dillan could ever love me. But there has to be someone out there for me, right? Otherwise, why even try to live? Why continue to fight?

"No!" I shake my head, and he arches a brow at me, thinking I'm answering his previous question, but I'm not. I refuse to even acknowledge it. "I want to stay here. With you." *With Dillan.* He's made me feel safe. He's shown me what it feels like to be wanted. Even if it is a lie.

"This is not up for discussion, Mia," he snaps, then takes in a deep breath. Lying down, he winces. "I need you to get the hell out of here and away from Bones."

Tears sting my eyes. Why? What did Dillan say to him about me? That I'm in the way? Something that he doesn't have time for? I know he's been busy between Kingdom and Glass, but it's not like I need a babysitter. I can take care of myself. He doesn't have to be with me all the time.

"If what he said was true, and the family is after you, then you need to hide."

"No," I choke out, the word *hide* making my throat close. I'm a fucking Bianchi, and a Bianchi doesn't hide in the dark. Not the ones that matter anyway. I'm so tired of not being noticed. Why my parents just didn't give me away as a baby, I'll never know.

"Yes," he grinds out through gritted teeth.

The door opens, and I turn, hoping to see Dillan, but it's Haven. "What the hell are you doing?" She rushes over to him.

"I need to get up," he tells her. "And get the fuck out of here."

"You've been in a coma, Luca," she growls at him. "You're not going anywhere."

"I'm not leaving." I meant to sound more assertive, but it comes out sounding squeaky due to the knot in my throat. He doesn't even hear it. Instead, he continues to argue with his wife. I clear my throat and raise my chin. "I'm not leaving," I say, fisting my hands this time.

They both look up at me, and before Luca can open his mouth to tell me what to do, I add, "I'm a grown-ass adult, and I'm tired of being treated like a child."

"Mia—"

"I'm going to do what I fucking want!" My voice rises. "And that is stay here in Las Vegas. And your ass can't make me leave." With that, I turn and storm out of his room. My heels clap on the floor while I make my way down the hallway and to the elevator.

I pull my cell out, prepared to call someone to come get me, and I decide on Jasmine's number. She seems to be the one who would keep me a secret. The others are married or engaged to a King.

The elevator dings, and the door slides open as I put the phone to my ear after hitting call on her number. It rings once, twice, three times. "Hey, you've reached Jasmine. Leave me a quick message."

"Hey, Jasmine, it's Mia. Can you give me a call when you get a chance, please?" I hang up, not wanting to give her very much information. I'm afraid she'll call Dillan before she calls me back.

Stepping onto the sidewalk outside the hospital, I think of my options. I could get an Uber to take me to Kink. Or have it take me to Luca's house, but I don't want to be caught there. He'll ship me off.

I can go to a hotel, but I don't have any money. Well, that's a lie. Dillan gave me a credit card, but he'd be able to track that. Which is probably why he gave it to me in the first place.

My best bet is Kink. If Jasmine isn't there, maybe Alexa can tell me where she is. As I step off the sidewalk to catch a cab, something presses into my back, making me pause. My body stiffens, my breath escaping my lungs.

A hand wraps around my hair and gently gathers it together before pushing it to lay over my left shoulder. Goose bumps cover my body when I feel lips on my right ear. "You look lost."

My eyes fall closed at the familiar voice, and I swallow the knot in my throat. "Matteo." I whisper his name.

"Where is your King?" he asks, the hard object pressed to my back, digging into my spine through my shirt. It's a gun. I know it.

Refusing to answer, I stay quiet. I will not give him the satisfaction of knowing where Dillan is. He'll have to do the work himself to figure that out. But we both know he's only one of two places—Kingdom or Glass. That's all he cares about.

"So it seems he's trained you well." He chuckles. "A perfect little puppet."

I spin around and slam my fists into his chest. His hand comes up, wrapping around my throat so tight it cuts my air off. I grip his forearm, trying to twist his skin to force him to let go, but it's useless. I start clawing at his face, listening to him laugh while I manage to tear his skin. I'll never beat him, but I'll go down fighting.

Within seconds, my body starts to convulse, begging for air, and my arms fall to my side, unable to hold them up anymore. He watches my lips part as I try to breathe but get nothing. He lowers the gun to his side, and he smiles at me, so cruel it makes my blood run cold. Tears blur my vision, and just when I think he can't hurt me, he says the one thing that terrifies me.

"It's okay, Mia. Father no longer cares about his Kingdom. He has decided on another way you can earn the Bianchi name."

My eyes grow heavy. My tense body relaxes, accepting its fate, and I welcome the darkness. It's better than the alternative.

His chuckle is the last thing I hear before everything goes black.

THIRTY-TWO
BONES

I 'M INSIDE THE meat locker, letting out my anger on a man who has been skimming money from us when the door opens, and Titan enters.

He props his back against the door, crossing his tatted arms over his chest. "What do you want?" I ask before punching the guy in the face.

Fuck, I'm in a horrible mood right now.

"I'll wait," he answers.

I punch the guy again, and he falls out of the chair. I chose not to tie him down. I'm in for the fight right now. I reach down and grab his shirt, yanking him to his feet and slamming his back into the wall. I go to hit him again, but he ducks, making my fist hit the wall. "Fuck," I hiss, and the guy shoves me back.

I hit the desk. Thankfully, it's bolted down, and as he runs for me, I lift my foot. My boot connects with his chest, knocking him off his feet. I yank him up and grip the back of his hair, slamming his face into the desk over and over until his body goes slack.

Letting go of him, he falls to the floor, knocked out. I turn to face

Titan, fisting my hand that hit the wall, trying to gauge if it's broken. "What?" I snap.

"Turner called me. Guess who was at the Airport?"

"I don't know." I sigh, not wanting to play this damn game. "Who the hell was it?"

"Matteo."

I frown. "Why the fuck would he be there?" I ask. Luca would be seen there, but not the others. They're too uptight for that environment. They're too good for the Mason brothers and the Airport.

He shrugs. "Turner said he was there watching a poker game but didn't stay long. Left after he got a phone call."

Someone knocks on the door, and Titan moves away to open it. Cross enters and looks at the passed-out guy on the floor. "You're not answering your cell." His eyes come to meet mine.

"I've been busy." I shut it off and left it in my car after I left the hospital. I didn't want to take the chance of Mia calling me and begging me to let her stay. I won't be able to walk away from her again. I've already done it twice.

"Haven called me. She said she's been trying to get ahold of you." Cross goes on.

"Is Luca okay?" Titan is the one who asks.

"Yeah," he answers but keeps his eyes on mine. "They can't find Mia."

I stiffen. "What do you mean they can't find Mia? She's with Nite." That's the only reason I left her there was because Luca said he wanted her to go with him.

Cross shakes his head. "Nite arrived at the hospital, and she's nowhere to be found. Luca immediately called Dr. Lane, and they were going to check the security cameras—"

I run past them and out the door of the meat locker, rushing to the elevator. "Fuck it," I growl, shoving open the door to the stairs and running up the one flight to the main lobby that is our private entrance. I push open the glass doors and run downstairs to the back

parking lot and my car. I catch sight of the Kings exiting as I squeal
my tires on the pavement.

———————

I ENTER THE MAIN OFFICE FOR THE HOSPITAL SECURITY.
"Where the fuck is she?" I demand.

Nite is standing in front of a few monitors. Haven stands next to
him with a hand over her mouth, and Luca sits in a wheelchair to the
right. A few machines that he's still connected to are on rollers next to
him. The room is dead silent at my entrance.

"Someone better fucking answer me," I demand through gritted
teeth.

Haven turns to face me, tears running down her face. "Matteo
has her."

"No." I breathe. Is she the real reason he's in town? If so, then
why even go to the Airport? Did he want us to know he was here
before he took her? "How would he ...?"

"It's on the cameras," Haven whispers. A security guard for the
hospital hits a button, and I see her enter the frame on one of the
screens. She's got her cell to her ear. You can see her speaking but
can't hear what she's saying.

You see Matteo enter the frame behind her, but she's oblivious to
his presence. He pulls open his suit jacket, removes his gun from his
shoulder holster, and points it at her back. My heart races as I watch
her body stiffen. Time seems to crawl as he speaks to her, and she
turns around. She hits his chest, but he wraps his hand around her
throat, choking her until she passes out. He lets her fall to the ground,
hitting her head on the sidewalk. He puts his gun back in his holster
before bending down to pick her up just as a car drives up. The back
door opens from the inside, and he gets in with her before driving off.
Leaving her cell on the ground behind him. The screen stops on the
back of the car.

"The tag?" I ask roughly. My mind trying to think of any way that would give us a hint as to where he took her.

"Came back stolen," the guard answers.

"Her phone..."

Haven turns around and holds it out to me.

"The last person she called was Jasmine." She sniffs as I take it in my shaking hand.

I hear the door open behind me, but I ignore it, knowing it's just the Kings. They weren't far behind me.

"Where would he have taken her?" Haven asks me, her watery eyes meeting mine.

How would I know? I had her location on her phone, but he left it behind. There's no way for me to find her now. For all I know, she's no longer even in the state of Nevada. Her father is in New York. So he could be taking her there or back to Italy.

"Shit." I hear Titan sigh as he plays the video back for them to get caught up.

"He'll call you, right?" Haven bites her bottom lip, still looking up at me expectantly. "They wanted her with you. So they'll call you."

At that, Luca turns his wheelchair around to glare up at me. "This is all your fault."

"Luca—"

"He did this!" Luce yells over Haven.

"It's not my brother's fault," Grave snaps at him. I didn't know he had come with Titan and Cross.

"He made her want to stay," Luca argues. "If she had left ..."

"Matteo would have found her no matter where she went," Titan tells him.

I place my hands on either side of his wheelchair and lean over into his face. "This is your family's fault. That includes you. And I promise you I'll find her, but I'm going to slaughter every one of them. You and Mia will be the only living Bianchis when I'm fucking done." And with that, I push off the chair and spin around, exiting the room.

MIA

I OPEN MY heavy eyes and instantly regret it. The bright lights hurt my sensitive eyes, and the smell of death makes me want to gag.

Blinking, I start to cough, making my already pounding head throb more. Lifting my face, I look around to see I'm in a large room. I'm seated in a chair, my wrists tied to the back legs with rope. My ankles are tied to the front legs with the same unforgiving material.

My head falls back, and I close my eyes, swallowing. The pain in my throat makes me flinch.

"It's about time you wake up." I hear Matteo in the distance. "I was afraid I killed you."

"That would be kind of you," I mumble.

His laughter fills the room. I lower my head and open my eyes to look at him. He pulls a chair to the center of the room to sit across from me. He spins it around backward and straddles it, placing his forearms across the back of it. He tilts his head to the side. "I've only got one question for you."

I just stare at him, trying to figure out where we are. I don't recognize it, but that's not surprising. I've been limited as to where I could go since I arrived back in Vegas.

"If I fucked you right now, would you still bleed on my cock?"

My teeth grind, but I refuse to answer that.

His laughter fills the room as he stands from the chair and walks over to me. I try to cower into the chair, but it's no use. There's nowhere for me to go.

He walks behind me and reaches over my shoulder, sliding his hand down into my shirt, stretching out my collar to grab a breast, and I start fighting my restraints.

I feel his lips by my ear. "I knew you'd be his little whore. It was inevitable."

"You're fucking sick!" I scream, trying to fight him off, but I am unsuccessful.

"Oh, sis." He chuckles, making the hairs on my neck rise. "You

253

have no idea how sick men can be. Not yet anyway, but you will." He pulls his hand out, and I slump into the chair, trying to catch my breath.

"Whatever you have planned, Dillan won't fall for it," I tell him, hoping I piss him off.

His laughter grows to the point it hurts my ears. "You think this has anything to do with Bones?" He shakes his head. "Dad doesn't want his Kingdom. Never did, actually."

My body tenses. "What do you mean? Never did?" I ask, getting a bad feeling.

He comes to stand in front of me. Placing both hands on my bare thighs, he digs his fingers into my skin, making me hiss in a breath as he places his face in front of mine. "The twins and I were just playing a trick on you, Mia."

"No—"

"I mean, it's not every day a King pays ten million for a piece of ass." He pushes off my legs, and they begin to shake. His black eyes run over my body tied to the chair, and he smirks, lowering his hands to his belt. He undoes it, and I start screaming and thrashing in the chair. His hand hitting my face quiets me. But only long enough to catch my breath. "Let's see if that pussy was worth it."

"Fuck you!" I scream, tears running down my face. "You motherfucker—"

He slaps me again, cutting me off.

"Matteo," a voice barks at him. "Leave her alone."

I suck in a long breath, watching Richard enter the room. *What the fuck?* I thought I'd never have to see him again after he slapped me around when he yanked me off that stage at the auction. "How? You're helping him?"

"How else do you think I knew who bought you?" Matteo asks with laughter.

"But." I drop my eyes to the floor, trying to figure out what I'm missing. "You shot Luca." I look back at Matteo. "You shot our brother to bring me back here. To force me back to Dillan."

254

"What happened to Luca was a misfortune, but I assure you, I didn't shoot him. And if I were to shoot our brother, I sure as fuck wouldn't do it because of you." He laughs at that.

Richard's phone dings, and he pulls it out of his pocket. He reads over a text and then looks at Matteo. "We've got three days."

My stomach sinks at that. Not sure what it means, but a gut feeling tells me it's nothing good. Matteo confirms it when he smiles at me. "We're about to find out just how much you're worth."

THIRTY-THREE
BONES

I STAND QUIETLY in the room of our hotel, staring out the floor-to-ceiling window that overlooks the city. I feel like Luca looked when he entered my office all those weeks ago—lost, confused, and one-hundred-percent terrified.

We searched Vegas high and low for Mia and found nothing. We contacted every person we've ever known—exhausted every contact to keep an eye out. To listen for anything that might lead us to her—and got nothing. We figured if anyone could help us, it'd be the Airport. So much goes on there that someone had to know something. But again, we only heard silence. So when I got a call from Tristan, who informed me of another auction in New York this weekend, the Kings and I jumped on my private jet and flew here.

"Luca's calling again." I hear Titan say.

I ignore him. I haven't spoken to Luca since I delivered my promise to kill every single member of his family. One by one, they will each pay for what they've done to her. Not only now but everything over the years.

I've got eyes and ears on their father, but I can't touch anyone just yet. Not until she's in my arms again. When I know she's safe, I'll go after them. And honestly, Luca's on my shit list too. He'll have to prove to me that he deserves to live after the part he's played in her life. Even if it is small compared to her other brothers. Nite is the only one who is safe at the moment, and that can always change.

"Bones?"

"Tell him to go to hell," I growl at Titan, turning my back to the window to face the room.

My brother sits on the couch, arms crossed over his chest, staring at me. I didn't want him to come. I told him to stay behind. I know it took a lot for him to leave April home alone after his recent meltdown at his dining room table. But he refused to listen to me, and Jasmine told us she'd stay with April so she's not alone while we're gone.

Titan sighs, pocketing his cell, but doesn't say anything else.

I go to exit the room, and my brother jumps to his feet. "Where are you going?"

"I need a shower." I walk down the hallway to the back bedroom. I enter the room, not bothering to turn on the light, and make my way to the adjoining bathroom. Stripping out of my clothes, I turn on the shower and step into the water before it even warms.

I place my hands on the wall and bow my head, the cold water making my body break out in goose bumps. My heart races, and my mind wanders to the worst. That video Luca had me watch plays over and over in my head once again. What they've done to her this time. Did they record her again? Have they beat her? Raped her? Anything is possible. She's no longer a virgin. I took that from her.

Her virginity was something they wanted to sell. Now that it's gone, will she be worth less? Will they take advantage of that and do as they please with her before she's sold once again? What if she's not here in New York and already gone?

I won't be able to live with myself if I lose her. I should have stood up to Luca and told him to fuck off when he told me to give her to Nite, but I was so pissed at myself. I have always had a plan and made sure to think before I acted. That hasn't been the case with her.

I've done things that I thought were best, but they turned out to be the worst.

Like going public with her. That was fucking stupid. She was the best-kept secret, and I showed her to the world. Did her father want that? Was that his plan all along? To show off his best weapon? Make her more desirable by being unavailable? Men will always want what they can't have. And Mia Rosa Bianchi is most definitely what every man wants.

Finishing up in the shower, I pull myself together, reminding myself that I need some rest. I haven't had much in months. And if I plan on saving her, I need to be on my A game.

I'm standing at the sink brushing my teeth with a towel wrapped around my hips when there's a knock on the bathroom door. "Yeah?" I ask with a mouthful of toothpaste.

It opens, and Titan steps inside, pocketing his phone. "Tristan just called."

"And?" I ask, the toothbrush pausing.

"He was just informed the auction is tomorrow night. And Mia is on it."

I drop the toothbrush and rinse my mouth before turning to face him. "How does he know for sure?"

He shrugs. "He didn't say. Just that he was read a list of names and hers was mentioned."

I run a hand through my damp hair, letting out a long sigh.

"This is good news, Bones. She's here in New York. And tomorrow night, she'll be yours again."

He turns, leaving me alone once again, and I place my hands on the edge of the countertop, gripping the black marble. He's right about one thing. Tomorrow night, I'll be buying Mia for the second time. And I'll pay whatever it takes to make sure she comes home with me for the last time.

MIA

I WAS DRAGGED onto a plane back in Vegas—Matteo's private jet —and brought to New York, where they've kept me at a warehouse. One that my father has used since before I was born to do his dirty work. A place the cops won't go because they're paid off. If they want to keep their family safe, they stay away.

This time is different from the last time I was being sold. There's no expensive hotel. There aren't any women who did my hair, makeup, or waxed me. I'm not dressed in an evening gown to show off what I could offer.

Instead, I stand in an oversized white T-shirt that hangs off one shoulder and falls down to my knees. I'm barefoot, and my hair is a tangled mess. Pieces fell across my bruised face. It still hurts. Like a throbbing pain that won't go away. I can feel a patch of hair stuck to my head where I was bleeding at one time. They haven't allowed me to shower. I guess they don't care about my appearance or if I stink.

Matteo wraps his fingers around my upper arm, pinching my skin, and I whimper. I try to pull away, but of course it doesn't work. I don't even know why I try at this point. I'm too weak to fight him right now. This morning, they fed me a few crackers and a bottle of water. They want me as weak as possible. They're no longer inter-ested in the fight. Just compliance.

"Does Dad know what you're doing?" I growl.

He snorts but doesn't answer. After what he said to me about our father back in Vegas, I'm not sure what is the truth or a lie anymore. Have Matteo and the twins been behind this the entire time? Was my father ever a part of it? Obviously, he allowed me to be sold the first time, but did he really want Kingdom? Was he after the Dillan and the Kings?

"Two more, and she's up," Richard announces, coming into view from around the corner. "Here." He holds out a device that resembles a plastic gun. It's black and has what looks like a very short needle on the end.

"Hold her." Matteo shoves me forward into Richard's arms. I

instantly start fighting, slamming my fists into his chest and face. Anything I can make contact with.

"Fuck, you're such a pain," he growls, grabbing my hair. I scream out as he pulls me away from him. Spinning me around, he shoves me face-first into the wall and yanks my arms behind my back. He slides something rough over them, and I feel the zip tie tighten around my skin.

I scream at the top of my lungs, pieces of my hair now in my mouth and my eyes closed to try holding the tears back. I hate for them to see me weak.

"Hold her still," Matteo barks.

A hand grips my hair, pulling it off my shoulder, and I feel something press into the base of my neck before a shooting pain has my knees buckling. I fall to the floor, my breath momentarily taken away as a lingering sting in my neck leaves me breathless.

"Get her up. She's next," my brother demands.

I'm yanked to my feet by my hair, and Richard has to throw me over his shoulder because I can't will my legs to work. I hope whatever they just did to me kills me because I can't go on like this—be their toy to toss around and use.

When I'm placed back on my feet, a hood is shoved over my head, and I'm thankful for the darkness. Even if it is a false sense of security because I don't want to see what's out there for me. I don't need to see the crowd or who is bidding. It won't be a handsome, tatted King coming to rescue me. Not this time.

Hands grip my shoulders, holding me in place, when I hear a voice whisper in my ear through the hood. "Go make us some money, whore."

I'm shoved forward just like last time, but I manage to remain standing. I won't be able to get up easily with my hands tied behind my back and a hood over my head. I'd hate to fall off a stage if that's even what I'm standing on.

I freeze. The blood rushing in my ears is so loud that I can only hear my heavy breathing. I'm sweating, my body cold and shaking. The hood is sticking to my skin along with my hair, and the snot running down my face mixed with the tears I'm now crying.

My legs tremble, and that pain at the base of my neck intensifies to a burning sensation. I want to scratch it but don't have that luxury.

It feels like hours that I stand frozen in place while men look at what I have to offer them. My shirt is grabbed, and I'm yanked backward into a hard body. The hood is ripped from my head, and I'm back in the hallway. I'm sucking in breath after breath, trying to calm my racing heart. I feel like I'm about to have a heart attack. Is that a thing? Can someone my age have one?

"Good job, little sis." Matteo grabs my chin roughly, forcing me to look up at him. "Be a good slut and show him a good time. Give him his money's worth. And when we decide he's had enough, we'll come and get you."

I spit in his face. Just like I did Richard. Fuck them and their sadistic mentality. Instead of slapping me, he laughs. "We'll be seeing you soon." He shoves the hood back over my head and grips my upper arm.

I'm pulled forward until yanked to a stop. "She's all yours."

I hold my breath.

"She better be worth it." I hear an unfamiliar voice say, and my heart stops. A part of me was praying, holding onto hope that Dillan would save me again. But whoever just spoke proves that I was just dreaming because that was not him.

"You'll have to let me know about that." Matteo laughs.

My shirt is grabbed once again, and I find myself walking forward.

I'm numb. My body accepts its fate of a life of servitude as a sex slave. I'm going to be sold over and over. Used for my brother's sick pleasure. A way to make money. It doesn't matter how much he already has because I can bring him more.

The man doesn't say anything to me. Instead, he leads me with the hood over my head. I hear the sound of a door creak as it opens, and then he's helping me into what I'm assuming is a car. Cool leather hits my legs as the shirt rides up while I sit down. Then the hood is ripped off my head.

THIRTY-FOUR
BONES

S ILVERY-BLUE EYES land on mine as I sit across from her in the limo.

"Mia." I rush over to her.

Her eyes fill with tears, but she doesn't say anything. Placing my hands on her shoulders, I pull her toward me so Tristan can cut the zip tie binding her wrists. He was texting me the entire time he was in there while she was on the stage. I hated that I couldn't be there, but we couldn't chance her brother seeing me. Since we knew he was behind this.

He cuts them free, and I sit her back into her seat. "Hey, you're okay." I cup her wet face. My eyes search hers, but she closes them, and her body starts to shake.

I wrap my arms around her and pull her off the seat. Sitting back in mine, I bring her onto my lap. "I've got you. I've got you, Mia."

Her arms come up to wrap around my neck, and I start to rock her back and forth softly, rubbing her back. She's got to be exhausted. I want to ask her what all she's been through in the last three days without me but refrain. Now is not the time.

"You ... left me." She sobs.

I hold her tighter. "I'm so sorry. I promise it will never happen again," I vow to her. The only way I will leave her is if they kill me, and I'd like to see them try.

She pulls away, and I let her. She remains sitting on my lap and brushes her hair from her wet face. "My neck," she says through sobbing.

"What's wrong with it?" I ask, my eyes falling to it. He had choked her out. Maybe he did it more than once.

"Matteo ..." She swallows. "He did something to the back of my neck." I allow her to crawl off my lap and sit beside me on the bench seat. Grabbing her hair to one side, she bends forward and holds her hair for me to see her neck. "Right here." Her free hand runs over the base of her neck.

"Tracking device," Tristan speaks.

I look over at him. "A tracking device?" I repeat. Is that how they found her the first time at my beach house? No. It can't be. If she had one then, Lane would have picked it up when he gave her a full body scan at the hospital after she showed up and passed out. Or ... she did say she passed out then. I guess they could have removed it while she was out.

Tristan nods. "That's their plan. To sell her. Kidnap her and sell her again." He looks at her, his eyes softening. "That way, they can get as much money out of her as possible. It happens a lot."

My hands fist. "How do we remove it?" Even as I ask the question, I know the answer.

He flips the knife open that he still holds from cutting the zip tie. "We cut it out."

"What?" she shrieks, letting go of her hair and sitting up straight. "No." Her wide eyes go to mine. "No. No. No."

"Mia—"

"Please. Don't," she begs, interrupting me.

"It has to come out, or they will find you again," I tell her.

Tears run down her bruised face, and she sniffs.

Tristan reaches into his suit jacket and pulls out a vial. Thankfully, she's too busy staring at her hands in her lap to care about what he's doing. He then grabs a glass tumbler and the scotch in the mini-bar. He pours both into the tumbler, then holds it out for me.

"Here," I hold out the glass, and her bloodshot eyes meet mine. "You must be thirsty." Handing it to her, she grips the cup in her hands and downs it. Some drips down her chin to her filthy T-shirt.

She sucks in a deep breath, and the cup falls from her hands at my feet. "What ...?"

Her wide eyes meet mine, and I cup her face. "It had to be done," I tell her, and then her eyes close. I catch her in my arms and pull her limp body into my lap. My eyes meet his.

He shrugs. "I was prepared to drug her if need be."

I told him what Luca once told me. *Do what you need to do.*

"Text Nite. Have him meet us ASAP."

He nods, flipping open the blade once again, and holds it out to me. Turning her onto her stomach the best I can, I take the knife while he pulls her hair off her neck.

I take my free hand and feel around her neck until I find the little bump. It's so small I would have never noticed it. I push the blade into her skin and make a small cut. Blood instantly starts pouring down the sides of her neck and onto my slacks.

Pushing my thumb and pointer finger into her open skin, I grab the device and pull it out. Tristan holds the empty cup out to me, and I drop it inside. Then I grab a shirt that we brought with us. Honestly, I expected her to be naked. Jasmine had packed Mia a bag while we had a meeting at my house yesterday and discussed our plans to bring Mia back with everyone. I made sure to grab an outfit from that bag for her this evening since her dress was ripped last time.

I press the shirt to the wound, applying pressure as the limo comes to a stop.

MIA

I WAKE IN an unfamiliar room. I sit up, gasping for a breath, panic gripping my chest. Getting to my feet, the room sways, and I hit my hip on the nightstand by the bed, making it rattle.

I hear a door open behind me, and I run toward the other one that I see at the opposite end of the room. Just as I reach the door handle, an arm snakes around my waist, practically picking me up off my feet. I let out a scream, but a hand slaps over my mouth, cutting me off. I start kicking and trying to grab at anything I can touch.

"Shh, you're okay." I hear a voice in my ear. "You're okay, Mia," it repeats.

My tired body goes limp in his arms, and he removes his hand from my mouth, allowing me a deep breath. Setting me on my feet, he spins me around, and I look up into a set of blue eyes. The ones I thought I'd never see again.

I slap him as hard as I can. Which probably isn't much.

"Mia—"

I do it again. "You drugged me. Again."

He grips both of my wrists and slams them up against the wall, pinning me to it with his body. His eyes narrowing down at me now. "I had no other choice."

"I didn't want—"

"To live?" He interrupts me. "That was our only option. And I didn't have time to argue with you about it." Letting go of me, he steps back and runs a hand through his dark hair. "Fuck!" he shouts. Then he pins his eyes on me once again. "It needed to be done. And we had a very short timeframe. I was either going to hold you down and force you to drink it or have you do it willingly."

I cross my arms over my chest and lean up against the wall. My legs are still wobbly, and the room is still spinning. I wouldn't have taken it on my own. I'm too stubborn for that, and we both know it.

Stepping into me, he cups my face, and his hard features soften just a bit. "How do you feel?"

I just stare up at him.

He sighs. "Please talk to me. You can be mad, but I need to know how you feel."

I lower my eyes to his Kingdom T-shirt that hugs his defined chest and broad shoulders. "I'm tired." I finally say. Fuck, I missed him so much. I hate that he outsmarted me. Once again, Dillan Reed saved me. Why? Why not just let me go? Was it another favor for Luca? I doubt it. Luca wanted me far away from a King.

"You need more rest. It's not out of your system yet." I hear him through my internal rambling.

"I want a shower," I argue, glaring up at him. I feel disgusting, and I stink.

"How about a bath? That way, I don't have to worry about you falling over in the shower." He offers.

"Fine."

I allow him to pull me into the bathroom, and I look around while he starts me a bath. We're obviously in an expensive hotel. I can tell by the white and gold tiles on the wall. The corner tub is massive, with three steps to even get into it. The shower is Roman-style with glass so you can see the black tiled wall on the inside that has three showerheads. The floor is white marble. It's what I expected from a King. But where are we? "How long have I been out?" I ask.

"Just a few hours. I didn't give you as much as last time."

"Thanks," I say dryly, rolling my eyes.

He stands to his full height, turning to face me. I still have my T-shirt on, and he stares at me expectantly. But I refuse to take it off until I'm alone. I'm ashamed of what I look like underneath. How fucking weak I was. How many times Matteo hit or slapped me.

Dillan's eyes drop to my wrists, and I hide them behind my back, hoping he won't see the marks from the restraints. I'm sure he already looked over me while I was unconscious, but something about having to look him in the eyes makes me nervous. He holds that kind of power over me.

Taking the hint, he walks over to me and leans in, giving me a soft kiss on the forehead. I hold my breath, knowing that I haven't brushed my teeth since I don't know when, and without another word, he exits the bathroom, shutting the door behind him and allowing me to bathe alone.

As I lower my bruised body into the scalding hot water, I let the first tear fall. This is the last time I will cry over my family. I'm more determined than ever to live up to the Bianchi name. And I have a feeling I'm going to have to do it behind Dillan's back. Otherwise, he may drug me again.

I SIT ON THE COUCH IN WHAT I KNOW NOW IS THEIR PENTHOUSE suite in downtown New York, freshly bathed and feeling like a new person. The fog from the drugs is long gone now. When I was done in the bath, I found a shirt and cotton shorts lying on the bed that I had woken up in. When I finally emerged from the bedroom, room service was being delivered. I sat and ate like an animal while the Kings watched me. I didn't care about my manners.

"What do we know?" Titan asks while sitting on the couch next to Cross. Grave stepped outside a second ago to take a phone call. Tristan, Dillan's friend, sits at the kitchen bar.

"We were wrong about my father," I say.

"Wrong how?" Cross is the one who asks.

"Matteo said that my father didn't care about Kingdom or the Kings." I look him in the eyes. A new me is here, and I'm not ashamed of her. "Said that he and the twins were just fucking with me. And that he realized I could make him more money over time than what he could get from you guys."

A silence falls over the room.

"Not like that changes anything." Titan breaks the tension. "If he's the one behind selling you, he's a problem."

"What do you mean if?" I ask softly.

Dillan speaks. "I don't trust Matteo. He could say your dad is behind it, but I'm not going to take his word for it."

"Was there anything about the auction that was like the last?" Tristan asks me.

"I'm not sure," I say honestly. "They had a hood over my head."

"They?" Dillan questions.

I nod. "Matteo and Richard."

"Richard was there?" He stands.

"Who is Richard? And how do you know him?" Grave asks, and I look over at the floor-to-ceiling windows, not realizing he has returned from his call.

"He's a fucking piece of shit. I don't know him personally, but he was in the video that Luca showed me. And he was at the first auction. I didn't think much of it before, but maybe he plays a bigger part in this than I thought."

My body tenses at Dillan's words. The video that Luca showed him? What is he talking about?

THIRTY-FIVE
BONES

"WHAT DO YOU want to do?" Titan asks me.

I sit back on the couch while Mia sits down next to me. She looks better than she did five hours ago when Tristan walked out of the auction with her. There's still a hint of sadness in her eyes, but that'll go away over time. I'll make sure of it.

The fact that Richard was involved this time makes me wonder what all happened to her. I watched him knock her around. Not to mention what all he did to her on the video that Luca showed me.

Leaning forward, I place my elbow on my knees. "Mia had a tracker in her. I removed it and handed it over to Nite, who got rid of it."

"Got rid of it how?" Cross questions.

"It's on a plane to France," I answer. We had to make up somewhat of a backstory for Tristan in order to get him into the auction. It wasn't like the one before, where names and personal information didn't matter. There was no need for suits and black leather books with important details about the women being sold. Tristan used an alias, and we gave them a lie about him residing in Paris.

"So how long do you think we have before they go and retrieve it?" Grave is the other one who speaks.

"I'd say five days. Tops," Tristan says. "The money was wired, so they received it immediately. No reason to make them wait," he adds. "I'd say we need to leave as early as tomorrow." Tristan nods at Mia, who sits silently beside me. "We return her to Vegas and then head on to France. Make them come right to us. They will never expect it."

"Too bad you couldn't have placed one on them. It would make it much easier to locate them."

I place my hand on her leg, and she pulls away from me. I frown over at her, and she narrows her eyes on me. What the fuck? Why is she mad at me? I just bought her. Again. Granted, it only cost me two million this time. Matteo isn't holding out for ten mill when he knows he's just going to take her back and sell her again.

"Mia—"

"What do you mean the video that Luca showed you?" she demands.

Fuck! Did I say that? "I don't know ..."

"What video did Luca have?" she growls, standing to her feet.

I look up at her and stand as well, not liking the fact she's looking down on me. "It's nothing."

"It isn't nothing, Dillan," she snaps. "I only know of one video with Richard and me in it. And when I showed it to you, you didn't mention that you had seen it before."

"Mia—"

"And Luca has been in a coma for weeks. So when the fuck did Luca show you a video of Richard and me?"

Silence falls over the room, and I can feel everyone's eyes on us. I didn't realize what I had said. But now I can't deny it. Or lie about it. "Before I bought you. The first time."

Her lips part, and her eyes widen. "What? Why? How did you...?"

"Luca barged into my office late one night and had the video.

Matteo had sent it to him, knowing Luca would want to save you. But he couldn't do it, so he brought it to me. I—"

She slaps me, cutting me off. "All this time." Taking a step back, she thins her lips up at me. "And you never told me."

"What did you expect me to say?" I growl.

"The truth," she snaps.

"You didn't even remember it. Why would I bring that up to you?" I never found it important to bring up something that she had no recollection of. Then when she watched it, she was distraught. How would her knowing that I've already seen it change anything?

"I can't believe this," she whispers to herself.

I reach out to her. "Mia."

"Don't touch me!" she shouts, pulling away. "You lied to me."

"I have saved you!" I shout. "Several times."

She snorts. "What do you want me to do, *Bones*?" She calls me by my nickname, and it makes my teeth grind. I've gotten so used to her calling me Dillan that I don't like her calling me Bones. He's a different man. And I feel like a part of me has changed for her. I'm just not sure if that's good or bad. "You keep reminding me of this like you want something in return. Want me to crawl to you?"

I snort. "Don't be ridiculous."

"Want me to kiss your feet? Show you how grateful I am?"

"You should be grateful." I step into her, and my eyes narrow. "If it wasn't for me, you'd be just another used-up whore. Passed around like your family intended."

Her face falls, and I instantly regret my words. I've never had to defend my actions or explain myself to anyone. It's going to take some getting used to.

She licks her lips and speaks softly. "You bought me. And you fucked me. Please explain to me how being your whore is any different?" And without waiting for an answer, she turns around and marches off to the master suite, slamming the door behind her.

"Fighting like a true couple." Grave chuckles to himself, and I narrow my eyes on him. "You two might have a chance at this after all."

MIA

HE HAD SEEN the video before I even knew it existed? It makes me feel violated all over. He saw me in such a vulnerable state and chose to keep it from me. What if Matteo had never sent it to me? Would Dillan just have never told me that it existed?

The door opens, hitting the interior wall, and I turn around to see him barge in behind me. "Get the fuck out!" I shout, pointing to it just as it slams shut.

He walks over to me, grabs my face with both hands, and forces me to look up at him. "I don't expect anything from you, Mia. The first time I saved you was because Luca begged me to."

"Great," I snap. "Now I'm your charity case. Don't do me any more favors." I try to pull away, but he keeps me in place.

"The second time was because I can't live without you."

My heart pounds at his words. And my eyes widen, staring up at him.

His gaze searches mine before speaking softly. "I have very few regrets, Mia. But the ones I do have, are you."

"What do you mean?" I whisper, afraid of the answer but needing to know.

"Walking away from you all those years ago. Believing you when you said you were no one." He lets go of my face and runs one hand through my hair. "Leaving you in California. And walking away from you when Luca told me to stay away."

My hands come up and grip his tatted forearms. "Dillan..."

"I didn't tell you about that video because I didn't want you to know it existed. Then when Matteo sent it to you, all I could think of was ways to save you."

"You have." I can't deny that he's done more for me than anyone else ever has. "But you have to expect something."

His eyes drop to my lips before he runs his thumb over my bottom one. I can feel my heart pounding, and my breathing picks up as I wait for his answer. "I can't lie to you," he says, making my heart stop. "I do want something."

I swallow. I can't pay him back. My family has money, but I don't personally. I have no home. No car. Hell, I wouldn't even have a cell phone if it wasn't for him. "What is it?" I whisper, afraid of what he'll say.

"You," he answers, and I feel tears sting my eyes. "All I want is you." He steps into me, pressing his hips into mine. "Give me the chance to do what I should have done eight years ago."

"What was that?"

"The chance to show you that you are someone."

Before I can say anything, he lowers his lips to mine. I don't hesitate. I wrap my arms around his neck and allow him to kiss me. His fingers dig into my thighs, and he picks me up off my feet. I wrap my legs around him, and he walks me backward before I feel him laying me down on the bed.

He pulls away long enough to remove my shirt, and then his lips are back on mine. I'm trying to shove my shorts down my legs when he pulls away once again to do it himself, making sure to take my underwear with them.

Then I'm yanking his shirt over his head and undoing his jeans. I can't get him naked fast enough. The need to have him inside me is too great. Which is crazy, considering I wanted to knock his head off just seconds ago. I've never experienced emotions like this before.

I'm already wet, and a quick look tells me he's hard. He takes his dick in his hand and pushes it into me. I arch my back, gasping at the feel of him stretching me wide to accommodate his size.

"Fuck, Mia." He groans in my ear, and it makes my breath hitch.

"Dillan." I'm gasping his name as my fingers dig into his muscular back.

Pulling away, he sits up, placing his arms under my knees and spreading my legs wider.

I grip my hair, crying out as he slams into me while he watches his cock slide in and out of my soaked pussy. My heavy eyes watch him bite his bottom lip, and his breathing picks up. Reaching out, I place my hands on his hard chest, enjoying the show. I could never get enough of him.

I went all my life thinking I'd die alone. But Dillan has taught me what it feels like to be wanted, and I could never go back. And that's what scares me. He's already walked away from me before, so what's keeping him from doing it again?

A sensation starts to build, and my eyes fall closed.

"Look at me, Mia," he orders roughly. The sound of his body slapping against mine fills the large room.

Opening my heavy eyes, I see him hovering over me. "I want you to watch me while you come."

My lips are parted, and I'm panting. His eyes drop from mine before running down my body. He licks his lips, and I dig my hands into the sheets on either side of my body as he holds my legs wide open for him.

I'm screaming his name while the heat licks over my skin, burning me alive. In the back of my mind, I realize that everyone in the suite can hear me, but I just can't care enough to be quiet.

I'm shaking uncontrollably when he smiles, looking between my legs. "I'll never get enough of seeing you come all over my cock."

I whimper.

He leans down, pressing his lips to mine while his hips pick up. He fucks me until he's stiffening, coming inside me. I close my eyes, unable to hold them open any longer.

THIRTY-SIX

BONES

S HE LIES NEXT to me with her eyes closed, sound asleep. I
cleaned her up after we were done, and she didn't even move.
The poor thing is still exhausted.

I get up out of bed, grab my cell out of my jeans pocket, and pull
up a number, sending a quick text. Once done, I get dressed and exit
the room, closing the door behind me.

Titan is on his phone sitting on the couch, Cross and Grave are
both standing in the kitchen, and Tristan is over at the floor-to-ceiling
windows. I walk over to him. "Thanks again for the help today."

He nods. "You know I'll help you however I can." His eyes go to
the closed master suite door and then back to me. "She has to go back
to Vegas."

"I know."

"Do you have men you can put on her? She's going to need
around-the-clock detail. Until we know who else is involved, we can't
risk her safety."

"The only person I trust who isn't here is Luca, and he's in no
condition to protect her." I sigh heavily. Nite is another option, but
he'll already be in France. He's got the tracker, and he's staying there

279

with it until we arrive. We couldn't just send a tracker and drop it off. It needs some sort of movement.

"I'll call Avery," he says, pulling his cell out of his slacks.

"Isn't he in Canada?" I ask. Avery is his older brother. I'm not as close with him as I am Tristan, though.

Tristan nods. "But you can trust him."

"I know where they are."

Tristan and I both turn around to see a sleepy-looking Mia standing outside the bedroom door, fully dressed once again.

"Who?" Grave asks, shoving a piece of pie into his mouth that he ordered from room service.

"My brother and Richard. I know where they are."

"Where?" Tristan beats me to it.

"When we arrived in New York, they took me to my father's warehouse. That's where they kept me until the auction. They're staying there."

"Did you see your father?" I ask, and she shakes her head.

I look over at Tristan, and he shrugs. "Might be our best bet," he states, understanding my silent question.

Running a hand through my hair, I sigh. "Text Nite. Tell him to drop the tracker and come right back," I order Titan, and he nods.

"But I thought we needed him to stay there with it," Grave argues.

"That was when we wanted them to come to us. If we can get to them before they leave New York, then there is no reason for him to be there. He needs to be here with Mia while we go after her brother and Richard."

She steps toward me. "Dillan, I can help."

"Absolutely not. You will stay here in the suite with Nite."

"But—"

"Your life is not up for debate, Mia," I interrupt her. She's had too many close calls as it is already. I'm not taking any chances. If they realize what we're up to and somehow get their hands on her, I'll never see her again. Matteo would kill her just to prove a point. And I wouldn't be able to live without her.

Her eyes dart around the room as if expecting someone to back her up. That won't happen. Not one man in this room would allow the woman they love to put themselves in danger to *help out*.

"Nite responded. He said he'll drop the tracker and come right back."

I nod. "We'll be ready."

MIA

I SIT ON the end of the bed while Dillan dresses in a pair of black jeans and a black T-shirt. My arms are folded over my chest, and my hair is wet from my recent shower. I'm wearing nothing but a towel. I tried to get some rest last night, but it didn't happen.

This is our second day here in New York. After he turned down my help, I was pissy. He kissed me good night, and I gave him my back. It only took him seconds before he was snoring away. I lay awake, staring up at the dark ceiling and thinking about the last twenty years of my life. Or lack thereof.

He doesn't know it, but I have a plan too. One that will show him I'm not so helpless. I want Dillan to know that I want him, not need him.

"It'll be okay," he says, and I glare up at him.

He thinks I'm concerned for his safety. I'm not. Not really, anyway. I have no doubt that Dillan will do what he sets out to do. I just hate that he wants to keep me wrapped in bubble wrap.

Walking over to me, he places his hands on either side of my body and leans his face down into mine. "You'll be safe here. Nite is staying behind. And as soon as we're done, I'll be right back."

I remain silent, and he sighs. Leaning forward, he gently kisses my forehead and then stands to his full height. "It'll all be over soon." With that, he turns and exits the bedroom.

Falling onto my back, I look up at the ceiling and close my eyes, taking in a deep breath. My clock has officially started ticking. Who knows how much time I have? Opening my eyes, I rush into the bathroom, knowing that it's now or never. I quickly tie my hair up in a high pony. Can't chance it getting in my way.

Going to the closet, I open the suitcase he had brought me. I dig around in it for some clothes when I see a small black Gucci bag hidden in a zipper compartment. Frowning, I open it up and smile when I see a note. "A girl can never be too careful." And I know exactly who put it there.

Once dressed, I crack open the bedroom door just in time to see Nite walk into another bedroom across the large living room. He's like all the rest—thinks I'm not going to fight back. That I'll just sit here and wait for Dillan to return. Taking care of my brother and Richard is only part of the problem. And I know what they are about to do will start a war. One that I'm not willing to chance. The Kings have too much to lose. Not only their Kingdom but also their loved ones. Too many people have already been hurt because of me. I'm the only one who can stop this.

Exiting the master suite, I softly close the door behind me so he thinks I've gone to bed. Then I tiptoe through the suite and slip out the front door, closing it as quietly as possible.

I make my way down the hallway to the elevator. Feeling my heart pound in my chest, I silently pray I can get out without Nite catching me. I wouldn't be surprised if Dillan put some kind of silent alarm on these damn doors.

Pushing the button for our private elevator, I watch over my shoulder for the penthouse door to open, but nothing happens.

The ping that alerts me the elevator has arrived makes me flinch, and I jump in, repeatedly pushing the button for the doors to shut until it closes me in. Once it does, I lean my back against it and close my eyes, once again preparing myself for what I have to do. Consequences be damned.

THIRTY-SEVEN
BONES

THE SUN HAS fallen, and I sit in the passenger seat of Tristan's car while he flies down the highway. Titan, Grave, and Cross are behind us in the Cadillac Escalade that we rented under Tristan's alias.

I cock the gun, chambering a bullet, and lay it on my thigh, feeling the heavy metal. It soothes me. It's been a long time since I've made something bleed for the greater good. It's usually work-related.

I wasn't lying when I told her my regrets involved her. Do I have others in my life? Of course. But they were ones that I had no control over. I chose to buy her and leave her. Twice.

Tristan takes an exit, and I watch the Kings follow in the side mirror.

He drives in silence for the next fifteen minutes as New York grows smaller in the rearview. The warehouse that Mr. Bianchi has is right on the ocean. Lots of ships import and export goods for John. The Mafia have their hands in everything and anything that can be sold.

I was terrified when I found out that Mia was in another auction here because I figured she'd go straight to the shipping yard after-

ward. That they'd place her in a shipping container, and that would
be that. She'd be gone forever with no way to track her.

"We're going to have to park and walk," I inform Tristan. "He's
got surveillance on the warehouse. Don't want to let them know we're
coming." Nite informed us of everything we needed to know about
the warehouse via text before he returned to New York.

He nods. "How far out?"

"I'd say at least a mile."

My cell rings, and I look down, thinking it will be Mia, but it's
Luca. I hit ignore. I'm still not speaking to him. He texts me immediately.

Luca: Answer your damn phone.

I GO TO TURN IT OFF BUT PAUSE. I CAN'T DO THAT, IN CASE MIA
or Nite needs me. Luca knows what I'm here to do, and he's not
trying to stop me. He just doesn't like that I'm blaming him for her
situation. The truth is, we're both responsible for it. I'm just the only
one who has decided to do something about it.

Tristan slows his car, pulling off onto a road where he brings it
around a brick building before stopping. It's dead silent out here. Not
even any buzzing streetlights.

Getting out of the car, I see Titan pull in behind us. They get out
and pop the hatch, grabbing what they'll need.

"Ready?" I ask, tucking my 9mm into the back of my jeans while
grabbing the Glock my brother hands me.

"Ready." They nod.

"Let's go," I say as Tristan slams his trunk, and we start to make
our walk, knowing I'm about to do something that I never thought
I'd do.

284

Isn't this how wars start, though? A man falls in love with someone he shouldn't.

Show me a man in love, and I'll show you his greatest weakness.

My father's words echo in my head, and I smile. He couldn't have been any more wrong. My cell starts to ring, and we all come to a stop. I pull it out, thinking it's Luca again but see it's Nite.

"What the fuck?" Grave asks, wondering why Nite is calling. The man chooses to be mute. We'll call him, but we never expect him to speak.

I hit answer and put him on speakerphone. "Nite—?"

He doesn't even let me finish before he rushes out. "Mia's gone."

MIA

I GET OUT of the cab and stand on the sidewalk of the busy Manhattan street. The thing about being a Don is that no one would ever fuck with you. And the police are paid off.

I enter the pizzeria with my head held high and shoulders back. This business has been handed down from my great-grandfather to my grandfather to my father. Luca or Nite will be the one who gets it next since I'm pretty sure they'll be the only two living Bianchis left.

The first twelve years of my life were spent in Las Vegas, but my parents did bring me to New York a couple of times. And I spent those rare days here, sitting in the corner booth with my nanny, where she taught me just enough to know that this wasn't the life I wanted to live.

The place is dead this late—after ten at night. I walk past the round red tables and to the back. Pushing the door open, I enter the office. Five men stand around a desk where my father sits.

"Mia?" he barks out when he sees me. "What the fuck are you doing here?" He looks behind me, and I wonder if he's expecting Dillan or Luca to be with me.

"I came to see you," I answer as his men glare at me. Two of them even have their hands on their guns tucked in their holsters. The other three don't see me as a threat. That's their mistake.

"Mia!" My mother jumps up from a worn-out leather couch, running to me. She wraps her arms around me, picking my feet up off the floor. "Oh my god." Setting me down, she pulls away and places both hands on my face. Her silvery-blue eyes that look just like mine fill with tears while they glance over the cuts and bruises as if she cares what I've been through. "Oh my God. My baby." She's crying now and sniffling.

I feel nothing for her. She might not have had a say in what kind of life I was raised to live, but she didn't do anything to protect me either. I begged her to let me stay in Vegas when my father and Luca told me it was best to go to Italy. Then I begged her to stay with me there, and she left me alone to come home and be with my father. If I'm ever lucky enough to have a child, I'll never leave him or her for my husband. But I'd also never marry a man who would make me choose.

"Sir?" one of his men questions. Clearly confused about how to handle my arrival.

"Leave us." He waves his hand in the air, and the men all exit the room, leaving me alone with my parents.

"What is it that you want, Mia?" he asks, sitting back in his chair with his arms crossed over his chest. "How did you manage to get out of Italy?"

That right there tells me he's had no clue what I've been through. He didn't order Matteo to kidnap me and sell me to a King. But to find out just exactly how much he does know, I ask, "Did you really expect me to get you Kingdom?"

He smirks. His black eyes drop to my Nikes and run up my bare legs, over my shorts, and then my chest. The way his smile grows makes goose bumps rise over my skin. Then they meet mine again. "There was a time when I was going to use you to get what I deserved." My eyes narrow on his. "But a King could never fall for a nobody. No matter how good the pussy is." When he stands, I take a step back toward the door to put some space between us.

I hate that my stomach sinks at his words. That he could make me second-guess Dillan's intentions with me. I've always been told I'm a nobody, so it's hard to believe otherwise. Even when a King tries to convince you that you're someone.

"Did you know Matteo sold me?" I ask and hate that my voice trembles.

He throws his head back, laughing, and I look over at my mother to see her reaction. She's got her head down, and arms crossed over her chest. I can see by the way her shoulders shake that she's silently crying.

She knew! I had a feeling she did, but I didn't want to believe it. "Why?" I scream, and tears sting my eyes. I hate that I care. And I hate it even more that he finds my lack of life entertaining.

"You were always meant to be nothing, Mia." He takes a step closer to me. "You can spread your legs for a million men." Another step. "But you'd still just be nothing."

He reaches me, and I feel the tears running down my face while I glare up at him.

"You should thank me." He tilts his head to the side.

"For selling me to the highest bidder?" I bark out.

"For making you worth something." Leaning into my face, he adds, "If not for the Bianchi name, you would have been given away for free."

I spit in his face, and he places his hand over my mouth, painfully gripping my cheeks and shoving me backward. My head hits the wall so hard that my vision blurs, and I fall to my knees as pain shoots down the back of my neck. In the distance, I hear my mother cry out while my head starts to pound like a drum.

I'm trying to catch my breath and blink away the dots and tears when I hear him laugh. "You should have let me kill her when I wanted to. She served us no purpose."

Lifting my head, I glare at his back as he starts to walk away from me.

"Thankfully, it's never too late to fix a problem," he adds.

I get to my feet, reach into the back pocket of my shorts, and slide my fingers into the metal holes of the bunny ears keychain I found packed in my bag. *Thank you, Jasmine.* This is my only chance. I knew coming here would end someone's life, and there was a possibility of it being mine.

Running, I let out a scream as I jump onto his back. He spins around, throwing my back into the wall, and the tight grip my legs have around his waist loosens just a bit at the contact.

"You fucking bitch!" he shouts. His hand reaches over his shoulder and manages to grab hold of my ponytail. He yanks on it, and I cry out.

I reach around and slap my hand over his face to try and obstruct his vision, and he trips into his desk. He tilts his head, and I take the opportunity to shove the metal bunny ears into his neck.

When I yank it out, blood sprays all over me. He falls to his knees, taking me with him. I stab him again. And again. Until my hand loses its grip because the keychain is slippery.

Screams pierce my ears, and I wonder if it's me. Something hard hits my body, and I'm on my back, looking up into a face that resembles mine. My mother is on top of me, hitting my face and chest.

"You ungrateful little bitch!" she screams, spit flying from her mouth to mix with my father's blood. "You killed him!" She slaps me. "Do you realized what you've done?" Of course, she chooses him. Always has. He was about to kill me, and she was going to stand by and just watch it happen. "You will die for this!" Her fist connects with my cheek, and I twist my body to lie on my side underneath her and see the keychain that had slipped from my grip. I reach out and grab it. Turning onto my back, I raise my hand and shove the ears up her neck into her throat.

Yanking it out, I feel more blood cover me and choke on it. Shoving her dead weight off me, I get to my hands and knees just as the door bangs open. I did it. No matter if I die right here or not, I at least did what I told myself I'd do. I stumble to my feet just as my father's guards enter.

"What the fuck did you do?" a guy shouts, charging at me.

I lift the keychain, and he hits my forearm with his, knocking it out of my hand. Gripping my throat, he lifts me off my feet. Placing his face in front of mine, he makes me gag from the smell of cigarette smoke.

I bare my teeth, and he lets go of my neck, but before I can even suck in a breath, he slams his fist into the side of my cheek.

Pain explodes up the side of my face and neck, and I'm then grabbed by my hair and slammed facedown onto my father's desk. His computer and papers go crashing to the floor. My breath is taken away once again from the impact. The taste of blood fills my mouth, and I spit it out onto the surface.

He holds me down with his large hand wrapped around the back of my neck. "Call Matteo," the man orders to one of the other guards who has now joined us.

The side of my face slides across the desk from the drool that runs out of the corner of my mouth. I spot two of the other guards checking my mother and father for a pulse. When they realize that's not a possibility, they move them to the corner. Throwing my mother's body on top of my father's.

A phone is placed next to me, and I see it's calling my brother on speakerphone.

"Hello?" I hear his voice, and my eyes fall shut. *He's supposed to be dead.*

"I've got a surprise for you," the guard states.

"You know how much I love those," Matteo jokes. "She better be a blonde with big fake tits."

I open my mouth to scream at him, but the guard slams the side of my face into the desk, making me moan instead while my vision goes in and out.

"More like a brunette with a flat chest." The man laughs. "Seriously, you'll never believe who showed up," the guy holding me down says cheerfully. They don't care that their boss is dead because they know my brother will now inherit it. They have job security.

"Who?" he asks.

"Your whore of a sister."

I try to wiggle out of his hold, but he tightens his fingers into the back of my neck. I grind my teeth, refusing to give him the satisfaction that he's hurting me.

"You-You have Mia?" he asks, sounding unsure. That makes sense, considering I'm supposed to be in France right now via the tracker he placed inside my neck.

"Talk, bitch!" the man growls while the other holds the phone up to my face.

I refuse to give them what they want. So the guy holding me down yanks my head up off the desk and the other holds a knife to my throat, his face in front of mine. "Tell your brother hi, or I'm going to cut up this pretty face of yours." He gives me a crooked-tooth smile. "They won't even be able to give you away."

I feel the cold blade pressed up against my skin, and I suck in a breath, hoping that will give me some space, but it doesn't work. His smile widens when he sees what I'm doing.

"She's really pretty, man," he adds, his eyes dropping to my parted lips while I hold my breath. "It's too bad she's nothing more than a whore now."

Baring my teeth, I snarl. "Go fuck yourself." And spit in his face. It's the only option I'm capable of.

The guy holding me down pulls me up and throws me across the room into the opposite wall.

Falling to the floor like a rag doll, I roll over, sucking in a deep breath, only to come face-to-face with my dead mother's body. Blood drips from her face, eyes open and on mine. I get up as fast as I can and scramble back against the wall, shoving the blood-covered hair from my now bruised face. My once high ponytail is now loose, hair falling all over my face.

"I'm on my way," Matteo growls.

"I can't promise she'll be in one piece." The guy holding the phone hangs up and then drops it to the floor before smashing it with his boot. He steps toward me, and the guy who threw me grabs him bringing him to a stop.

"We don't touch her until Matteo arrives." He glances over at me. "Whatever you have planned for her, he'll make sure it's ten times worse once he sees what she's done."

"That doesn't mean we can't play with her, right?" he asks, smiling.

One of the guards who hasn't said a word goes over to the desk and opens a drawer. He pulls out some zip ties, and I get up to run but am met by another guard. He picks me up and tosses me back onto the desk, where my arms are pulled behind my back and secured. I can't help the tears that run down my face. Matteo is going to kill me. But when he sees what I've done, it'll be a slow and painful death.

Why is he alive? Where are Dillan and the Kings? I begin to cry.

"It's going to be okay, whore," one of the guards says. "We're not going to kill you. Just play with you." They all laugh at the situation I've put myself in.

They are not why I'm crying. It's the fact that I didn't get to tell Dillan how I felt about him before I left. He was going to start a war over me, and I've ruined everything. At this point, all I can do is pray that he and the Kings forget about me because there's no way I'll survive. I once told him I was not worth it, and I meant every word.

THIRTY-EIGHT
BONES

W E PULL UP to the pizzeria just as Matteo walks in.

"You think she's here?" Tristan asks.

"She has to be." After we got the call from Nite, we turned around and were headed back to our cars to go to the hotel and look for her when we decided our best bet was to wait on Matteo and see what he did. Sure enough, it wasn't ten minutes later, and he was in his car and driving into town.

Mia left for a reason. And I'm praying he takes us right to her.

The door to the pizzeria opens, and two guards step outside. Both cross their arms over their chest and look around. They've got blood on their hands, and it's obvious it's not theirs. Tristan looks over at me. "Ready?"

"Let's go." I open the door and get out of the car. They raise their guns when they spot us, but we're faster. I've already got a shot off to one of them in the head. Tristan gets the other with a shot to the chest. Both of them drop dead.

"Cross?" I call out, walking toward the front door.

"Got 'em," he answers, coming up with Grave and Titan behind us.

293

We enter the pizzeria, and the three of them drag the two guards into the building, immediately going to work. I wanted to make Matteo and Richard suffer, but that won't be happening. This is a rescue mission now. Get in, save Mia, and get the fuck out. Kill anyone who stands in my way as quick as possible.

Tristan and I make our way to the closed door with our guns ready. I step back and look at him. He nods and then kicks the door open.

I enter with my gun raised and kill a guard. Another one jumps in front of me, and I shoot him too. Aiming my gun, I go to shoot again but realize who's in front of it. Mia.

She stands in front of a desk with Matteo's arm wrapped around her throat, while he hides behind her small frame. A quick look around shows me her father and mother are dead. And I understand why we're here—she killed them.

Good for her.

I lift the gun, aiming it right at his face, but he moves her to where it's on her. "Let her go," I demand.

She's shaking, covered in blood, and her arms are behind her back. I want to be pissed and yell at her, but it has to wait. I need her alive in order to do that.

"Di—llan." She chokes out my name. "I'm sorry."

I ignore her, refusing to even take my eyes off her brother. He removes his arm from around her throat and instead places his hand over her mouth, muffling her cries. "Where's Richard?" I ask him instead. We're not sure where the fuck he's at.

Matteo laughs. "Luca showed you the video of her, right?"

I tighten the hold on my gun.

Matteo licks up the side of her face, making her scream out and close her eyes. "I bet he didn't send you the one where he played with her unconscious body."

I tense.

"Of course, he didn't fuck her." He laughs. "A used-up whore is worth much less."

"Let. Her. Go," I demand, the gun now shaking in my hands. I could take the shot, but I'd chance hitting her.

I hear a gunshot coming from inside the pizzeria, meaning the Kings took out another guard. I wonder how many there are.

Stepping to my left, Tristan goes to his right. Both of us try to get a better shot. If we can slowly move to stand on either side of him, one of us could get one.

He steps back, yanking her with him. Letting go of her mouth, he grips her hair, pulling her head back. Forcing her to look up at the ceiling, he places a knife to her neck. I watch her swallow and glance at Tristan. He nods once.

"Why are you here, Bones?" he asks, laughing maniacally. "Because of her?" Another laugh. "Don't tell me that you fell in love with her?" Matteo doesn't let me answer. "Did your father teach you nothing about pussy?"

Titan, Cross, and Grave all enter the room, guns raised and pointed at Matteo and Mia. Matteo looks from the three of them to me and smiles.

"Last chance, Matteo," I add. "You're outnumbered and have nowhere to go." He knows it. The question is, will he take her down with him?

I get my answer when he starts pushing the knife into her neck, making her scream out into the room. Blood drips down her neck and shirt, the material soaking it up.

"Tristan, now!" I shout.

A gun goes off, hitting Matteo in the shoulder.

He shoves her away from him to the floor, and we all start shooting. His body shakes as bullets fill it. The shooting stops, and silence follows. The sound of ringing fills my ears as his lifeless body falls into the chair behind the desk.

I lower my gun and run to where she lies on the floor. Cross cuts the zip tie, and I apply pressure to her neck. She's unconscious but breathing. Wrapping her neck the best I can, I pick her up in my arms. "She needs a doctor."

295

"I've got one." Tristan helps me apply pressure to the wound while I get to my feet and carry her out.

MIA

I OPEN MY eyes to another unfamiliar room. I'm in a large bed with cool white sheets that smell like lavender. The walls are a light gray and the carpet is white. Looking around, I see sheer curtains hanging in front of floor-to-ceiling windows overlooking a balcony.

I stretch, and a pain shoots up my back. I place my hand on my neck to feel some kind of bandage. Getting out of the bed, I look down and notice I'm still dressed in bloodstained clothes.

I killed my parents. But what happened to Matteo? Dillan? The Kings? Who won that fight? I remember seeing my brother enter the office and knowing it was over. But then Dillan was there. Saving me.

Hearing something on the other side of the bedroom door, I make my way over to it on shaky legs. I open it up and step out into a hall. Nothing about this house is familiar. It makes me wonder if it's another one of Dillan's houses.

I make my way down the hall to an open living room. My breath catches in my lungs when I see him standing with his back to me, looking up at the TV that hangs on the wall. Titan and Grave sit on a couch, also facing away from me. Tristan and Cross are midconversation, but it pauses when they spot me.

"Bones." Tristan gets his attention and then nods to me.

I want to walk over to him, but the TV has my feet planted where I'm at. It's the pizzeria. The one that my parents own. It's up in flames, well, what's left of it, which isn't much. Everything looks melted while firefighters try to put it out, but it's lighting up the midnight sky. "What—what happened?" I manage to ask.

My eyes meet Dillan's, and he walks over to me. Reaching out, he cups my cheek gently. His pretty blue eyes soften before he speaks. "We had to make sure no evidence was left behind."

"So you burned it?" I ask, making sure I understand. As I watch Cross flip a Zippo open and closed, something tells me he was the one to light it all up.

"How do you feel?" Dillan asks, his eyes falling to my neck.

I take a step back, and his hand falls. "But why?" I ask, my eyes going back to the TV.

"Even though your family has the police in their pocket, we didn't want to chance anyone finding your prints or blood at the scene. It was the only way to guarantee everything was destroyed." Grave is the one who answers.

Dillan steps back into me, gently cupping both of my cheeks and forcing me to look at him. "How do you feel?"

I feel tears sting my eyes. Twenty years and I've only ever had Luca on my side. And even he had his limits on how much he could protect me.

"Mia." He sighs my name.

"Just tired," I rush out. Trying to not get emotional. I'm finally free. But what now? Where do I go? What do I do? My breathing picks up, and my throat tightens.

"Mia, look at me," he demands.

Tears fill my eyes to where it distorts my vision, and my chest starts to heave.

"Mia." I hear him, but he sounds far away.

I've waited all my life for this, but I can't help but think I made a mistake. Now Dillan has no reason to keep me. To protect me. I told him I wasn't a charity case, but that's exactly what I was to him.

"Mia." He gives me a little shake, and I manage to focus on his eyes. "You're okay. They're gone, Mia. They can't hurt you anymore."

Of course, that's what he's thinking. Why would I be upset that they're dead? That I've wished for something all my life, and now that I have it, I'm not sure I want it. He's going to leave me, and I'll be all alone again. Luca won't speak to me after what I've done. So many people have died because of me. Shouldn't I be next?

"Mia!" Dillan snaps in my face, and I blink as fresh tears roll down my throbbing cheeks. "I'm not going anywhere," he states. Placing his forehead on mine, he lets out a long breath. My hands come up and grip his muscular arms, refusing to let go of him. "I'm right here, Mia. I promise you. I'm right here."

EPILOGUE

BONES

I'M GETTING IN my car to leave Kingdom when I get a text.

Nite: We have a problem.

I SIGH. IT'S ALWAYS FUCKING SOMETHING. I NEVER CARED TO leave this place before. Hell, I've lived here. The home I built with the Kings has stayed vacant for months at a time. Now I can't wait to go home. Because that's where she is. The woman I'm in love with.

Me: Where are you at?

. . .

Nite: Kink.

I THROW MY CAR IN GEAR AND SQUEAL MY TIRES HEADING THAT way. Fifteen minutes later, I enter the club through the front door to see Alexa and Cross arguing about what most couples argue about—money.

"That's too much, Cross," she growls, placing her hands on her hips while looking down at the marble flooring he's added to the stage.

His lips twitch, and he starts laughing. "You can't be serious right now."

"I told you that you're not going to pay for all of this," she argues. "Plus, who in the fuck puts marble in a club? Laminate or tile is best."

"I told you—" He spots me walking across what will be the dance floor and nods to me.

I nod back and make my way down to the basement, letting them have their argument. She's been fighting him all the way. Alexa and Jasmine went into business together. They both own the club and Kink. Alexa was to pay to remodel the club, and Jasmine was spending her inheritance on Kink. Then there was an accident at the bar Alexa originally owned here, and Cross stepped in to rebuild it better than it ever was. Alexa's remodel was supposed to be done with a small budget. Cross took over, paying for everything one hundred percent, and he doesn't do anything small, let alone cheap.

"I said absolutely not." I hear Jasmine snap.

Seems everyone is in a mood tonight. "What's going on?" I come up behind her in the hallway.

She spins around, eyes narrowing on me before she glares over at Nite. "Are you serious? You texted him?"

He crosses his arms over his chest, staring down at her.

"You fucking tattled," she shouts.

"What's going on?" I repeat, turning to ask the man that stands to her right. I know Nite isn't going to answer me. Maybe he'll help me understand what the fuck she's so pissed about.

"She's refusing my services." He points at her, and she snorts, shoving his hand away from her face.

"Fucking children. All of you." She steps into him, and Nite grabs her arm, yanking her back.

"Office," I demand, and Nite drags her away. "Give us ten minutes," I tell the man I had called earlier this morning, and he lets out a huff but nods.

We enter the office, and Nite places her down in the chair at her desk. Nite and I both sit down across from her.

"This has to be a joke." She glares at me.

"Look, I've spoken to Hooke—" She rolls her eyes at the mention of his name. He owns the Kink location in New York. I don't blame her for hating the sexist bastard, but his club is successful. And even though I'm Alexa and Jasmine's silent partner—on paper—I'm not going to profit off this. I want it to be successful for her and Alexa too. "We need these security cameras."

"Are you even listening to yourself? We can't put cameras inside of a sex club, Bones. It's a lawsuit waiting to happen."

I shake my head. "They will only be in the hallways. Not in the rooms."

"No!"

My teeth grind. "This is to save our own asses, Jasmine." I try to reason with her.

"They sign NDAs," she argues.

"Yes, they do, but only the members. Not the company they bring with them," I remind her. "And we need those cameras to prove someone willingly walks down a hallway and into a room." Hooke recently had a lawsuit from a third party who entered and tried to say they were brought there against their will. The cameras he had installed show otherwise. Hooke won, and the accuser had to pay him.

She tilts her head to the side in thought. Her short red hair covers a part of her face. Just when I think she finally gets it, she says, "No."

Nite slams his hands down on the table, and it rattles from his force, making her jump. He stands to his feet. "This isn't a fucking debate! The cameras are being installed, and that is that!"

Silence follows his outburst. I watch the anger leave her face as it pales. Nite slowly lowers back down into his seat, and her wide eyes go to mine. I think she expected me to be as surprised that he spoke because that anger returns to her face and her narrowed eyes go back to his.

She stands, reaching across her desk, and slaps him across the face. "You son of a bitch!" she screams at him. Then she gets up and exits the office, slamming the door shut behind him.

I sit back in my seat, running a hand down my face. I'm exhausted. And I've still got one more place to go to after this. "You didn't have to say anything," I tell him.

He surprises me again by adding, "I know that woman, and you weren't going to win." He stands and turns toward the door to exit, mumbling under his breath, "She's as stubborn as they come."

Checking my watch, I see it's almost one o'clock in the morning when I enter Luca's hospital room to see him sitting up in his bed. He's looking better than when I saw him last. I haven't spoken to him since I informed him I was going to kill his family. He eventually stopped texting and calling me.

He mutes the TV and glances at the clock on the wall after seeing me enter. "Little late for visiting hours, don't you think?"

"I knew you'd be awake." You don't spend all your life working throughout the night and then automatically sleep. Our bodies aren't programmed that way. "All alone?" I look over at the bed they have in here for Haven and notice she's not there.

"She's at your house."

"Oh, yeah. Girls' night." Mia had reminded me twice this week. Things have been crazy since we returned from New York last week. The fact that we set the pizzeria on fire has kept things to a minimum when it comes to the shit show I was expecting. But we've still got a lot going on. And Luca has a long recovery ahead of him. With John and Matteo dead, Nite will take over the family business. No one has any clue right now as to where the twins are. Probably in a penthouse suite somewhere snorting cocaine off women's asses—doing what they do best.

I toss a small black bag onto his bed, and he reaches inside, pulling out a small box. His body tenses, knowing exactly what it is. Setting it back in the sack, he looks up at me. "Is this you coming to ask my permission to marry my sister?"

I snort. "As a friend and business partner, I respect you, Luca. As a brother to the woman I love, I don't." His jaw sharpens. "I'm not asking. I'm here to tell you I'll be asking Mia to marry me." I thought he deserved at least that.

He lays his head back on his pillow and lets out a sigh. "I didn't want this life for her." Tilting his face, he meets my eyes. "She deserves better."

I can't argue with that. "I agree. And I'm going to give it to her." I pick up the sack and turn my back to him as he speaks again, making me pause.

"My father had the police in his pocket. They may never find out what happened to him and my mother, but once they realize their checks aren't going to arrive, they will keep looking for an answer."

I turn back to face him. "It's taken care of." And with that, I exit his room.

MIA

It's been two weeks since we returned to Vegas from New York. The girls and I have been spending all day at a spa getting ready for tonight. Grave has a fight at Kingdom. It's weird for life to seem so normal. Or at least what I think normal is.

I get to pick up my phone and call any one of them whenever I want. Just yesterday, I was cooking dinner, and there was a knock at the door. It was Alexa bringing over a bottle of wine she thought I might like to try. And she was right. It was pretty good.

It's like a dream. Better than a dream, really. Dillan has been giving me driving lessons, and I think I'm starting to change his mind about a chauffeur.

It feels good to be free. To get to make my own decisions.

We pull up to Kingdom in the limo that the Kings had sent to pick us up. We thank the valet workers and make our way up the stairs and through the glass doors. Alexa and April are laughing about something Jasmine said, and I'm holding hands with Haven, who is smiling over at me.

I take a quick look over the large lobby and its grand staircase. It has black carpet littered with gold flecks that match the floor. The railing is also black, and a chandelier that looks like falling stars hangs down from the second-floor ceiling in the center of the staircase. The gold circle and K in the center are underneath my Gucci heels. I've been here more times than I can count over the past couple of weeks, but I've never seen it look like this.

Red roses are everywhere. So many, the smell of them is overwhelming. I love it. It reminds me of April's flower shop. Petals are sitting on the floor and stairs. They also look to be wrapped around the railing that leads up the staircase.

"Like it?" Jasmine asks me.

"It's gorgeous," I say and look at her to see she's already staring at April. "You did this?" I ask her, and she nods. She's been so busy for the past few days that I haven't gotten to spend much time with her. "It's stunning."

"I was hoping you'd approve," she says. Her purple-painted lips are smiling so wide that it shows off her glowing white teeth.

I frown. "Why?"

All of their heads turn to look up at the stairs, and mine follow at their silence. My breath gets caught in my lungs when I see Dillan standing at the top dressed in a black button-up with the sleeves rolled up to show off his tatted arms and matching slacks with his hands tucked in the front pockets. He's so gorgeous.

Lights start to flash from cell phones and cameras as people gather around. I take a quick look around and then focus my attention back on him when he starts making his way down the stairs. He takes the last step, and I realize my heart is pounding.

"Mia." He takes my hands, and I hold my breath. The room is too silent for how many people have gathered around.

"Dillan." I manage to breathe his name.

He shows me that smile that gives me butterflies in my stomach and makes my knees weak. "I'm sorry."

I frown at the apology. My legs start wobbling while my brain tries to process what the hell is going on and why everyone is watching us.

"I once walked away from you." He takes a step back, letting go of my right hand, and it drops to my side like a boulder off a cliff. "But if you give me the chance." He reaches into the pocket of his slacks with his free hand and then drops to his knee. I hear someone gasp, but I'm not even breathing. "I promise I'll spend the rest of my life by your side." Letting go of my other hand, he pops open the black box in his hand, and I see the large red pear-shaped diamond in the center with a diamond halo around it.

This time, I gasp as my hands fly to my mouth. "Dillan." His name is spoken softly on my trembling lips.

"I told you that you'd get to choose, Mia. I'm just hoping that you choose me." He gives me a soft smile, before adding, "I love you, Mia. Will you—"

"Yes!" I shout, nodding my head quickly as I feel tears running down my face.

People start hollering, some laughing at how impatient I was and cutting him off. But he just gives me a big smile and slides the ring on my finger. He then stands, picks me up, and spins me around before placing his lips on mine and kissing me. My hands tangle in his hair, and I let him devour me as I moan into his mouth.

He pulls away too quickly and sets me back on my heels. "I can't believe it." I sniff, looking around at the flowers once again that he had the lobby decorated with. "All these people ..." Flashes are going off while they take pictures, and some are recording us. I never thought Dillan would be the kind of guy who would put on a show for others.

He reaches up, pushing a piece of hair behind my ear. "I want everyone to see how much you're loved, Mia. You are my someone, and I wanted the world to know that."

My body melts even more into his, and he wraps his free arm around my waist to hold me up. After spending a life in the dark, this King will show me what it's like to be seen for who I am—his.

EPILOGUE TWO

BONES

MIA: When will you be home?

Me: In about an hour.

I type out the response to my fiancée and then pocket my cell. Looking up, I watch the man secured to the chair in the middle of the room. He thrashes in it, trying to break the rope that Titan tied him up with.

"You've been a busy man," I say.

He glares up at me, baring his teeth. "You have no idea. Is this supposed to scare me?"

Grave laughs, and Cross smirks, flipping his Zippo open and closed. I ignore his question. "But I do have an idea of what you've been up to." He stiffens at my words.

"It shouldn't have taken me as long to put the pieces together, but

307

the moment I did, they made perfect sense." I take a step toward the chair.

"You know nothing," he growls.

"You were the only one who knew I had bought Mia. You were the one who handed her over to me." His eyes narrow at that. "I had Tristan pull up his surveillance footage that night of the auction, and what would you know? You followed me to his house and, I'm guessing, to the private airfield. But how did you know where I went?"

He snorts, refusing to answer.

"Cross," I say, and he pushes off the wall, walking over to us. He flips the Zippo open again and lights it up before placing it in Richard's face.

He pulls away the best he can, watching it out of the corner of his eyes. "Wait. Wait. Wait," Richard rushes out.

Cross looks at me, and I shrug. Why not let the man speak. Cross closes the Zippo and takes a step back from the chair.

"Speak," Grave growls.

"From the beginning," I add. I know quite a bit from the messages in Matteo's phone that we had taken from his pocket before we set the pizzeria on fire, but some things are still missing.

"I—" Richard licks his lips. "Matteo called me and said his father told him to get rid of Mia however he saw fit." I fist my hands. "I said I would take her." He stops, and the silence drags on. Cross lights his Zippo again, and Richard rushes to finish. "He didn't acknowledge my offer. So I asked why her father was waiting until now to get rid of her. He said that your father had promised John an arranged marriage, but since he passed away recently, there was no way it would happen. So she was no longer needed."

I feel my brother's eyes on me, but I can't look away from Richard. I have no doubt that my father made such an agreement. He was always willing to do something to make a buck. And I'm sure that John was offering a pretty penny for it.

"I told him not to kill her. That there was a way to profit off her name ..." He trails off.

"The auction." Titan finishes his sentence.

Richard nods quickly. "I knew who you were the moment I saw you sitting in the crowd. I called Matteo, and he said to keep an eye on you."

"So you followed him afterward." Grave snorts.

"But you didn't know where I went. So how did you know where she was?" I wonder. He had to have been the one to tell her brothers she was at my beach house.

He stays silent, and Cross sighs. Instead of pulling out his Zippo this time, he slams Richard's face into the table. "Keep going," he demands.

Richard takes in a sharp breath, blood running down his face now. "Matteo just went down the list of the properties you own." He licks his busted lips, and I close my eyes. Of course he did. Fuck, I was so fucking stupid. "He watched her for a couple of weeks, waiting for you to return." He laughs at that. "He really thought that you'd hit that ass that first night. But when you never returned, and she hadn't seen a single person, he decided he needed some reinforcements."

"And when she didn't run right back to Bones, you helped by shooting Luca." Titan guesses how things played out after her brothers knocked her around.

He bows his head, and his laughter fills the room. "You couldn't be more wrong."

I step forward and punch him in the face, making his head snap back. "Then make us understand," I shout, not in the mood for this shit.

Fresh blood pours down his face. His eyes blink to clear the fog. "Matteo called me and said he was sending her back to you. He knew she'd go running like a scared little bitch." He spits blood at me, and it lands on my shirt. "I told him you'd never fall for it. She was useless, and that he got your money, and he should just give her to me. Otherwise, he should just kill her."

I hit him again, and the inked skin covering my busted knuckles splits from the breaking bone. Cross grips his hair and yanks his head back, forcing him to look up at me. "Luca?" I demand through gritted teeth, needing more.

He gives me a bloody smile. "I was there for you. I wanted you dead." His left eye is swollen shut, but his right one narrows up at me.

"If she didn't return to Bones, you could take her." Grave is the one who speaks.

"But you weren't there," he spits out angrily. "I knew Luca was the one who called you and sent you to save her because Matteo said that he had sent him the video of us. I thought I'd go ahead and take care of him."

"Take care of me later." I nod, understanding.

"How'd you keep the Bianchis from knowing you were the one who shot Luca?" Titan wonders. "They would have killed you on the spot."

He shakes his head, trying to free his hair from Cross's hold, but it does no good. When he doesn't answer right away, Cross shoves his face into the table again. "Matteo didn't care." He cries out but manages to continue. "With Luca out of the way, he would be next in line to take over. Plus, he knew Luca had too many enemies to count, and Matteo was more focused on Mia." His one good eye finds mine. "He was obsessed with the two of you." He grits his bloody teeth. "And you fell for the bait. She was the best-kept secret until you ruined her!" he shouts at me. "Paraded her around like the fucking whipped whore she was—"

"You mean you could take her against her will, and no one would look for her because no one knew she existed," Grave growls, interrupting him. "And those who did, didn't care."

"John was just going to kill her. I saved her!" he screams.

"You helped kidnap her and sell her!" I scream back in his face before punching him again, feeling more bones break.

Cross steps back, and Richard starts laughing maniacally. The sound bounces off the concrete box we stand in, making the hairs on my neck rise. I'm so angry I'm shaking. "You think you had her first?" He looks up at me through his lashes. The good eye is starting to swell now too. "You might have fucked her first, but I was the first one to touch her." He laughs once again, his busted lips turning up in a bloody smile. "Drugged and naked...the bitch never even knew."

Grave pushes off the wall, heading for him, but I place my hand out, hitting his chest and pushing him to a stop. Richard is mine. Although I'm thankful my brother wants to stick up for his future sister-in-law, no one touches him but me.

His eye falls to Grave, then back at me. "Remember that the next time you fuck that useless cunt."

The blood rushes in my ears at his words. Matteo had mentioned another video, but I never found one on his phone. Probably a good thing. The one I did see haunted me for weeks and still does at times.

My legs start to move, and I realize I'm walking toward him. Placing both hands on either side of the chair, I lean down and ram my face into his, knocking it back. His blood covers my face, and I get an instant headache. "Load him in the car," I order, pushing off the chair and turning my back to him. We'll bury him in the desert tonight. "I've heard enough."

His laughter fills the room, making me pause, and I turn back to face him. Leaning over the best he can, he spits blood onto the concrete floor. "But I've got so much more to say."

"Nothing worth listening to," I say, turning and opening the door.

"How's your arm doing?" he asks.

I pause again, listening to his laughter growing louder.

"What about his fucking arm?" Titan demands, and I turn to see he's got his hand wrapped around Richard's neck. "Huh?" He shouts in his face, then pulls away, punching him. "Fucking speak!"

Richard's head lolls back while he sucks in a breath before lowering it to look at me. "You think those guys randomly chose to follow you that night?" He smiles up at Titan. "I was a little disappointed. I would have fucked his bitch too."

I feel all the Kings' eyes on me, but I ignore them. My heart is pounding in my chest. How does he know this? We've never told anyone. I don't talk about what happened that night. None of us do.

"Come on," I say, wrapping my arm around Emilee, trying to keep her up. She's wasted. I only had water. I have a tournament this weekend and have to be up and at the field early in the morning. She's been begging me to go to this concert for weeks, so I figured why not? It couldn't hurt to go out. I'm not much of a partier, but I do like the band that was playing.

"We can't go to my house, Bones ..." Hiccup. "My parents are home."

"We'll go to mine." My father doesn't give a fuck what I do. Plus, he's in New York right now meeting with Mr. Bianchi. He said something about the future of Kingdom, but I wasn't really listening to him. I hope he fucking sells his shares so I don't have to worry about it.

I'm a senior in college. Emilee is a sophomore. Her parents still think she's a virgin. There's not a hole I haven't fucked on her body. I open my passenger side door for her, and she falls into it.

I shut it and walk around to the driver's side. Starting it up, I pull out of the parking spot, and she's already leaning over, unzipping my jeans. "Wait," I tell her, pushing her away. We're not far from my house.

Sitting up, she sighs heavily. The last thing I need is her puking all over us. "You—"

The side of my car is hit, cutting off her words, followed by a scream. I smell smoke, and my face stings. I reach out for her, but I hear the sound of metal grinding to my left. Then there are hands on me. I'm pulled from the car. I can't see. Everything blurry. My eyes burn. I can hear Emilee screaming in the far distance, but I can't get to her. "Em—"

Pain explodes up the side of my arm, and I roll away from it. Something hits me in the back, taking what little breath I had left away. Blood fills my mouth, and I start to cough. What feels like hands grab at me, and I hear a snap, followed by unimaginable pain. Then everything goes black.

Richard's laughter brings me back to the present. "You never did find those guys who dragged you out of your car and beat the shit out of you, did you?" he asks.

No. I woke up in the hospital after emergency surgery, found out I had a broken arm among other injuries. But it was over. The one thing I ever wanted was no longer a possibility. My baseball career had ended. As far as I knew, so had my life.

"Funny what you'll do for money," he adds, smiling up at me. "Your father paid those men five hundred dollars. Total. To take you out."

Silence follows. My heart picks up at his words. I always knew I was a target that night. I just didn't know why. I thought maybe it was someone from college. Or I'd fucked one of them up before and it was retaliation. But I never thought my own father was behind it.

His laughter fills the room. "You think he gave a fuck about your baseball career? He had a hundred million on the line with John. You were worth nothing to him unless you took your place at Kingdom and married the Mafia princess. Then the bastard died. And well, John knew his chance at Kingdom was over."

Cross steps back into him. The lit Zippo at his neck once again. "It was you. You were the one who called in the anonymous tip to Marsha." That was who the news reported Mia to be—Mafia princess. "But why? You said she was the best-kept secret? Why would you out her to the world?"

He clenches his mouth, refusing to answer that.

"Enemies." Grave is the one who speaks. "If the world knew who Bones was with, it would put a target on his head. Every enemy he ever had would come after him, knowing she would be his weakness."

Richard wanted me dead so he could take my Queen. That's the only way he was going to get her. Over my dead body. I'll never give her up. And I don't plan on dying any time soon to give him that opportunity. So I'll do what needs to be done.

"Bones?" Grave gets my attention, placing his hand on my shoulder, and I jump back.

Richard laughs at my unease, knowing he's gotten to me. It's time to end this. My queen is waiting for me at our house, in our bed. And I want to be there, holding her, fucking her. Reminding myself that I may have failed her before, but it won't happen again. I will be the one she can count on.

Going over to the cabinet, I open it up and grab what I need before going to stand behind Richard. He's trying to look over his shoulder to see me on either side but is unsuccessful. I grip the concertina wire at each end and then start wrapping it around his neck.

He's shouting, blood instantly running down his neck and chest as I wrap it around three times. Once satisfied that I've done it enough, I hold the ends, feeling the sharp blades digging into my palms. But I don't let go. Instead, I pull on it harder, watching them cut up his neck like it is my hands. "I'm going to hold this here until you slit your own throat." I growl through gritted teeth.

"If I was you, I'd make it quick," Titan adds, and Grave laughs.

His body thrashes in the chair for only a minute before he stops, and then it sags. I let go of the wire, and it doesn't move, the blades now embedded into his neck doing exactly what I intended.

"Christ, Bones." Grave sighs, looking down at my hands.

I drop my eyes to look at them as well and see blood. "I'm fine," I say, wiping them on my jeans, ready to get the fuck out of here.

"Go." Titan nods to the door, reading my mind. "We'll take care of him."

Normally, I wouldn't leave the Kings to clean up my mess, but for once, I have a reason to want to go home. I mumble my thanks and rush out the door.

I make it home in less than fifteen minutes. I enter the house and go straight to the shower. Turning on the water, I get undressed and step inside. Just as I turn to let the water wash off the blood, I spot Mia entering the bathroom, rubbing her sleepy eyes. I woke her up.

"Dillan?" She yanks the door open and steps inside, not even bothering to remove her Kingdom T-shirt. "Are you okay?" Her wide, silvery-blue eyes drop to my bloody hands before meeting mine. "What happened?"

"I'm fine," I say, reaching out to her, and she doesn't flinch when I grip her hips with my bleeding hands and pull her body flush with mine.

"But—"

I lower my lips to hers, and she doesn't hesitate to kiss me back. I spin her around, pressing her back into the wall. My cut and bloodied hands gripping the hem of her T-shirt, needing her naked and my cock inside her. Needing to remind myself she belongs to me. Tonight, tomorrow, and the rest of my life.

Twelve years old

"No self-respecting man marries for love, Dillan," he states while sitting across from me at the table.

"Then why get married?" I wonder.

"For power. Wealth." Leaning back in his chair, his eyes meet mine. "You will one day marry, but it will be who I choose for you. Think of it as a business transaction."

"And if I don't want to?" I ask.

His eyes harden on mine before he answers. "The Reeds aren't weak, son. You're not a motherfucking sheep. You're a goddamn King. And a King does whatever it takes in order to run his Kingdom, do you understand?"

"Yes, sir."

Pulling away, I watch her open her heavy eyes, and for once since my father died, I wish he was still alive. He never brought up marriage again. It was as if we had never had that conversation, and I now realize why. Somewhere along the line, he found the woman he would force me to marry. Too bad the fucking bastard isn't here to see how much I love her.

He was right about one thing. I'm a fucking King, and I will rule my Kingdom with my Queen. But she will come first, even if that means destroying everything I have for her.

"I love you," I tell her.

Her eyes search mine, the concern in them evident. "I love you," she whispers, her eyes dropping to my bare chest, and I lower my lips to hers again, ready to prove to her just how much.

THE END

Thank you for taking the time to read **Bones.**

Want to dive into The Lords World? Continue reading for a sneak peek of *The Ritual*

THE DARK KINGDOM

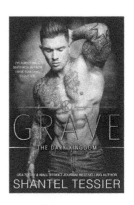

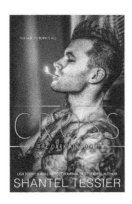

THE RITUAL

USA TODAY & WALL STREET JOURNAL BESTSELLING AUTHOR

SHANTEL TESSIER

PROLOGUE

L.O.R.D.

A LORD TAKES his oath seriously. Only blood will solidify their commitment to serve those who demand their complete devotion.

He is a **Leader**, believes in **Order**, knows when to **Rule**, and is a **Deity**.

A Lord must be initiated in order to become a member but can be removed at any time for any reason. If he makes it past the three trials of initiation, he will forever know power and wealth. But not all Lords are built the same. Some are stronger, smarter, hungrier than others.

They are challenged just to see how far their **loyalty** will go.

They are pushed to their limits in order to prove their **devotion**.

They are willing to show their **commitment**.

Nothing except their life will suffice.

Limits will be tested, and morals forgotten.

A Lord can be a judge, jury, and executioner. He holds power that is unmatched by anyone, other than his brother.

If they manage to complete all trials of initiation, he will be granted a reward—a chosen one. She is his gift for his servitude.

RYAT

Freshman year at Barrington University

I KNEEL IN the middle of the darkly lit room along with twenty other men. My hands are secured tightly behind my back with a pair of handcuffs. My shirt is torn, and blood drips from my busted lips. I'm panting, still trying to catch my breath while my heart beats like a drum in my chest. It's hard to hear over the blood rushing in my ears, and I'm sweating profusely.

We were dragged out of our beds in the middle of the night to serve. Our freshman classes at Barrington University start in two weeks, but we already have to show our loyalty to the Lords.

"You will always have to prove yourself," my father once told me.

"You were each given a task," the man calls out as he paces in front of us. His black combat boots slap against the concrete floor with each step, the sound echoing off the walls. "Kill or be killed. Now how many of you can fulfill it?"

"I can," I state, lifting my head to stick my chin out in the warm and sticky air. Sweat covers my brow after the fight. It's rigged. You

323

are supposed to lose. The point is to wear you down. See just how much you have to give. How far you can go. I made sure to win mine. No matter what it took.

He smirks down at me like I'm fucking joking. "Ryat. You seem so confident in yourself."

"I know what I'm capable of handling," I say through gritted teeth. I don't like being second-guessed. We were each raised for this —to be a Lord.

Wealth got us here.

Yet our determination will separate us by the time it's over.

The man looks at the guy on my left and nods. The guy walks behind me and yanks me to stand by the back of my shirt. He undoes the cuffs, and I rip the shredded material up and over my head before dropping my hands to my sides when what I really want to do is rub my sore wrists.

Never show weakness. A Lord does not feel. He's a machine.

The man steps up to me with a knife in hand. He holds it out handle first to me, his black eyes almost glowing with excitement. "Show us what you can do."

Taking it from him, I walk over to the chair bolted to the floor. I yank the bloody sheet off the chair to reveal a man tied to it. His hands are cuffed behind his back, and his feet are spread wide and secured to the chair legs.

I'm not surprised I know him—he's a Lord. Or was. The fact that he's restrained tells me he's not anymore. But that doesn't change my orders.

Kill without questions.

You want to be powerful? Then you realize you are a threat to those who want your position. In order to succeed, you don't have to be stronger, just deadlier.

The man shakes his head, his brown eyes pleading with me to spare his life. Multiple layers of duct tape are placed over his mouth —those who spill secrets will be silenced. He thrashes in his chair.

Walking behind him, I look down at his cuffed wrists. He wears a ring on his right hand; it's a circle with three horizontal lines across the middle. It stands for power.

Not just anyone would know what it means, but I do. Because I wear the same one. Everyone in this room does. But just because you get one doesn't mean you'll keep it.

I reach down and grab his hand. He begins to shout behind the tape as he tries to fight me, but I remove the ring easily and walk back around to stand in front of him.

"You don't deserve this," I say to him, placing it in my pocket. "You betrayed us, your brothers, yourself. The payment for that is death."

When he throws his head back and screams into the tape, I press the knife to his neck, right below his jawline. His breathing fills the room, and his body strains, waiting for the first cut.

A Lord does not show mercy. Blood and tears are what we demand from those who betray us.

I press the tip of the knife into his neck, puncturing his skin enough for a thin line of blood to drip from the wound.

He begins to cry, tears running down his already bloody face.

"I uphold my duty. For I am a Lord. I know no boundaries when it comes to my servitude. I will obey, serve, and dominate," I recite our oath. "For my brother, I am a friend. I shall lay my life down for thee or take it." I stab the knife into his right thigh, forcing a muffled scream from his taped lips before yanking it out, letting the blood soak into his jeans while it drips off the end of the knife onto the concrete floor. "For we are what others wish to be." Circling him, I run the tip down his forearm, splitting the skin like I did his neck. "We will be held accountable for our actions." I stab him in the left thigh and tug it out as his sobbing continues. "For they represent who we truly are."

Jerking on the collar of his shirt, I rip it down the middle to expose his chest and stomach. The same crest that's on our rings is burned into his chest. It's what we are given once we pass our trials. Gripping the skin, I pull on it as far as I can with my right hand,

325

then slide the blade through it with my left, cutting it from his body.

He sobs, snot flying out of his nose as the blood pours from the gaping hole in his skin. His body begins to shake while he fists his hands and thrashes in his chair. I throw the skin to the floor to rest at his feet. A souvenir for later.

I walk behind him. The only sound in the room is his cries muffled by the duct tape. I grab his hair, yanking his head back, and force his hips off the chair. His Adam's apple bobs when he swallows. I look down into his tear-filled eyes. "And you, my brother ... are a traitor." Then I slice the blade across his neck, splitting it wide open. His body goes slack in the chair as the blood pours from the open wound like a waterfall, drenching his clothes instantly.

"Impressive." The man who handed me the knife begins to clap while silence now fills the room. Walking over to me, I throw the bloody knife up in the air, catching it by the tip of the blade and holding it out to him.

He comes to a stop and gives me a devious smile. "I knew you'd be one to watch." With that, he takes the knife, then turns and walks away.

I stand, still breathing heavily, now covered in not only my blood but a fellow brother's. Lifting my head, I look up at the two-way mirror on the second-floor balcony, knowing I'm being watched and knowing that I just passed my first test with flying colors.

WANT TO DIVE INTO THE LORDS WORLD?

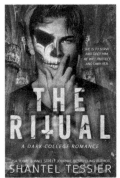

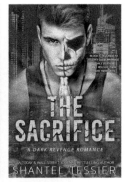

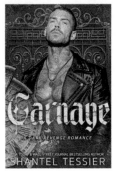

CONTACT ME

Facebook Reader Group: Shantel's Sinful Side

Goodreads: Shantel Tessier

Instagram: shantel_tessierauthor

Website: Shanteltessier.com

Facebook Page: Shantel Tessier Author

TikTok: shantel_tessier_author

Store: shanteltessierstore.com

Shantel Tessier's Spoiler Room. Please note that I have one spoiler room for all books, and you may come across spoilers from book(s) you have not had the chance to read yet. You must answer both questions in order to be approved.

Milton Keynes UK
Ingram Content Group UK Ltd.
UKHW020751241123
433194UK00015B/941